# "That boy is a Kincaid.

"I knew it the minute I saw him," Brock continued. "He looks like a Kincaid, through and through. You can't deny it."

"What are you insinuating?"

"I'm not insinuating anything. I'm stating a fact. Jonathon is either Caleb's or Will's...or mine."

*Caleb's or Will's!* Indignant at the insult, Abby shot from her seat and swung her right hand toward Brock's face. Too swiftly, he caught her wrist and held it fast. His strong grip held her close and a disturbing light flared in his eyes.

"Why did you marry Jed Watson?"

"I don't have to explain anything to you!" She managed to get past her growing fury. "I don't owe you a thing."

"I have a lot of time, Abby." His hold relaxed a measure. "I've come to Whitehorn to stay. I can sit here all day, every day, and wait for you to tell me the truth."

\* \* \*

*The Gunslinger's Bride*
Harlequin Historical #577—September 2001

## Acclaim for Cheryl St.John

"...a style reminiscent of LaVyrle Spencer's
earliest books."
—*New York Times* bestselling author Linda Howard

### The Doctor's Wife
"...Cheryl St.John gives testimony to the blessings
of family and the healing powers of love."
—*Romantic Times Magazine*

### The Mistaken Widow
"Cheryl St.John has woven a beautiful tale.
The characters are endearing. The attraction...
leaps off the pages. A winner!"
—*Affaire de Coeur*

### Joe's Wife
"Ms. St.John knows what the readers want
and keeps on giving it."
—*Rendezvous*

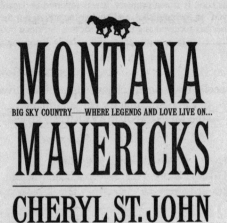

# MONTANA

BIG SKY COUNTRY——WHERE LEGENDS AND LOVE LIVE ON...

# MAVERICKS

## CHERYL ST. JOHN

# THE GUNSLINGER'S *Bride*

# HARLEQUIN®

TORONTO • NEW YORK • LONDON
AMSTERDAM • PARIS • SYDNEY • HAMBURG
STOCKHOLM • ATHENS • TOKYO • MILAN • MADRID
PRAGUE • WARSAW • BUDAPEST • AUCKLAND

Special thanks and acknowledgment are given
to Cheryl St.John for her contribution
to the MONTANA MAVERICKS series.

ISBN 0-373-29177-9

THE GUNSLINGER'S BRIDE

Copyright © 2001 by Harlequin Books S.A.

This edition published by arrangement with Harlequin Books S.A.

Visit us at www.eHarlequin.com

**Printed in U.S.A.**

*Available from Harlequin Historicals and*
*CHERYL ST.JOHN*

*Rain Shadow* #212
*Heaven Can Wait* #240
*Land of Dreams* #265
*Saint or Sinner* #288
*Badlands Bride* #327
*The Mistaken Widow* #429
*Joe's Wife* #451
*The Doctor's Wife* #481
*Sweet Annie* #548
*The Gunslinger's Bride* #577

**Other works include:**

Silhouette Intimate Moments

*A Husband by Any Other Name* #756
*The Truth About Toby* #810

Silhouette Yours Truly

*For This Week I Thee Wed*

Silhouette Books

*Montana Mavericks Big Sky Brides*
"Isabelle"

*Montana Mavericks*
The Magnificent Seven

Please address questions and book requests to:
Harlequin Reader Service
U.S.: 3010 Walden Ave., P.O. Box 1325, Buffalo, NY 14269
Canadian: P.O. Box 609, Fort Erie, Ont. L2A 5X3

This book is dedicated to:
Bernadette Duquette
Debra Hines
Barb Hunt
& Donna Knoell
who not only can eat as much chocolate as I can,
but who always help me write the best possible story.
Thanks, again.

And to our newest baby:
Jared

# Chapter One

*January 1897*

Brock Kincaid squinted at the slate-gray clouds that had been shifting down from the Crazy Mountains since he'd broken camp that morning, and pulled his sheepskin collar around his neck against the bitter wind. Born and raised in Montana, he found that seven years away hadn't dimmed his ability to smell a blizzard coming from the north. He built a fire and melted snow for the horses. There were two: one he rode; the other carried his bedroll and supplies, as well as gifts carefully chosen for the brothers he hadn't seen since he'd left the Kincaid ranch behind.

Caleb, the oldest, would be there, running the ranch, but Will had been gone when Brock left, having headed out after repeated disagreements with Caleb. Brock had no idea where he was now, just as they hadn't a clue where he'd been or what he'd been doing. For their protection, he'd been careful to hide his identity...and his whereabouts.

Cooling the water with a handful of snow and holding the dented pail for his mount to drink, Brock scratched the animal's bony forehead and yawned. Imagining his brother's reaction to his return had kept him awake most of the night, and he'd started out after only a couple hours' sleep.

After the horses were finished, he stowed the pail, then bent and scooped snow to scrub across his tired face. A few more hours and he'd reach Whitehorn, where he could board the animals and get a night's rest before heading to the ranch. He wanted to be alert and prepared before facing Caleb.

With a creak of cold leather, Brock mounted and let the gray pick its way around overgrown scrub and drifted snow. The packhorse whinnied and shook its head, and Brock paused to gather the slack from the lead rope until it calmed. Wolf tracks and bright red blood spattered on the pristine snow several yards to his right told him he didn't want to be around after dark. He drew his .44 Winchester from the scabbard on his saddle and rested it across his thighs. Damn, but a warm bed would feel good tonight. It had been a long time since he'd been comfortable.

A minute later, the crust of snow on the ground crunched beneath the horses' hooves as he nudged his mount forward, the only sound, save the horses' snorts in the bitter air.

He'd cut all ties with his acquaintances of the last few years, transferred funds, changed horses and saddles, bought new clothes and taken a painstakingly slow, roundabout trail to reach Montana. He'd covered his tracks with as much caution as humanly possible.

The only personal possessions he still owned were the pair of carved, ivory-handled .45 Peacemakers in the holsters strapped to his thighs, as much a living part of him as his arms or his legs. They'd saved his life more times than he could count, and leaving them behind would make him more vulnerable than he could afford to be and still live.

Brock blinked against the snow glinting pink and gold from the mountains, and adjusted his hat brim to shade his eyes. By late afternoon, he'd skirted the outlying ranches and made his way toward town. With luck, no one would recognize him, and he'd have time to prepare himself for the only showdown he'd ever had doubts about.

A tinny bell clanged, and the door of the schoolhouse flew open. Brock halted the horses in a stand of bare-branched cottonwoods and watched bundled children charge out the door and down the wooden stairs of the structure, which had been built on the outskirts of Whitehorn since his departure. The grays, actually black-skinned with white hairs, and chosen for their light coloring against a snowy landscape, stood silent.

A few parents near the building waited with wagons or horses. Brock let his gaze scan the students.

Was his nephew Zeke among the children? Brock did a quick calculation and figured the boy would be eight by now. Was someone from the Kincaid ranch down there to meet the child? Heart chugging nervously, he studied those waiting, but none struck him as familiar. From this distance he couldn't make out brands on the horses.

None of those departing headed for the Kincaid ranch, but several children ran toward town.

Brock observed the willowy, dark-haired woman who locked the schoolhouse door and trudged through the snow toward the main street.

Once the area was clear, he rode out of his secluded spot and followed. Whitehorn looked much the same as it had the last time he'd seen it, false-fronted buildings with signs proclaiming the businesses: the telegraph office, a dressmaking shop, the No Bull Meat Market, the

Double Deuce Saloon, *Whitehorn News,* Watson Hardware, the bank. Big Mike's Music Hall and Opera House was new, as was a structure that looked to be made of oil cans bearing a sign advertising Fish for Sale.

He passed Old Lady Harroun's boarding house and the Centennial Saloon before stopping at the livery. Lionel Briggs, a long-faced fellow, emerged from the warmth of the forge and greeted him. "How long you stayin', mister?"

"I'm not sure," Brock said, keeping his hat pulled low. "I'll pay for tonight. They need feed and rest." He pulled his glove from his numb fingers and reached inside his coat for silver coins.

"I'll treat 'em good. Check their feet?"

Brock nodded and paid him.

The man stared suspiciously, a frown and then recognition registering on his face. "Brock Kincaid! I'll be damned! Thought I recognized that voice."

"I'd be obliged if you didn't mention that you'd seen me," Brock said. "I'd like to get some rest before I visit the ghosts."

"Where ya been all this time?" the man asked. "Some said you was workin' with Bill Cody. Others claimed you'd settled down in New Mexico."

"I saw some of New Mexico," he replied noncommittally, pulling down his rifle and unstrapping his gear. "Can I leave my bedroll in a stall?"

"Certain you can."

"Still get a decent meal and room at the Carlton?"

Lionel nodded. "Amos still runs a good place. That hasn't changed. Wife's sickly now, though."

Thanking the livery man, Brock threw his saddlebags over his shoulder. His boots clomped across the boardwalk as he headed for the hotel. He'd reached the wide dock that fronted the hardware store when a couple of laughing boys wrapped in heavy coats, wool caps and scarves shot out the door and ran into his legs, knocking him sideways. Groping for balance, he dropped his gear and grabbed a wooden post.

"Jonathon! Zeke! Apologize to the gentleman. You weren't even looking where you were going."

A slender, russet-haired young woman without a coat appeared in the doorway, a white apron covering her plain dress and calling attention to her curvy figure.

"Thorry, mithter," the shorter of the two said with an endearing lisp. "We wathn't lookin' where we wath goin'."

The other boy struggled to pick up Brock's cumbersome saddlebags and hand them back to him. "Didn't mean no harm," he said. The wool cap he'd worn tumbled off his head and he turned to grab it, knocking into the smaller boy. Both of them landed on their butts on the icy loading dock.

Chuckling, Brock bent over and plucked both of them up and steadied them on their feet. The youngest one gazed up, dark blue eyes wary of the stranger. A wisp of wavy blond hair escaped his cap. Was this a Kincaid nephew? Brock glanced at the other boy, also fair-haired and blue-eyed.

Then he turned and saw the young woman for the first time.

She was staring at him, her complexion gone pale, a sprinkling of freckles standing out against the pink rising in her cheeks. "Abby?" he asked uncertainly.

A combination of things had driven him away from this town. The constant discord in the Kincaid house was surely part of it. The other part—the bigger part—was the fact that he'd killed this woman's young brother.

She stared at him still, as though not believing what her eyes were telling her. Once his identity registered, her expression quickly changed to one of cool hostility. "Come inside, boys," she said curtly.

"But we didn't get licorith yet," the younger one complained.

"We didn't mean to knock the man down," the other added.

"No harm done," Brock said kindly, stooping to pick up his leather bags. He couldn't help casting another hungry look at the boys, who reminded him so much of him and his brothers at that age.

"One of you Zeke Kincaid?" he asked.

The taller boy's eyes widened. "How'd you know that?"

"Come inside *now,* boys!" Abby told them sharply.

"Are you Zeke?"

The lad nodded, then gave Abby a quick look. Caleb's son. Brock's nephew. Brock looked him over hungrily, all the years away from here seeming so wasted and lonely. Caleb had had more children and Brock had missed their births. Abby must be watching them for Marie.

"Come in *immediately,*" Abby ordered.

"Aw, Ma," the younger boy said unhappily.

*Ma?* The address hung in the air like the report of a bullet. Brock's gaze shot to Abby's face. Shuttered and distant, her expression revealed only her disdain. "*Your* son?" he managed to ask past a dry throat.

"That's right. Jonathon is *my* son. Now excuse us." She nearly pushed the boys inside the store and slammed the door so hard the glass panes rattled and the bell inside clanged.

Her son? But that child was unquestionably a Kincaid. Had Marie died and Caleb married Abby? Had Will come back and married Abby?

Snow had begun falling in earnest, blowing up across the dock and dusting Brock's boots. He wasn't sure how long he stood there in confusion, contemplating the shocking information and the possibilities. Of course, life here had gone on without him; why had he imagined everything would still be the same?

Through the square panes of window glass, he could see that the hardware store held a few customers. What Abby Franklin was doing in there he had no idea, but he didn't want the entire town to know he was here before he'd had a chance to see Caleb, and the stove at the hardware store was the social gathering place on winter afternoons such as this.

Tamping down his questions and his eagerness to see his nephews, he adjusted the heavy bags over his shoulder and hurried through the snow to the hotel.

Abby Watson stared out the window at Brock's tall, long-legged form retreating through the swirling snow. She bit her lip and pressed a shaky hand to her thundering heart. Surely she'd expected that he'd be back one day. He owned a share of Kincaid land, for heaven's sake! Both of his brothers were here, Caleb running the ranch, Will having returned and made his amends a year ago. He now ran the bank.

At the time of Will's return, she'd been forced to think of Brock—to wonder where he was and whether or not he, too, would make his way back to Whitehorn and his family home. She'd considered selling the store and leaving before that became a reality, but her roots had grown deep into this land. Her father and brother were dead now, but Jonathon had family here, even though he didn't know it. She owned her father's ranch as well as a thriving business, and she felt good about being a respected citizen.

Caleb couldn't acknowledge Jonathon publicly without shaming Abby, because Abby had married Jedediah Watson, and the older man had accepted the boy as his own. Caleb had seen to it that Zeke and Jonathon spent plenty of time together, though, especially since Jed's death two years ago. Zeke coming home with Jonathon after school every day had begun as much to keep the boys together as to spare Zeke the tension of his unhappy home life, Abby suspected. Now that Zeke's home life had changed for the better, he still came here every day.

Abby glanced back at her handsome, fair-haired son brushing snow from his pants, and a sick feeling curled in her belly. What would happen when Brock learned the truth? Would he even care? He hadn't seemed to in all these years, so she couldn't imagine that he'd suddenly develop a conscience.

She brought her worried gaze back to the window. Men like Brock Kincaid thought only of their prowess with a gun, to the exclusion of family and loved ones. Men like him had no loved ones. And they robbed other people of theirs, as well.

A shiver ran through her body.

"What're you lookin' at out there, Miz Watson?" Harry Talbert, the barber, called from his favorite chair beside the stove. "That snow is gonna come down whether or not you keep an eye on it."

More than seven years ago Brock Kincaid had shot and killed her brother, then ridden out of town without a backward glance.

Now he was back. And about to find out he had a son.

Brock awoke at first light, placed his feet on the frigid floorboards and strode naked to the window. From the second story, he could see much of the frozen, rutted street, the shops with mounds of snow drifted across the boardwalk and against their doors, a few animal tracks leading in and out of the alleyways, and smoke drifting from chimneys.

The brick smokestack at Watson's Hardware belched a steady gray cloud. He'd watched until dark and Abby hadn't left the place. Caleb had come with a team and wagon and taken one of the boys away. If Abby'd left, it had been late, or she'd exited by a rear door, but Brock couldn't imagine why she would bother.

He dressed and continued his vigil at the window. One by one, lamps came on in the businesses below. Merchants arrived and shoveled boardwalks. Shades rose. A man with a key entered the hardware store, a man too young and fit to be Jedediah Watson.

A team and buckboard pulled up alongside the dock that fronted the hardware store, and the driver climbed the stairs and tried the door. He knocked. Lights came on and the door opened to admit the customer.

Sometime later, the rancher came out, followed by the man who'd entered earlier, and together they carried boxes, rolled barrels across the dock and loaded the supplies into the wagon bed.

Abby appeared at the doorway, wearing a white apron. She waved as the rancher pulled away. The young man entered the store behind her and the door closed. She looked as though she belonged there. If the man was her husband, why had he just arrived, when it was apparent she'd been there all night? If she worked there, perhaps she had a room over the store. Brock glanced at the lace curtains at the upper windows.

He could stand here supposing all day, but he had business to see to with his brother, so he packed his bags and left.

Lionel had fed and groomed the horses, and Brock paid him an extra dollar for their care, loaded his belongings and rode out. He followed the ice-crusted creek, from time to time spotting wolves sunning themselves on outcroppings that jutted from the rock walls of the foothills. The horses startled an occasional deer or rabbit. He'd missed the wide-open spaces of this country, missed a sense of belonging and of family, more and more as the years passed.

At the time, leaving had seemed like the best thing— the only thing—he could do. Caleb had married Marie, a pampered young woman who'd been expecting his child, and her immediate withdrawal had confused everyone. Unhappy in his marriage, Caleb had turned cold and distant, and Will's competitive badgering wore on him. Will had resented Caleb being groomed to take over the ranch, and his jealously drove a rift between them.

Brock had been torn between his two older brothers. Though he'd been the troublemaker in his youth, he had kept his tomfoolery away from the ranch, wreaking havoc in the saloons and streets instead. As he'd been the youngest, his irresponsibility had been overlooked. Frustrated by his lack of position in the family and on the ranch, as well as by the constant rivalry between his siblings, Brock had taken a devil-may-care attitude. When Will stole money from Caleb's safe and headed East, his actions had stabbed Brock like a knife to the heart.

That hadn't been the final straw, however. He probably could have stuck it out, moved to town perhaps, away from Caleb and Marie, though he adored their fair-haired baby, Zeke. No, the event that had driven him to pack his bags and ride toward the horizon had taken place the day he'd shot and killed the boy—Abby's brother.

Brock sat his horse in a flurry of swirling spindrift and gazed at his family home, at the well-kept barns and corrals and the cattle on the nearby hills. Caleb had done well. So well that he wouldn't welcome Brock's return?

He nudged the gray and headed forward.

A figure on horseback emerged from the concealment of trees to the north and rode swiftly toward the barns. Brock recognized the brown-and-white skewbald and the figure atop as John Whitefeather, half Cheyenne and a friend of Caleb's.

Before Brock reached the yard, the tall, broad figure of his brother, dressed in denims and a flannel shirt, appeared in the open doorway of the barn. Shaggy, dark blond hair blew back from his face in the cold wind. But despite the wind and the frigid air, he stepped away from the shelter of the building and ran forward.

Brock reined in the gray several yards away and dismounted, closing the final steps that brought him face-to-face with his brother.

Caleb looked older, still muscled from hard work, his gray-blue eyes not revealing the thoughts or feelings behind them. He looked so much like their father that a wave of odd familiarity swept Brock, then disappeared when Caleb's mouth turned up in a grin. "Little brother," he said calmly. Those steely eyes scanned the mountains and the sky. "Some time of year you picked for traveling."

"Yeah, well, you know I never had much sense when it came to practical things."

Caleb's gaze moved to Brock and seemed to warm with his assessment of what he saw. "Your room's still there. Don't think the shirts are going to fit, though. You've grown some."

Brock took that as a welcome, and the reticence that had created a stone wall around his heart cracked.

"Bet you could use a bath and a hot meal."

The crack widened and a thread of hope snaked through. "Sure could. Who's cooking?"

Caleb reached for the reins and took them from Brock's gloved hand, then led the animals toward the barn.

"Things have changed around here. We have a lot to catch up on."

Brock walked beside him. "I'm looking forward to it."

The gray-blue eyes that met his held an unmistakable sheen. "Me, too, little brother."

After unsaddling and brushing the horses, then throwing down hay for them, the two men walked toward the house, where a familiar dark-skinned woman with a glossy black braid met them at the back door and led them into the warm humid kitchen. She rested a chubby, dark-haired baby on her hip.

"Ruth is my wife now. This is our son, Barton." At Brock's puzzled expression, Caleb added, "I told you there was a lot to catch up on. Marie's dead," he explained, referring to his first wife. "She was thrown from a horse and stayed in a coma until she died."

Brock was at a loss for words. "I'm sorry" didn't seem adequate, yet he couldn't help thinking guiltily how miserable Caleb had been with his first wife and how he was better off without her.

"I'm glad you're home, Brock," Ruth said with a warm smile, teeth white against her dark skin. "And don't let your brother fool you, he's glad you're here, too."

Ruth was John Whitefeather's sister, and she had stayed with them for a time many years ago.

Brock nodded. "I'm glad to be back."

"Dada!" the baby burbled, and flapped a chubby arm at his father.

With a wide smile, Caleb took the boy from his mother and tossed him in the air. The baby chortled and a string of drool hit Caleb on the chin. He shook his shaggy head and grimaced, which only made the baby giggle harder. Caleb brought the boy to rest against his wide chest and wiped his face with his shirtsleeve.

Ruth laughed and the couple exchanged looks of affection and pride. She turned to Brock then and said, "Let's get you settled. I'll heat water for a bath."

"Do I smell?" he asked with a grin.

She laughed good-naturedly. "The first thing your brother wants to do after he returns from a trip is clean up."

"Well, you're right about that. I stayed at the hotel last night, but I didn't take time for the niceties."

"You were in town overnight?" A furrow dipped between Caleb's brows.

"Yes. I needed a little time to collect myself. I wasn't sure—well, I wasn't sure how you were going to react to seeing me."

"Ruth's right. I'm glad to see you. About damned time is all I have to say." Caleb handed the baby back to his wife. "We'll talk at supper."

With that, he turned and left the house, the door banging shut in a gust of wind.

"He doesn't have a coat on," Ruth commented.

"I think he was a little distracted," Brock replied.

"He *is* glad you're here."

"I hope so." For some reason it seemed easier to talk to this woman than to his brother. "I spent too long on the trail and I'm ready to settle in somewhere. Make up for the lost years, if I can."

"Well, you're welcome here. This is your home."

He didn't know if she'd feel the same if she knew what he'd been doing all those years, if she knew the things he had to put behind him: the violence and the bloodshed and the wavering line between right and wrong that he'd walked for so long. Too long.

Brock didn't know if it was possible to put all that behind him, if the man he'd become could be the man he wanted to be. Even if he cut himself off from every person

who'd known him or known of him, and started over,
could he ever live at peace with himself?

"I'll have the tub and water brought to your room."

Brock thanked his new sister-in-law and climbed the
stairs, his gun hand riding the glossy banister.

Catching up took Brock and Caleb most of the day,
half a bottle of rum and several cigars. Ruth prepared
lunch, something she claimed to enjoy, since Caleb normally ate in the bunkhouse with the hands at noon.

After telling the story of his and Ruth's romance, Caleb
related how Will had come home a year ago, wanting to
return the gold. Caleb hadn't wanted it, didn't want
money to be a factor between them, so they'd secretly
buried it in a cornerstone of the Double Deuce Saloon,
which Caleb owned.

"That doesn't sound like the Caleb I remember,"
Brock told him. "I can't picture you doing something like
that."

Caleb grinned. "Hopefully I've changed—for the better."

"I saw Zeke yesterday," Brock told him.

Caleb slapped a hand against his thigh. "Are you the
stranger he saw outside the hardware store?"

Brock grinned. "That's me."

"He was taken with the revolvers you wore. I see you
don't have 'em on today."

And he had no idea how difficult it was for Brock to
leave them in his room, even while in this house.

Caleb's eyes narrowed and he pierced Brock with a
look he remembered too well, a look that said he'd see
through him if he tried to lie. "So what have *you* been
doing all these years, little brother?"

## Chapter Two

Brock brushed his fingertips across the empty space on his denim-clad thigh where his holster should have been. The absence of that familiar weight kept surprising him. "I hired on in a range war in Wyoming after I left here. Occasionally I rode shotgun for Wells Fargo on special runs. But the ranchers kept hiring me to do their dirty work, and they paid too well to say no. After a while it seemed I was getting so many offers that I could choose."

Brock stood and stretched his legs, striding to the window and gazing out at the snow-covered mountains. "I traveled with army details to recover stolen horses. Took a couple of U.S. Marshal jobs. Things like that."

"You never wrote."

The words hung in the air, more of a hurt-revealing question than an accusation.

Brock hadn't written because he hadn't wanted his enemies to be able to track him to his family. The sugar-coated version of the past he was feeding his brother was enough. The less Caleb knew, the better. "I didn't know what to say."

"You could have said you were okay."

"You were mad that I left, weren't you?"

"I was mad at your hotheaded foolishness that got that boy killed."

Brock stiffened and turned his gaze to Caleb. "I didn't go looking for that kid, he came gunning for me."

"Because you dishonored his sister!"

"What happened between me and Abby was our business."

"Something like that becomes family business, Brock. Her father would have come after you himself if he'd known first. But it was Guy who found out and Guy who tried to protect his sister's honor."

"I never even had a chance to make it right," Brock argued.

"What would you have done? Married Abby?"

The question sucked the tension from Brock's body. He drew a palm over his face, then hung his thumb in his belt. "I don't know."

"You wouldn't have," Caleb answered for him.

"I was young."

"You were a hothead."

"Maybe I was, but I didn't want to kill Guy."

"I know that." Those words were laced with sincerity and regret. "And things were ugly here, too. I knew why you left. I always knew. It wasn't just the boy. You'd have been found innocent of his death—there were witnesses. You were protecting yourself. Guy was just the last straw."

"I was all mixed up. You and Will were fighting…and then he left with the gold."

"Don't forget Marie," Caleb added.

"And Marie," he agreed with a nod. Caleb's understanding eased away the burden of Brock's worries. His brother had changed, and it was a change Brock liked. "You're different now than before I left."

"Maybe that's why I understand that you're different,

too. It's been a long time. We all change. And grow. Thank God.''

"And Zeke is so big, I can hardly believe it. He looks like you did."

Caleb grinned and agreed.

Brock's thoughts switched to the other boy he'd seen the day before. "What is Abby doing at Watson's Hardware, anyway? Working there? Seems like an unlikely place for a female."

"Might be an unlikely place for a female, but she's been doing a fine job of running it since Jed passed on."

"Running it? What for?"

"She owns the store now. She's Jedediah Watson's widow."

*Widow.* The prickly news didn't want to settle nicely in Brock's mind. It poked around nervously, leaving stinging wounds. His breath grew short and he had a difficult time drawing air into his lungs. "She married Jedediah Watson?"

"Yep."

"He's an old man."

"*Was.* And I don't think he was over fifty when he died."

"What the hell did she marry him for?"

"Why do most women marry? Security maybe."

"She said the other boy is hers—the boy I saw with Zeke."

"Jonathon. Smart as a whip, that one."

"I thought he was yours."

Caleb looked at him in surprise. "Mine? Why would you think that?"

"I saw him with Zeke. The two look like brothers, don't they?"

Caleb's expression closed before he pulled out a pocket

knife and worked at a sliver in his thumb. "There's a resemblance."

"I was sure that boy was a Kincaid."

"Hmm."

Brock didn't like his brother's avoidance one bit. It made him nervous as hell. "Don't you think it's odd?"

"What?"

"That he looks so much like…"

"Like what?"

"Like we did." His heart kicked in an unsteady rhythm as the pieces came together in his mind. "Caleb, how old is Jonathon?"

His brother folded the blade away and studied his knife. "About seven, I guess."

Brock took a few frantic steps toward the chair where Caleb sat, the weight of wonder growing heavier on his chest. "When's his birthday?"

"I don't remember."

"Caleb—"

"Brock, these questions are for Abby. Go talk to her."

The tension inside Brock had built until he felt sick to his stomach. "You know something, don't you?"

Caleb stood and drilled his blue-gray gaze into Caleb's. The room around them took on an odd gray-tinged bleakness. "I don't know any more than you do. Go ask Abby. And that's all I'm saying about it."

Brock couldn't leave the room fast enough.

Abby tied up a brown paper package with a length of twine and handed it to Etta Larimer, her first customer in an hour.

"Did you hear there's a gunslinger in town?" Etta asked. There was an edge of excitement in the reedy voice of the newspaper man's wife.

"No, I hadn't heard."

"He got off the stage yesterday, all dressed in black. Fancy clothes and fancy guns. Henry Hill saw him and says he wears silver-plated six-shooters in silver-studded holsters and a scarlet silk neckerchief."

"Henry noticed his neckerchief?"

"Well, it would be a striking contrast to the dress in this town. People are saying he's that Jack Spade fellow."

Abby had heard the rumors of the famous Jack Spade being in the area for some time now. Her fiancé, Everett Matthews, worked at the telegraph office, and he'd been seeing conflicting reports of the dime novel hero's supposed whereabouts. Her immediate thought was of Jonathon at the schoolhouse, but she dismissed her motherly fears as being intensified by the appearance of Brock Kincaid yesterday. "Those kind of men are trouble wherever they go, and I hope Sheriff Kincaid sends him on his way immediately. We don't need his kind in Whitehorn."

Etta's expression grew subdued. "Of course, you're right, dear." She lowered her voice. "I just hope I get to see him before he leaves."

"Not me. I hope I don't have to set an eye on him or anyone like him."

The front door opened, and even clear across the cavernous interior of the fully stocked store, Abby could feel the cold snake in and wrap around her ankles. She thanked Etta for her business and moved to add more fuel to the fire in the stove. She was poking the coals with an iron tool when boot heels sounded loudly behind her.

"I was wondering where all the customers were this after—" She stopped abruptly as she turned, the sight of Brock Kincaid's formidable figure in a long, snow-dusted coat bringing her up short. His dark blue eyes radiated as much heat as the stove behind her. She set the tool aside. "What do you want?"

"I want to talk to you."

"This isn't the place or the time."

"I think it is."

Abby glanced around. Her only customer had departed, and Sam Rowland, her hired man, was gone for the day, since his wife was expecting a baby soon and hadn't been feeling well. A shiver of fear slipped up her spine. Rarely was she frightened to be alone here where men gathered and shopped. They held a healthy respect for the widow of Jedediah Watson, but this man wasn't one of them. He was a stranger now. A killer. "I don't have anything to say to you."

"You'll answer my questions."

A statement. *A threat?* She made herself look at him again.

He was bigger than she remembered, taller, with wider shoulders and the expressionless face of a hard man. She would not let him see the sudden rush of fear that sent a cold chill through her blood. She seated herself abruptly on one of the worn wooden chairs near the stove and folded her hands in her lap. "Hurry then. I run a business here."

Brock took his time removing his sheepskin coat, hanging it on one of the brass hooks that protruded from the nearby post for just that purpose. A pair of embossed leather holsters were strapped to the length of his thighs, ivory-handled revolvers gleaming deadly in the light. Her heart slowed to almost no beat, then raced alarmingly. She drew a shaky breath and quickly looked down at the floor.

His boots left puddles of melted snow on the scratched varnish. He stepped closer and she closed her eyes in keen trepidation of the inevitable.

"How old is Jonathon?"

She swallowed, knowing what was coming, dreading it from the depths of her wounded soul. Countless sleepless nights and innumerable days of wondering and waiting had culminated in this moment. She felt light-headed and disconnected, as though this was happening to someone else and not to her. "Seven."

"When's his birthday?"

"What difference does it make to you?"

"It makes a difference."

"I don't think it's any of your business."

"I think it is." His voice was quiet, but held a tone that brooked no argument.

She argued, anyway. This was her life at stake. "I don't have to tell you."

"Then I'll ask him."

She opened her eyes finally, her head clearing and her protective instincts on full alert, and brought her gaze up to his. "You stay away from him."

"What are you afraid of?"

He was calm, too calm for a man tearing someone's life apart. His cool detachment frightened her more. "I mean it! Stay away from him."

"He's a Kincaid." He said it with deadly calm.

Was her heart still beating? Of course. That was what the deafening drumbeat in her ears was all about. She fought to keep her expression bland.

"I knew it the minute I saw him. He looks like a Kincaid through and through. You can't deny it."

"What are you insinuating?"

"I'm not insinuating anything. I'm stating a fact. He's either Caleb's or Will's...or mine."

*Caleb's or Will's!* Indignant at the insult, Abby shot from her seat and swung her right hand toward his face. Too swiftly, he caught her wrist and held it fast, her braid whipping across her shoulder and smacking him in the chest. She struggled against his hold and raised her other hand, but he grabbed her upper arm.

"Leave us alone!" she managed to bite out past the mounting fury.

"Why did you marry Jed Watson?" he said, staring down into her face.

Her entire body trembled with anxiety, and she hated that he could feel her weakness. "He was kind. He was good to me and to Jonathon."

His strong hands gripped her painfully. A disturbing light flared in his eyes. "Why did you marry him?"

"I don't have to explain anything to you. I don't owe you a thing."

"I have a lot of time, Abby." His hold relaxed a measure. "I've come to Whitehorn to stay. I can sit here all day, every day, and wait for you to tell me the truth." And he demonstrated by releasing her.

She almost fell at the loss of support, bumping into a counter and sending a tool flying with a clang, then catching her balance. She wrapped her arms around herself, massaging the places on her arms where she could still feel his biting touch.

He sat on a chair, propped his feet on another and rested his arms behind his head in an infuriatingly nonchalant pose. How dare he come back here after all this time and act as though he had any rights whatsoever! This man had taken every girlish dream she'd ever had, shot them full of holes and left them to die an agonizing death.

Anger boiled up and she wanted to throw something at him. She glanced around at the rows of tools and boxes of springs and bolts. The bell over the door clanged, saving her from a violent act she would have regretted.

Brock looked up and gave her a cruel grin. "You have a customer."

She wouldn't cry. She wouldn't. She would not give the malicious man the satisfaction. She'd shown weakness once before, but she'd learned a harsh lesson. She turned away, composed her quaking chin and picked up a cast-iron utensil that had been knocked off a shelf, replacing it with trembling fingers.

"I'll wait right here," he said from behind her.

The "customer" was Harry Talbert, the barber. He made his way past spools of wire and down the long row of silver-nickled, dome-top, coal-burning stoves. "The coffee doesn't smell burnt yet."

"No, no, it's still drinkable."

He took his stained mug from the rack on a nearby shelf and poured himself a cup of dark brew, turning slowly to see who occupied the chair. Coffee sloshed onto the stovetop and hissed. "Brock Kincaid? Good Lord, you haven't been in these parts for—how long? Five, six years?"

"Almost eight."

The words grated along Abby's nerves like a shiver.

"Has it been that long? Well, I guess so. Since that day—" His gaze shot to where Abby stood. The day Brock had killed Guy was what he didn't finish saying.

She turned and hurried away, checking the orders she had started writing the day before. She overheard bits and pieces of their conversation as they discussed cattle and snow, and Harry brought Brock up to date on some of Whitehorn's residents and businesses. The low rumble of Brock's laughter grated on her nerves. The nerve of the man to make himself comfortable in her establishment, at the expense of her peace of mind.

She moved on to dusting oil lamps and the endless length of glass showcases, and then inventoried the kegs of nails she'd already counted that morning. Brock could afford to sit about and converse merrily. He hadn't a care in the world, save the killing of innocent men, which obviously didn't worry his conscience a whit.

Harry stayed over an hour, before he called out a good-bye and the bell rang. Abby had waited on a few customers in the meantime, all of them raising eyebrows or asking her about the man occupying a seat near her stove. Ready to order him out, she stomped back to where he sat calmly twining a scrap of fuse around his index finger.

"You were about to tell me why you married old Jed."

His words and his insolence were intolerable. "Don't call him that! He was a decent man! A responsible man willing to marry a woman and provide for her—and her son!"

"*Her* son. But not his."

She clenched and unclenched her hands in raged frustration. "I don't owe you an explanation. I don't owe you anything. And I don't want anything from you. Except for you to leave us alone."

"I can't do that, Abby." His voice was as hard and cold as his steely blue eyes. "I want the truth."

She shook her head and her own voice came out annoyingly weak. "Why are you doing this?"

"I don't want to hurt you. Abby, I never wanted to hurt you."

"You killed Guy!"

"What should I have done? Let him kill me?"

"He wouldn't have killed you—he was a poor shot, as you found out. He was a stupid angry boy, but he didn't deserve to die!" Tears stung behind her eyes and she fought to keep them back.

"He shouldn't have come after me with a loaded Colt. He didn't leave me any choice."

"Just leave me alone, Brock," she pleaded again. "Please."

Heat radiated off the iron stove. A rafter in the lofty ceiling creaked.

"He's my son, isn't he?" His gaze dropped to her breasts, to her belly, as though he imagined her with his child growing there.

A never-soothed ache swelled and burned in her chest. Abby had an empty feeling that a lot more people suspected the truth than had ever let on. They had pitied her, and she had married a respected businessman, so the truth had been overlooked. Caleb found ways to help and to get the boys together without embarrassing her. Never once had he asked her about Jonathon's parentage. But he knew. And she had accepted his help and the tie to the family, because it was the truth.

Brock brought his attention back to her face, which burned anew with humiliation. "Say it, Abby. Say he's my son. Tell me the truth."

She stared at him long and hard, remembering all the days and nights after he'd ridden away. Remembering her father's outrage at discovering her condition and his insistence that she marry Jed. She remembered her fear and her loneliness and her final resignation. When dreams died, they died hard. "The truth?" She looked him in the eye. "You want the truth, Brock? Jonathon is your son. And I despise you more than words can say."

Countless times, Brock had stared into eyes that radiated hatred and he'd stared back, unfazed. Uncaring. Unfeeling. Not caring or feeling had kept him alive. Being quick on the draw wasn't the only critical factor in winning a showdown. Most victories were won by gaining the upper hand before a gun ever cleared a holster. Mental strategy, confidence and a complete lack of emotion had given him the edge.

This time, God help him, he cared. The two facts struck like poison arrows and spread numbness through his chest and belly.

Jonathon was his son.

Abby hated him.

He'd missed seven years of his son's life. Missed seeing the squalling infant come into the world, missed his first smiles and first teeth. Brock had spent his life on trains and horseback, in saloons and jails, taking pay to do things men were afraid to do for themselves. He'd been sleeping in strange hotel rooms and beside campfires, while Abby had been raising his son.

"Who does he think his father is?"

"He called Jed papa."

Brock swallowed a groan and let the piercing hurt sink in. "Jed knew he was my son?"

"He knew I was expecting Jonathon before he married me."

"Why did you marry him, Abby?" He still couldn't comprehend her reasoning.

"My father arranged it. He was furious when he discovered I was going to have a baby. I didn't have a choice."

"Surely there was something—"

"Such as what? My father had just buried a son, if you'll recall. Guy didn't tell him about us, and I was too afraid. I never told him anything, but when he knew I was getting sick in the mornings, he figured it out. He made all the arrangements, then he hauled me off to Whitehorn, watched Reverend McWhirter marry us, and rode back to the ranch without a backward glance."

Brock imagined Abby, young, afraid, bearing her father's anger, mourning her brother's death, and married to a stranger.

"What did you do?"

She raised her chin and met his eyes. "I cooked and cleaned and learned about hardware, and I had a baby. There wasn't anywhere for *me* to run."

He had no explanation that would change her mind about him. He'd been young and confused, but she'd been young and confused, too. Nothing he said now would change what had happened back then. She was acting as though he'd had a lot of choices. Even if he'd wanted to make it right, he couldn't have. If he'd asked her to marry him then and there, she would have refused. Even if he'd known he had a son, still he couldn't have come back. "I want to see him."

"No. I forbid it."

"You can't forbid me from seeing my son."

"You won't do anything to hurt him. You have that much decency. If people caught on, they would treat him cruelly, and you don't want that. You've left us alone all these years. Why should that change now?"

"Because now I know."

"You'd have known back then if you had stayed and faced what you'd done."

"We both know it was self-defense."

"I have a feeling that everything is self-defense with you," she said in a tone meant to inflict injury. "Have you ever taken responsibility for anything?"

Those words penetrated armor that bullets had never pierced. It was easy for her to blame him, easy for her to think the worst of him. Brock had never intended to kill her brother; he'd never even wanted to hurt him. The boy had drawn first, moved into the bullet. But he was dead all the same.

Little did she know Brock had taken responsibility for her safety and that of the son he hadn't known existed—as well as his entire family—by staying away.

All the things she took for granted, things like a good night's sleep in a familiar bed, like eating a meal without looking over her shoulder, like being able to live here, were the things he'd lost.

"I won't do anything to hurt him. But I will see him."

Fear clouded her expressive eyes. Did she think he would hurt her? Did she think he'd take the boy and disappear? She hadn't tried to hide her contempt, but she'd done a poor job of covering other emotions. She thought he was a monster. Let her think it. Utilizing fear had always given him an edge.

"I want to know my son. It can be as hard or as easy as you make it, but a boy needs a father."

"As usual, your feelings are the only ones that count," she said with cool accusation. "Not mine. Not Jonathon's."

The bell over the door rang, echoing across the expansive interior and sparing him a reply.

A small figure dropped a scarf away from her head, revealing jet black hair, parted down the middle and pulled away from her oval face. She made her way toward the seating area near the stove, shaking the wool scarf as she went. "It is starting to snow again."

Abby glanced uncomfortably from the girl to Brock.

He coolly lifted one brow.

"Am I interrupting a sale?" the young woman asked.

Up close, Brock observed her dark, almond-shaped eyes and obviously Asian features. She was exceptionally pretty, with an open, friendly face.

"I was just leaving." He reached for his coat.

"We haven't yet met," she said, ignoring the dark look Abby shot her. "You are either the infamous Jack Spade that everyone is talking about—"

Brock wore the expressionless mask he'd perfected and didn't so much as flicker a lash.

"—or you are the Kincaid brother who has been gone for years. You don't look to me like the gunfighter everyone talks about."

"Brock Kincaid," he said easily.

"I'm Shan Laine Mei."

"How do you do, Shan Laine Mei," he said, uncertain of how to address her properly. "Is it Miss Shan?"

She smiled broadly. "It is. The Shan family runs the fish market."

"The structure made of…oil cans?"

She nodded. "Cans are filled with stones and dirt. Fireproof. Bulletproof, too."

He hadn't thought of that. "How is business this time of year?"

"My father and brother cut wood to sell during the winter. I sell canned vegetables that I garden during the growing season. Come by if you want good squash."

"I will." He situated his hat on his head and touched the brim. "Pleasure to meet you."

"And you, Mr. Brock."

He gave Abby a strong look. "I'll be back."

She pursed her lips and looked away.

The bell over the door clanged at his exit.

"Laine, how could you stand there and converse with the man as though he were a *gentleman?*" Abby said to her friend in irritation.

"Mr. Brock is not a gentleman?"

"No, he most certainly is not. He's a selfish, infuriating, cold-blooded killer, that's what he is."

Laine's dark eyes widened. "You know this for a fact, Abby?"

Abby turned and placed a kettle of water on the stove. "I watched him shoot and kill my brother."

Slowly Laine removed her coat and hung it up. "You have not told me of this before."

Abby rubbed her palms together. Few people in town associated with Laine socially, so she'd never been filled in on the gossip surrounding Brock Kincaid. "I don't like to talk about it."

"If he murdered your brother, why isn't he in jail? Or why wasn't he hanged?"

Abby grew flustered at the question. "Guy had his gun drawn. It looked like self-defense."

"The law said it was self-defense?"

"But Guy was seventeen years old. Just a boy."

"I am sorry. I knew your brother died young, but I did not know the circumstances. Mr. Brock, he is sorry for his part in your brother's death?"

"He thinks of nothing but himself."

"You know he was not sorry? He has said so?"

"He didn't take time to say anything. He turned and ran."

"But you said Guy had his gun out. Did he mean to shoot Mr. Brock?"

Now look what she'd done. She'd opened a can of worms she didn't want to discuss, and her friend wasn't one to back down. Abby chastised herself for letting her anger place her in this uncomfortable position, and measured tea into a metal strainer. "My brother was furious with Brock—for good reason. He was doing what he thought was right. Brock, on the other hand, was doing what he always did—wearing a gun and looking for a reason to fire it."

Laine came and stood beside her. "You knew Mr. Brock well?"

Abby closed her eyes, and the anguish of those days washed over her in an oppressive wave. Tears burned her throat. How could she answer that question and not lie?

Laine's hand touched her shoulder in a comforting gesture.

Did Abby want to deny the truth any longer?

# Chapter Three

"Abby, are you all right?"

She nodded silently, but her cheeks blazed with the heat of humiliation. She had never shared what had happened with anyone. She'd been too ashamed and embarrassed. For nearly eight years she'd held her silence about what had been a painful and life-changing turn of events.

Brock's return had resurrected old hurts, all those chaotic feelings of confusion and apprehension. His insistence on seeing Jonathon endangered the secure life she'd grown comfortable with. She would go crazy if she couldn't release the tension by at last telling someone.

Opening her eyes, she turned, seated herself upon a chair and patted the one beside her. She couldn't carry this burden alone any longer. "I foolishly fancied myself enamored with him when I was young," she confessed matter-of-factly, knowing her confidence was well placed in Laine.

"You had feelings for Mr. Brock?" Her friend sat beside her, their skirts touching.

Abby nodded, incredibly relieved to make the confession at last. "But he barely gave me a second glance. I always knew when he was at a gathering because I watched for him and observed his every move. I knew the way he walked and the way he smiled and how he held a partner on the dance floor. When he looked my way I could barely breathe.'' She shook her head at her childishness.

"So you see, it was a one-sided admiration. Until one summer all those years ago.'' She paused to think about that particular year, and could still remember the scent of the pines in the high country, the vivid splashes of paint-brush streaking the mountainsides and the unique paleness of pink sunsets. That summer had defined all that was beautiful—and what had happened had characterized all that was ugly.

"He was miserable at home. His brother Caleb was married to an insufferable woman. Brock had no father or mother by this time, and his brothers fought all the time. He used to ride into town with the ranch hands and shoot up the saloons, then sleep off the liquor in jail.''

Laine gave her a puzzled look. "And you were sweet on this young man?''

"I knew him before all that,'' Abby replied with a dismissive shrug. "I remembered him from when his mother was alive and our families were friends. Obviously I had an image of him that wasn't the real person. I thought he was misunderstood. Humph.'' Again she shook her head at her youthful foolishness. "I was the one who misunderstood. I thought he possessed redeemable qualities.''

Laine took Abby's hand. "What happened the day your brother died?''

Abby studied their fingers. "It was night. And he was murdered.''

"How?''

"Brock had asked me to meet him in the foothills by the river. It was our secret place. I took a horse like I always did.'' She turned a pleading gaze on Laine. "I was so in love with him. I thought he felt the same. I thought…''

''What?''

''Well, I thought our—relationship was quite romantic and forbidden and exciting. He was the most handsome young man—those sad blue eyes and that wavy hair—and he had this…this *appeal*. I can't explain it.''

''I think I understand.'' Laine's sympathetic eyes said as much, too. ''But what about Guy? He did not like you with Mr. Brock?''

''Afterward he found the note Brock had written, asking me to meet him. He knew I'd been taking a horse and disappearing for hours at a time.''

''And he was angry.''

''He was very angry. He set out to avenge a wrong he thought had been done to me. I rode after him. I got to town in time to see Brock pull his gun and shoot Guy.''

''He seems like such a nice man. You said your brother had gone after him. Did Guy shoot at Mr. Brock?''

Those words seemed traitorous to Abby. She stared at Laine. ''A nice man? He killed my brother!''

''Did he not have cause to draw his gun? If he was a cold-blooded murderer, he would be in jail right now, would he not?''

''If there was any justice!'' Abby replied, tears forming in spite of her anger.

''I am sorry, my friend.''

Abby shook her head and blinked away the moisture. ''I blamed myself for not getting there in time, for losing my head and making such an awful mistake.''

''You weren't to blame for your brother's death.''

''I wanted Brock so much that I didn't think of the consequences.''

''And he wanted you?''

In all these years Abby had never allowed herself to

think of Brock—to remember the feelings and the passion and the wonder—because their time together had so swiftly turned ugly. But she had to face it now. "He is Jonathon's father."

The confession had been so easy to say. Part of the tension inside her abated and she took an easy breath, not realizing she'd been holding herself rigid and barely breathing.

Laine's eyes widened in surprise. "Jonathon's father! Who knows of this? Your husband knew of this?"

The rest came easily now that that had been revealed. "We never spoke of it, but he knew. No one has ever spoken of it until now. Until Brock came and asked me. That was the first time I'd ever heard the words aloud. Saying them to him—to you—have been the first times I've heard the truth other than in my head."

"It must feel good to have the truth out in the open."

Abby gave her head a quick shake. "I'm glad I've told you, but it's not good that he knows. It frightens me what he'll do."

"What do you want him to do?"

"I want him to go away and leave us alone."

"You still have feelings for him," Laine stated.

Abby's stomach clenched at the accusing words. "I have no feeling beyond contempt for a cold-blooded killer!"

"You have made excuses for his behavior. His parents were gone, he was miserable with his fighting brothers. You think he is handsome."

"I do not."

"You do. You describe his hair and his eyes and his— what did you call it? Appeal."

"That was a long time ago! He's not the man I thought he was."

"Same hair. Same eyes." Laine pressed her small

hands against her breast. "Same attraction. And you have a son together. Jonathon is a tie that binds."

Abby clenched her fists in her lap. "I am not attracted to that man." At her friend's skeptical look, she protested more emphatically, "I'm not! And as far as I'm concerned he is not the kind of father Jonathon needs. His influence can be nothing but harmful."

"A boy needs a father."

"Perhaps, but not a father who is a murderer. Whose side are you on?"

"If sides are drawn, I will stand on yours, of course."

Having a sympathetic confidante was new to Abby, and she was grateful for Laine's caring and loyalty. "Thank you."

"You're welcome."

Abby swallowed her indignation and gave her outspoken friend a half smile. Laine's old-fashioned father believed she should be silent, bowing to the decisions and wishes of the males in her family. Because she respected her father, Laine did her best to oblige them and be an obedient daughter, but her Americanized thinking had her in hot water more often than not. She had been born and raised in a Western mining camp, not in her father's native land of China, and she loved to share her opinions.

Laine returned the smile.

Abby leaned toward her and the two embraced.

"I am glad you told me," Laine said.

"Me, too. I'm sorry I didn't know how to say it before. I didn't want you to think badly of me."

"I could not think badly of you."

"Others would."

"Others should not matter, but I know they do. You know you have my confidence."

"I know."

"Now come. Sell me some lamp oil."

* * *

That afternoon, when Jonathon and Zeke arrived at the hardware store after school, Abby hung their coats and poured them mugs of milk she'd warmed. She'd thought of little else but Brock's visit and his warnings all day.

As Jonathon sipped his milk beside the stove and bit into a raisin cookie, she studied his dear, familiar face with its delicate nose and spray of freckles. The freckles and nose were hers; every other feature he'd inherited from his father.

His hair, as fine as a baby's, had turned thick and wavy. If it were longer, it would curl over his collar like Brock's did.

Jonathan had never known any other home but this one, any other life but that of playing between barrels and kegs and wheelbarrows. They lived overhead, their quarters taking up only half of the huge expanse. The hardware store was three levels. The lower level was partially underground and filled with bins of coal and stacks of lumber. The middle level was the retail area, and the upper floor was divided into living sections. One side had always been rented to Asa and Daisy Spencer, which made Abby feel safer than if she were completely alone.

Jed had made his home above the store for as long as Abby could remember. Coming from a ranch, she had felt it confining at first, but she'd learned to appreciate the convenience of working and sleeping in the same building, without braving the harsh Montana elements in the winter. And Jonathon knew nothing else.

"Me and Theke wanna play marbleth, Ma," he said, raising those irresistible blue eyes. "We got jarth and jarth of 'em and no dirt."

"No dirt is a problem," she said, and her mind tossed around possibilities. The ground was frozen too hard to loosen enough dirt to bring inside, but come this summer she could make them a ring in a frame somehow. For now… "How about something that would slow the marbles down, like dirt does, something like…fabric? Canvas maybe. We could cut a circle and nail it to the floor."

"Think it would work?"

"We can try." She found shears and set to cutting a length of tarpaulin.

When John Whitefeather came for Zeke, the boy didn't want to leave.

"Look, Uncle John! We're playin' marbles." Zeke showed him excitedly.

"Your ma has a fine roast and a cinnamon cake ready," he replied. "And your pa needs some help stacking wood."

Zeke shot up and ran for his coat. "Bye, Jonathon. My ma makes the best cinnamon cake in the world and I gotta help my pa!"

Abby helped bundle him into his coat and hat and mittens, and waved them off. Jonathon climbed on a bench and watched through the square panes of glass. "Theke hath hith own horth, Ma. Look, that'th him there. John brought him for Theke to ride home. Ain't he purty? Hith pa teached him how to ride and they do work together."

With an ache in her chest, Abby stood behind her son, smoothed down the cowlick that sprang right back up, and watched the riders on the street. "Looks like a fine horse."

"Did you have a horth when you were a little tyke, Mama?"

"We had a lot of horses where I grew up. It was a ranch."

"But one of your own…did you have one of your own that you named and everything?"

She heard the wistful tone in his young voice. "No. Nothing that special."

"Did my grandpa teach you to ride?"

Good memories of her father were tainted by the recent ones, and the sad-sweet twinge of retrospection tugged at her already aching heart. She blinked back tears—for herself—and for her son, who believed he was fatherless. "Yes, he did."

"I'm gonna have me a horth when I get bigger. One like Theke'th."

"You have to pay to board a horse when you live in town," she told him.

"Oh, I ain't gonna live in town. I'm gonna live on a ranch."

"Oh." Abby rubbed his shoulder. "Well, come help me get ready to close up. If someone comes late, they can ring the outside bell and I'll come down and help them."

Jonathon stood to inherit the hardware store, as well as the Franklin ranch. Abby hadn't wanted to sell it, and had leased the land to a young rancher eager to build his own herd. She guessed it would be Jonathon's choice what he wanted to do when the time came.

A shiver of anxiety left her uneasy as she thought about her boy's future. He was still young, but if he had his heart set on being a rancher, that was fine by her. What effect would Brock Kincaid have on their lives now that he was back? He wanted to be a part of Jonathon's life, and that would probably mean passing down a share of Kincaid land, as well. Jonathon could easily grow to be one of the wealthiest men in Montana.

Her responsibility to raise him to be an upright, honest man had never been so clear. And she had never been so afraid or felt so alone.

Brock planned his trip to town for supplies on Saturday, when Jonathon would be out of school. When he arrived at the hardware store, he stopped the wagon beside another that sat at the loading dock. The man he'd seen from the window at the hotel was helping Matt Darby roll barrels into the back of a springboard. Brock set the brake, jumped down and climbed the stairs.

"Hey, Brock," Darby said, thumbing back his hat and straightening. His gaze dropped to the revolvers slung low on Brock's hips. "I heard you were back."

"Matt." Brock strode forward and shook the rancher's hand.

"You in Whitehorn for good?"

"I am."

The other man approached. "Sam Rowland," he offered. "I work for Mrs. Watson."

*Mrs. Watson.* The name sounded ill-fitting. Brock shook his gloved hand. "Brock Kincaid."

"I know who you are."

Brock glanced from one man to the other. "I'll bet you do. The stories are flying right now, eh?"

Matt grinned. "Biggest news since Will came back. Some folks even think you're Jack Spade."

Brock had spent the previous evening with Will and Caleb, catching up on their lives, hearing Will's side of the story about the gold. Will had related the rumors circulating through town. "What do you think, Matt?"

The man tugged his gloves a little tighter. "I think if you were a famous gunslinger you'd be crazy to come back here, and I don't think you'd put your family in danger like that."

Brock didn't flicker an eyelash.

"My bet is on Linc Manley," Matt added.

"The man in black who arrived on the stage and set tongues to wagging?"

"That's how he's registered at the hotel," Sam explained.

Brock nodded, and the men turned back to their task.

He looked Sam Rowland over—a sturdy enough fellow with a lean face and more than capable demeanor. Working daily with Abby, he was bound to have formed a working relationship with her. Brock wondered if there was anything more to it.

He entered the store and pulled a wrinkled list from his pocket. Caleb had been glad to turn over the run into town, and Brock had a feeling the chore would be his from now on. Harry Talbert called a greeting from his spot beside the stove, and Brock sauntered back to say hello, wondering with amusement how the man ever managed to give a haircut when he was always here.

An elderly gentleman that Brock didn't recognize sat with a cane leaned against his bony knee and a coffee mug resting on the other. He squinted at Brock from beneath wispy white eyebrows. "Mighty fancy Peacemakers ya got there."

His interest seemed genuine, not critical. Brock slid one of the ivory-handled six-shooters from its leather sheath and displayed the carved eagle for his inspection.

"Man who carries a gun like that knows how to use it. Them's either peacemakers or troublemakers." The old gent ran shaky fingers over the ivory in admiration.

Brock exchanged a look with Harry, but the man seemed more amused than curious. "I've done some peacemaking. Marshaled in Nevada, South Dakota."

"Bringin' criminals to justice, eh? Meet any of the Earp boys, did ya?"

"Saw them in passing."

"Mr. Kincaid!"

Brock turned, the gun sliding automatically into his palm.

Abby faced him, her face flushed with anger. She shot her fiery gaze to the revolver in his grip. "I would appreciate it if you would keep your weapons out of sight in my establishment. My customers have no reason to shoot one another.''

''I was just showing the gentleman—''

''Golly!'' a child's voice interrupted. ''Can I thee it, Mithter?'' Jonathon ran forward, his face alight with admiration.

''No!'' Abby shouted, stopping him with a forearm across his upper chest. The length of her thick braid swung forward and draped her arm to her elbow. ''You may not.''

''But, Ma!''

''Guns serve only one purpose, Jonathon, and no son of mine will be a killer.''

''Man needs a gun in this country, Miz Watson,'' the old man said. ''Man can get hisself killed without one.''

''If everyone got along peaceably, there would be no use for violence,'' she argued.

''This ain't fairyland,'' the old gent said with a laugh. ''Or even Boston. This here's Montana, and a body needs to protect his home and his family.''

''Killing isn't a solution to every problem.'' Indignant, she straightened and glared from Brock to the old man.

Harry cleared his throat. ''I think I have to give a haircut.''

''Might not be a solution to every problem, but it sure shuts up the criminals,'' the old man continued with a gleeful cackle.

Harry grabbed his coat, plunged his hat down over his head and bolted for the door.

''Mr. Waverly, please refrain from placing barbarous ideas in my son's head.''

Brock had holstered his .45, and he removed his coat and hung it up. ''Here's a list of supplies. Jonathon, will you show me the rope, please?''

She took the slip of paper with a frown. "I can show you—"

Brock raised a palm to stop her in her tracks. "Jonathon will show me."

Her green eyes spat fire, but she bit her tongue. She followed them with a worried frown as Jonathon led Brock to the other side of the store.

"Thith here'th the rope."

Brock made a choice. "Do you know who I am?" he asked.

Jonathon gazed up with round blue eyes and nodded. "You're Mithter Brock. Theke'th uncle."

Brock surveyed the elfin face with a light sprinkling of freckles and let his gaze caress the hair so like his own. The urge to touch that baby-soft skin and wavy hair was so strong, he clamped his hand on the length of rope. "Y-yes," he said, his voice breaking so that he had to say it again.

"Theke thaid you been gone a long time. You wath off fightin' bad guyth. That right?"

"Something like that."

"Did you thoot 'em with your gun?"

Brock understood Abby's protectiveness. He did. He would rather take a beating than expose this child to the ugliness in the world. If only it were reasonable to think Jonathon could be protected from reality. But that wasn't possible. Or even wise. He would need to know how to protect himself.

"We all have to do things that we don't want to do sometimes," was all he said, and it sounded trite.

When they returned to the stove several minutes later, the old man was sipping coffee. He grunted and shook his head.

Brock followed Jonathon to where Abby stood beside a counter, calculating a stack of figures. "Do you want this on the ranch account?'' she asked in a businesslike tone.

''Yes.''

''Sam will help you carry out the kegs.''

''I'd just as soon wait awhile, so I can visit with Jonathon.''

Her hesitation was evident in the way she paused over the numbers, in the way her chin lifted slightly.

''Or I can take him back to the ranch with me, and he can play with Zeke and help me put things away.''

Unfairly, he'd suggested it in front of the boy, and Jonathon shot forward, raising a small hand to place it on the counter by her paper. ''Can I, Mama? Can I go play with Theke? Brock wanth me to help him!''

Abby's gaze lifted and struck Brock with as much force as a bullet. Anger simmered there, but the fear in her eyes took him aback. Why it should bother him, he didn't know. He had her where he wanted her. She was afraid to let her son go, but she was afraid Brock would tell Jonathon the truth if she didn't comply.

He looked down. ''Let me talk to your ma alone for a minute, okay?''

''Okay!'' The child shot away and disappeared into the depths of the store.

''I'm not going to snatch him and ride off,'' he assured her. ''You don't have to fear that. I told you I would get to know him. This seems like a good way. He's used to Zeke and Caleb. What would people think if I sat around your store all day long?''

He had her there. She cared very much what people thought. And she obviously cared very little for his tactics. ''If you sank any lower, you wouldn't have to open the door to slide out of here,'' she said in a venomous tone.

He took a step toward her.

Her heartbeat fluttered at her throat. The soft scent of

lilacs floated to his nostrils, striking an unexpected chord of familiarity.

"You didn't mind me so much once," he said, his voice as even and insinuating as he could make it.

She released the pencil she'd been holding and dropped her hand to her side, taking a step back and coming up against the cool glass display case. "I was a fool."

He inched closer. Her green gaze focused on his shoulder, and she refused to meet his eyes.

"We all make mistakes, don't we, Abby?"

Her chin lifted a notch. "Some more than others."

He remembered now their brief, heated encounters, his anger and mental chaos and her warm welcoming embrace that soothed and satisfied. He had sought comfort in her arms, taken her virginity, knowing she was smitten with him but also knowing he wasn't of a mind to be making decisions or commitments. He couldn't truthfully say what would have happened if Guy's actions hadn't forced him to defend himself.

"I won't hurt our son. I make you that promise."

At those words, her gaze rose to his, hurt, bewildered.

"Have I ever made you a promise before?" he asked.

She gave a jerky little shake of her head and whispered, "No."

"So you see, I've never broken a promise to you, either. You're going to have to trust me."

"I will never trust you until you take off those guns and admit your guilt."

Guilt because of Guy? Or his guilt over her? If that was what made her mad, it was sure funny that she didn't remember her part in their carryings on, as if he'd seduced an unwilling partner. Hardly. He remembered then how she'd claimed to hate him. "Then you're never going to trust me."

She blinked.

"But you don't have a choice that I can see, now do you?"

She tightened her lips as though she was clamping them shut against a torrent of raging words. "You're despicable," she hissed.

"No," he replied with stern denial. "Rape is despicable. You came to me willingly." He lowered his voice and added, "Eagerly."

Her face flamed.

"Stealing is despicable. I only took what you offered."

Tears glistened and she blinked them back.

"Denying a child is despicable. I acknowledge my son. I want to know him and teach him and be a father to him."

Holding herself so rigidly like that, she'd shatter into a million pieces if he pushed her over, he imagined. "Murder is despicable," she accused.

For a confused moment, he thought perhaps she knew more about him than he'd revealed, but that couldn't be. He'd been too careful. She meant Guy. "He drew on me first, Abby, and you know it. You're just too stubborn to admit it." He stood a step back, giving her space, distancing himself so he wouldn't be tempted to grab her and shake some sense into her. "I'll return Jonathon before dark."

Before Brock's return, Abby had never in her life wanted to hit someone, and the fact that she again wanted more than anything to strike out at this man shocked her. She stood by helplessly, rooted to the floor, as Brock called her son. She stood fast while she watched Jonathon bring his coat and hat, despite the fact that her fingers itched to help while Brock bundled him up.

Watching them prepare to leave, she felt a chasm yawn in her chest. Her breath came in shallow, painful gasps, and she wanted to run to Jonathon and clasp him safely to her, protect him from the truth and the man who threatened the sanctuary of this home she'd made for them.

Brock had donned his own coat, but he knelt, one knee touching the worn wood floor, and said something to Jonathon.

Her son's blond head turned her way, and without hesitation he darted toward her and hugged her around the waist. "Bye, Mama. I'll be back before dark."

Abby loosened his slender arms and knelt to fold him in a desperate hug. She petted his shiny hair and inhaled his unique little-boy scent. "Goodbye, darling. I love you."

"I love you, too, Mama." Pulling away, he ran to join the tall man who waited patiently.

He raised his gaze to Brock's, and Brock looked down. Jonathon trustingly placed his mittened hand in Brock's huge, gloved palm, and they walked away. The bell over the door clanged a finale to the heart-wrenching scene. Abby's chest felt as though a lead weight were pressing down upon it. She drew a staggered breath and placed her hand over her heart, where the real ache gnawed.

Stinging tears bit her eyes and she closed the lids tightly.

The bell rang again.

He'd changed his mind! Her eyes flew open.

Her fiancé, Everett Matthews, stood in the doorway, looking over his shoulder, and she knew he was watching Jonathon depart with the stranger.

Stupefied, he turned and met her gaze. "What is going on, Abby?"

## Chapter Four

Not now! Why now, of all times, did Everett have to show up? The tears Abby held inside threatened to burst through her defenses and engulf her, but she couldn't allow Everett to see them, to sense even a glimpse of her torment. He would surely suspect something was wrong if she behaved the least bit odd.

Turning as he removed his coat, she plucked up the pencil and held it over the paper as if she could actually see or think to figure. "Oh, hello, Everett." He wore a neat, brown serge suit and vest, and a matching bow tie at his neck. The perfect gentleman. "What brings you out today?"

He walked forward with his coat folded over his arm. "Why is Jonathon leaving with Brock Kincaid? What's going on?"

"Jonathon's going to play with Zeke for the afternoon. He'll be home before dark," she said, forcing lightness into her voice.

"I've never seen you let that boy out of your sight except to go to school."

"Why, that's not so. He's gone to play with Zeke before. The winter days are so long. He needs a change of scenery now and again.''

"But *Brock Kincaid?*" Everett stepped closer, and she was forced to look up, somehow managing a tight smile. "You hate that man!"

Abby's eyes wanted to clamp shut tight. She wanted to roll into a ball and disappear under the counter like a clump of dust. She would love to pound the floor and kick and scream that she did, in fact, hate that insufferable man.

She didn't want to stand here all sweet faced and pretend to her betrothed that she didn't loathe the man who had just walked out with her child! Instead, she scrambled for something—anything logical to say to prevent him from suspecting the worst. "All that was a long time ago. Caleb and Ruth are our friends, after all, and Jonathon and Zeke are best friends." She took Everett's coat and hung it on a brass hook. "Jonathon loves to play with him. Besides, Brock is Caleb's brother, so I might as well let bygones be bygones."

Had she said that? Had that atrocious lie rolled from her tongue? Abby tasted acrid bitterness and decided that, indeed, it had. She couldn't abide deceptiveness, and here she was lying to the man she was going to marry. Once again, because of Brock Kincaid, she was going against her principles.

Everett shook his head of thick, neatly trimmed brown hair. One dark brow rose now, and coffee-colored eyes bored into hers in disbelief. "Pinch me to wake me up, because I can't believe my ears. I must be dreaming, because I thought you just excused the man."

"You're not dreaming, silly. It's not healthy for a person to go around with hard feelings locked up inside. I've decided to let the feud go. That's all.''

"That's all? That's all, Abby? Did he apologize?" he

asked in amazement. "Did Kincaid say he was sorry about your brother?"

"Oh, yes." She told the bald-faced lie and turned to carry a lantern back to its shelf. "He regrets that they ever had a misunderstanding and that things got out of control so quickly. He's a changed man." Changed from bad to worse, anyway.

"I never really understood what it was they fought over," Everett said, following.

"I don't think anyone really remembers," she said dismissively, as though the worst event of her life was of no importance. "It was a long time ago and they were probably too drunk to know what they were doing."

"This is quite a change of heart for you," her fiancé said, still seeming to have trouble understanding.

"Yes," she agreed sweetly. "People are allowed to change."

Abby glanced aside to note that Mr. Waverly, who still sat by the stove with his cane against his knee, watched her in silence, a shrewd expression on his grizzled face. He couldn't have overheard her earlier restrained conversation with Brock, but he'd heard their original exchange and was now getting an earful of this one—and the two sure didn't line up.

"Do we need a fresh pot of coffee, Mr. Waverly?" she asked.

"Couldn't hurt. I lost m'spoon in the last cup."

"I'll get some water."

She went about carrying the pot to the back room to rinse and fill. Everett waited while she stoked the fire and set the pot to boiling.

Taking her elbow, he led her aside, away from the old man's curious gaze. "This is all such a…a surprise," he said carefully once they were hidden in an aisle of garden tools. "I've never seen anything but scorn from you when the man's name was mentioned, and now this sudden act of forgiveness."

"Don't concern yourself with it. It was time to lay things aside, that's all." She looked up and gave him a warm smile to distract him. She pulled her elbow from his gentle grasp and placed her hand on his forearm. "Have you heard any interesting news?"

Everett worked at the telegraph office. News passed through his fingers daily, and he loved to share what he'd learned. His curious demeanor seemed to change at her touch. "Seems they have a few cases of measles over toward Billings."

Abby pretended interest. "Oh, really?"

"And the surrounding marshals have been alerted to watch for Jack Spade. No one's sure where he headed, but he was reported crossing the Missouri at Helena and coming this way."

She grew uneasier at that report. "Some are saying he's the man who's been in the saloons the last few nights."

"I confess I stopped at the Four Kings last night to have a look-see."

She cast him a playful frown. "Am I engaged to a drinking man, then?"

"You know better than that. I had a couple of rounds and a cigar, waiting to see if anything happened."

"And what would you have done if it had?" Suddenly genuinely interested, she withdrew her hand and went on. "Those places are nothing but trouble. You could've been shot if guns had been fired."

Everett didn't carry a gun, one of the things she appreciated most about him. He didn't try to charm her or intimidate her, either; in fact, Everett was everything Brock Kincaid wasn't. Stable, levelheaded, responsible. He would make an adequate husband and a good father for Jonathon.

Her heart tugged with fresh insecurity at that thought.

She'd believed for the last year that she was making a wise choice for Jonathon's well-being by saying she'd marry Everett. "A boy needs a father," Brock and Laine had both said, and she knew that was a fact. But a father like Everett, not one like Brock.

"I would never want to worry you," Everett said with a repentant tilt of his head. Moving forward, he took both her hands and clasped her fingers in his. "I'm looking forward to our dinner tonight. I would like to treat you to a meal at the hotel. You shouldn't have to cook for me after you've worked hard all day."

"That's a tempting offer."

"What have you planned for Jonathan?"

"I've planned for him to stay with the Spencers. They love his company."

"Then you'll have dinner with me at the Carlton."

Abby didn't have to think twice about not cooking their meal. "All right," she agreed with a nod.

"Very well then." He leaned forward and brushed a quick kiss against her cheek. Rarely did he kiss her on the lips, and whenever she turned her face to deliberately make that happen, he seemed embarrassed. "I'll come for you at six-thirty."

"I'll be ready."

Everett released her hands and hurried away to get his coat.

Mr. Waverly eventually headed for home, but not after observing her closely for another hour. He lived alone in a tiny room behind the livery, so he divided his days between watching Lionel Briggs at his forge and drinking coffee at the hardware store. Ordinarily Abby welcomed his presence. Today's annoyance with his eavesdropping had been unusual.

She counted the day's earnings, placed the money in a

strongbox in the back room and swept the floor, starting on one side and working her way across the front of the building. The store was too big to do it all at once, so she made a point of cleaning a section each evening.

The sky had just begun to turn dark when a forceful knock sounded. Running forward, Abby opened the front door. Jonathon stepped in, followed by Brock, who helped the boy remove his neck scarf and hat.

"Come look, Mama!" Jonathon said, pointing through the windowpanes. "Brock din't bring the wagon thith time. He rode me on hith horth! Ain't it big?"

Abby observed the handsome gray tethered to the dock. "He's big for sure."

"Brock'th gonna teach me to ride all by mythelf. Won't that be thomethin'?"

"That'll be something, all right."

"I'm gonna take 'im up and thow 'im my carved horth-eth."

"Jonathon, you need to wash up and eat. I'm having dinner out tonight, remember?"

"I already ate at Theke'th, Ma. Come on, Brock." He took the man's gloved hand, and Abby got a catch in her throat, seeing the familiarity, the worshipful expression on her boy's face, the proud smile Brock couldn't hide. A casual onlooker would think they'd known each other forever.

Abby tasted a grim measure of fear. "But I have to get ready."

"We won't bother you," Brock said. "I'll keep an eye on the boy while you get ready."

"Come on, the thepth ith back here."

Speechless, Abby watched her son tow Brock into the back room toward the stairs that led to their living quarters above. Anger simmering at Brock's audacity, she yanked down the shades and locked the front door. After double-checking the banked fire in the potbellied stove and pouring a pail of hot water, she headed up the stairs.

Jonathon was excitedly showing Brock his carved horses when she entered her own kitchen, feeling like an intruder. She carried the bucket past them into her room. Seeing them like that, their heads together and their hair the same shimmering fair shade, her chest got tight. Jonathon deserved a father.

A simple cotton curtain separated the bedroom from the living area, and the sounds from the kitchen carried down the hall. Abby shrugged out of her work dress. Having no door on her bedroom had never bothered her until now. Now she wished for something more than flimsy fabric between her vulnerable undressed state and that unscrupulous man out there.

She bathed self-consciously in the water she'd poured into her basin. Her gaze was constantly drawn to the curtain, and every little sound nearly made her jump. Hurrying, she slopped water on the floor and spent several minutes cleaning it up. Finally dry and dusted with talcum powder, she selected her rose-colored wool skirt and cotton blouse with ruffled cap sleeves and ruffled waistline, because she felt competent and attractive in them. She brushed out her hair, rebraiding the thick length into order. An upswept curled style would be more fashionable, but her heavy straight hair never cooperated with current fashion.

Abby buttoned her boots, picked up her reticule and pushed past the curtain. Taking a deep breath, she hurried down the narrow hall. Jonathon and Brock still sat in the kitchen, their heads bent together over a small wooden horse.

Jonathon looked up. "You look pretty, Mama!"

"Thank you."

Brock's blue gaze traveled over her clothing, face and

hair. "If you'd told me you had plans for the evening, I'd have kept the boy at the ranch."

"Aw, Ma!" Jonathon whined. "I coulda thayed at the ranch!"

"You always have a good time with the Spencers," she said. "And Asa looks forward to your company."

"I think that'th 'cuz Mizz Thpencer ain't a very good checker player," Jonathon confided to his new friend.

Amusement turned up one corner of Brock's full lips, giving Abby another hitch in her chest. "Is that so?" he asked.

"This way Jonathon only goes across the hall, and I don't have to take him out in the cold to bring him home and put him to bed."

"I can see the advantage to that," he replied. Relief flowed through Abby, since she'd been fully expecting Brock to insist on staying or on taking Jonathon back to the Kincaid ranch. Surprisingly, he seemed to have accepted her explanation and her wishes. "Do you have a room all your own?" he asked the boy.

"Yup. Wanna thee it?"

Brock stood, his revolvers coming into view above the tabletop and making Abby queasy. He'd hung his coat over the back of a chair as if he'd been invited to stay. "Sure do."

Jonathon cheerfully ran ahead and flung aside the pleated fabric that covered his doorway. "Here'th my bed an' my chetht o' drawerth and my box o' writin' paper an' them are bookth I'm learnin' to read."

Abby's gaze followed Brock's broad back as he dwarfed their kitchen, the hall and the doorway to Jonathon's room with his height and breadth. His intrusion into their home, their life, made her feel helpless, and she hated the feeling. He had her over a barrel and he knew it. They both knew it.

So she stood, waiting nervously for him to decide that he'd done enough bullying for one day and be gone.

A knock sounded on the outside door behind her, and she stifled a startled shriek. She opened the door to Everett, who stood at the top of the stairs, his wool collar pulled up around his ears against the wind.

"I thought you had a customer, but it's all dark downstairs."

"No, I closed up."

"There's a horse out front."

Boots sounded on the floor of the hall. Everett's dark gaze traveled beyond Abby's shoulder. He hid his surprise well, turning and gently closing the door behind him.

"Don't think we've met," Brock said, striding forward and stating his name.

"Everett Matthews," he said, removing his glove to take the hand Brock offered.

"Everett is my fiancé," Abby managed to say, then watched Brock for a reaction.

"Well," he said, his face void of emotion. He took his coat from the chair. "I'll be going now. Have a nice evening."

"Where'th your hat, Brock?" Jonathon asked.

"Left it on my saddle, half-pint."

"Thank you for lettin' me ride your horth."

"You're welcome. We'll do it again."

Jonathon grinned jubilantly. "Hear that, Mama? Brock'th gonna let me ride hith horth again!"

"Yes, I heard. Gather your things to take to the Spencers now."

"G'night." Brock nodded at Abby and exited onto the outside stairs.

She could tell Everett didn't know what to say. He studied the door for a moment, then turned his dark gaze, almost accusingly, on Abby.

Jonathon appeared with his bundle, and Abby walked him across the hall to the Spencers.

"There's my checker buddy!" Asa called from beside the hard-coal heater identical to the one that kept Abby and Jonathon's quarters cozily warm.

"I made Jonathon some bread pudding," Daisy said with a cheerful smile.

"You spoil him," Abby admonished.

"Well, we have to have somebody to spoil, don't we? Have a good time."

"Thank you."

Everett walked ahead as they descended the narrow stairs, and Abby clutched his shoulder for support in the dark. They reached the ground and walked toward the hotel, several buildings away and across the street.

Once inside the Carlton, Everett hung their coats, and the two of them were promptly seated in the dining room. Most of the tables were full, but Amos Carlton had extra help on Saturday evenings.

"News has it Amos's wife is barely hanging on," Everett reported. "He wired her sister back East."

"Poor thing." The woman had been ill for some time. "I'll make a point to send her a little something."

Abby knew everything on the menu, but read it anyway, avoiding the subject she knew Everett would bring up next, though the queries were inevitable. When the waitress took their orders, Everett ordered pot roast, potatoes and carrots, as she knew he would. Pot roast was the special, and Everett was frugal.

"I was quite surprised to see Kincaid in your home," he said finally.

Not any more surprised than she was to have him there. Her stomach fluttered nervously. "I'm sure you were. Jonathon wanted to show him his horse collection."

"I don't know if it's wise, allowing Jonathon to get friendly with the man."

Abby was certain it wasn't wise, but she was helpless to keep Brock from his son. She shrugged.

"I can't see as how this will do anything except confuse our relationship," Everett pressed. "Jonathan has to get used to a new father."

Her heart raced at his words, and her mind went blank for a moment.

"Kincaid's presence is only going to muddy the waters while I'm trying to be his father."

Of course he didn't know Brock was Jonathon's father. He was referring to himself! The waitress brought strong tea and she laced hers with cream, something about the thought of Everett being Jonathon's father making her uneasy. She wanted a father for him, so she should just be thankful for his concern and willingness to take on a ready-made family.

"You could be referring to half the population of Whitehorn when you refer to him as Kincaid," she said lightly, without touching the subject.

"No one even knows where he's been all these years," Everett continued quietly, flattening a palm on the tabletop.

Abby finally found her voice. "I heard him mention he'd been a U.S. Marshal."

"There's a fine line between marshals and hired guns," he replied.

His comment brought even more awkwardness to their meal. Their food arrived and Abby tasted her glazed chicken.

Several minutes later, Everett laid down his fork with a clank. She turned her head and followed his scowling gaze to the patrons being seated several tables away. Accompanying Will and Lizzie Kincaid was Brock. Big as you please, he folded himself onto a chair directly facing their table. The three Kincaids got settled, greeted neighbors on either side of their table and glanced around.

Brock's gaze unerringly met Abby's. One side of his mouth inched up in that provocatively irritating manner, and he gave her an exaggerated nod.

Her heart jumped.

Abby didn't want to greet him civilly, but Everett was watching her reaction, so she returned the nod with a stiff smile and jerked her head back to their own table. The nerve of the man! He'd known she was going out to dinner and he'd deliberately come here to torment her!

Her chicken tasted like sawdust, and she had trouble swallowing the delicately browned potatoes. All she had to do was turn her head and she'd find him staring at her. Using every ounce of her resolve, she ate her entire meal without glancing over once. Why did he have the power to make her heart race so erratically, then stop altogether? Why did she want to know where he was looking and who he was talking to? That he held so much control over her was a revelation she would have rather never faced.

The waitress cleared their plates and brought them fresh tea, and Abby sipped hers as though she hadn't a care in the world.

"He's making himself right at home," Everett said.

"Whitehorn *is* his home," she replied, hoping Everett hadn't noted her wry tone. And Whitehorn being Brock's home *was* the problem. Most of the problem, anyway. She could have continued her life the way it had been, married Everett and been perfectly happy to never set eyes on Brock again. Instead he'd come back and deliberately turned her world upside down at every opportunity. Where was this going from here? She couldn't begin to imagine. She gave Everett a sweet smile for no reason, and he became flustered under her gaze.

They finished their tea and sat speaking about the weather and the telegraph news for nearly half an hour, as though Everett, too, was loath to let Brock run them off. Finally, Everett pushed his chair back and stood, coming around to assist Abby.

She refused to look again, though she could feel Brock's gaze on her back the whole time she walked to the foyer and slipped into her coat. The cold night air felt gloriously refreshing on her heated skin. Everett took her arm and guided her over the treacherously icy boardwalks.

"Thank you for dinner," she told him at the top of the stairs. "Would you like to come in?"

"Just for a moment. It's getting late."

It wasn't late at all, but rarely did he come inside to be alone with her. She had always appreciated his thoughtfulness, knowing he was protecting her reputation, but she grew lonely, too, and craved adult company on these long winter nights. Her relationship with Jed had been warm, but never passionate or truly personal. Sometimes she imagined a man who would wrap his strong arms around her, kiss her with more than duty or perfunctoriness.

They stood inside the door in their coats, and Everett leaned toward her as was expected of him. Abby raised her face and accepted his kiss. She was older now, wiser and more mature. Not having to hide her relationship with Everett stole the excitement she'd known in her impetuous youth. Those were factors in the lack of passion they shared, and she was glad for it. Not being crazy in love allowed her to make better choices. What was passion compared to stability, anyway?

When they pulled apart, he kissed her cheek and went down the stairs. His form disappeared into the darkness beyond the gas lamp, and she closed the door, leaning her forehead against the cool wood and blotting out acute disappointment. She had herself to blame. She'd allowed

Brock liberties before marriage. She had never been courted properly, and the proper way was slowly. Everett was a gentleman.

Abby remained at the Spencers' for over an hour, since Jonathon wouldn't let Asa stop reading to him. Daisy chatted to Abby about this and that.

Descriptive words caught her attention, and she realized the story Asa read was one of the many dime novels glorifying Jack Spade, the legendary gunfighter. She had never told Asa not to read such a book to her son, so he wasn't going against her directions, but the man should know better than to fill a boy's head with such violent tales!

"Mama, did you know how Jack Thpade got that name? Cauth he leavth a jack of thpadeth on the body of the bad men he killth."

She had never heard about the gunman leaving a jack of spades on his victims, and she didn't think Jonathon had needed to know it, either. She would talk to Asa the following day and let him know she disapproved of his bedtime stories.

"Jack Thpade ith in town, Mama, did you know that?"

She took her son home and put him to bed, then undressed herself and climbed beneath her heavy quilt. An hour later, she had barely begun to doze when Jonathon's cough woke her. She checked on him, finding his skin warm and his hair damp. After bathing his face with cool water, she sat at his side until he slept peacefully, then tiredly lay down beside him.

The following morning, Jonathon was still warm and the cough nagged. Abby went to get Daisy, who'd been preparing for church, to sit with Jonathon while she went to Laine's. The town council had been looking for a new doctor since Dr. Leland's death. Harry Talbert took care of teeth and boils and the like, but Abby had complete confidence in her Chinese friend's herbal remedies.

"I will come," Laine said after Abby woke her and told her of Jonathon's symptoms. She packed several small cloth bags and a few tiny bottles in a basket, and they trudged along the paths in the shin-deep snow and up the flight of stairs.

"It's nothing serious," she told Abby, after checking Jonathon over, looking in his eyes and mouth, and listening to his heart and lungs. "The fever will run its course and he will feel better. I will make a tonic for his cough, though. He will sleep better, then."

"Thank you, Laine. You've attended Jonathon through all his childhood ailments, and I wouldn't trust a licensed physician as much as you."

"Thank goodness many of the families in Whitehorn feel the same." Laine grinned. "And my father is none the wiser about the nice nest egg I have set aside."

Her father didn't approve of her practicing herbal medicine on the townspeople, so over the last few years she had deposited her earnings in the bank without his knowledge.

Abby sat at the kitchen table while Laine crushed herbs into a fine power and added tinctures from her bag. "You and I aren't like most women this far West," Abby told her. "We aren't dependent on a man for our livelihood."

"Your inheritance is not a secret, however." Laine added a few drops of boiling water to her mixture. "My savings are. But my father did not force me into the marriage he wanted for me, and for that I am thankful. I work as hard as my brother, and unlike many fathers, mine sees my value." She poured the mixture into a bottle and corked it. "Your father forced you to marry your husband?" she asked quietly.

Abby nodded.

"I cannot imagine how difficult that must have been for you."

"Doing what I did, I didn't give him much choice, I guess," she replied with a shrug.

"You believe you lost your head with Mr. Brock because you were young and foolish?" her friend asked.

"Definitely young and foolish," Abby agreed. "Stupid."

"And if you could live it over, you would do it differently?"

"I would do it differently. But I'm not sorry about Jonathon. He's the best thing that ever happened to me."

"Is it not the same regarding Mr. Brock?"

Abby frowned. "What do you mean?"

"Was he not young and foolish, too?"

"I didn't carry a gun and look for trouble," she said.

"If he had it to live over, would he not do it differently?"

"He *still* flaunts those guns," Abby declared. "He never learned anything!"

"Abby, most every man I see carries a gun. This land where we live requires them to do so for protection."

"Using them against bears and cougars is one thing," Abby protested. "Shooting people is different."

"We need protection from people as well as animals." Laine sighed. "I am talking about you and Mr. Brock, and you are avoiding the discussion by talking about guns."

Abby stood and pulled out ingredients to bake bread. "I'm not going to agree with you, so stop trying to make me change my mind."

Laine shrugged. "All right. Let me show you how to give this to Jonathon."

They dropped the subject, and Laine stayed for another

hour, helping Abby knead dough and entertaining Jonathon. Finally, she said her goodbyes and hurried out.

While the dough was rising, Abby heated water and washed her hair, then sat before the stove, drying the heavy length.

A light tap sounded on the outside door, startling her into dropping her brush with a clatter. She picked it up and hurried forward, expecting Laine to have returned. Instead, Brock stood in the cold, wearing a stern expression she had begun to recognize and resent. His handsomely carved features softened slightly as he took in her loose hair flowing over her shoulders and down her back.

"What do you want?" she asked.

"I came to see Jonathon. I heard he was sick."

"How on earth could you have heard that?"

"Daisy told Will and Lizzie, and they told me when they got home from church."

"Of course," Abby said, throwing up the hand with the hairbrush.

Brock glanced at the brush and back at her hair, and her face grew warm, remembering. He'd loved her hair. All those years ago, he'd loosened her braid and run his fingers through the tresses, bringing them to his face, touching her skin through her hair.

He obviously remembered, too, the recognition changing his features and darkening the blue of his eyes.

Abby's pulse beat faster. She became aware of her femininity as she hadn't for a long time, feeling his gaze touch her hair and face and infuse her with sudden heat.

As she moved back and allowed him to shut out the cold, the rustle of her skirts seemed loud, the fit of her modest dress suddenly revealing a woman's body.

And he noticed. Lord help her, he noticed.

## Chapter Five

Brock allowed the warmth of the room, the yeasty smell in the air and the seductive beauty of the woman to silence him for a full minute. Seven years had changed her. Her shape had blossomed; her breasts beneath the plain fabric dress had become more rounded and womanly than he recalled. Her face had lost its charming girlish roundness, and now delicately modeled bone structure and pearly skin characterized her haunting beauty.

And that hair. The shining, fragrant mass aroused memories whose erotic images shot a reaction from his brain to his loins. His palms itched with the urge to touch the silken skein and know if it still felt the way he remembered.

Her luminous green eyes were shimmering with a combination of confusion and something he could have sworn was desire, and when he focused his attention on her mouth, he thought her breathing stopped.

He'd never forgotten the softness of those lips, the heated passion of the young woman or the exquisite pleasure of hot slick intimacy with her. Her nearness still had the same disturbing effect on him. For a split second he fought light-headedness, until his thoughts were under control. His body didn't obey as quickly, so he stoically ignored it.

"What's wrong with him?" he demanded, more roughly than he'd intended.

She blinked and licked her lips. He refocused his gaze on her shoulder, but it was covered by that glorious hair and didn't provide much distraction. "Nothing serious. Laine made him some medicine."

"Laine? What's she doing giving him medicine?"

"She has treated Jonathon and me both since he was very small. She's an herbal healer. There's no doctor in Whitehorn."

"I could ride to Butte for a doctor."

"That's not necessary. I trust her implicitly."

"She's done this before?"

"Many times."

"I want to see him."

"He's resting now—"

"Mama, who'th here?"

Brock shrugged out of his coat and hooked it on a peg beside the door. His hat followed.

He turned to find her frowning. "Something wrong?"

"I believe you should have respect for my wishes when you're in my home. If you insist on coming here and seeing Jonathon, then I would prefer that you didn't wear those weapons."

Brock's hand went to the butt of one revolver in its holster. She had every right to ask him to remove them in her home. She simply didn't know what she was asking. He'd have been more comfortable removing his clothing.

But knowing how she felt, and knowing, too, that her strong feelings involved a fear for Jonathon, Brock unfastened the buckle and removed the holster. He was perfectly justified in doing so, he told himself, but he never knew when he would need the .45s, and their weighty assurance had been a constant companion for years.

Brock hung the holster over a hook beside his coat, still in plain reach if he had to grab a revolver in a hurry, but out of reach for a little boy.

"Thank you," she said softly. The lilac scent of her hair surrounded him like a fragrant, sensual cloud as he moved past her and entered the hallway, then Jonathon's room.

The child lay on his bed, covers pulled to his armpits, and he wore a dismal expression of boredom.

"Hey, half-pint. How ya doing?"

"Not too good. Mama thayth I have to be in bed all day. I told her I feel better. Laine gave me thtuff and I ain't coughing too much now."

Brock felt the boy's forehead and found it warm but not alarmingly so. "Your mother knows best," he assured him. "Rest is what you need."

"But it'th boring!"

"I know, partner."

"Will you thtay and play with me?"

"Sure." He seated himself on the bed. "It's been a lot of years since I played, so you'll have to remind me how."

Jonathon sat up. "Yippee!" Immediately a cough attacked him.

Brock gently pushed him back against his pillows. "Don't get excited, you're supposed to be resting."

"You won't go nowhere, right?"

"Right."

"We could pretend theth are wild," Jonathon said, reaching for the carved horses beside his bed. Brock stretched an arm and easily retrieved the figures for him. "And that we're cowboyth who hafta round 'em up!"

"Okay." It wasn't so difficult playing once Jonathon

slipped into his imagination mode and Brock figured out he was supposed to change his voice from one cowboy to the next and call commands to Jonathon's pretend cowboy characters. Somehow he became the leader of a trail drive, and was supposed to show the horses where to eat and sleep.

One of Jonathon's wild horses got away, and he made all kinds of whinnies and shouts in getting him back to the herd on the patchwork quilt.

Brock laughed at the boy's creative antics, mesmerized by his freckles, delicate ears and small hands, captivated by blue eyes that sparkled with delight and mischief, and completely charmed by his creativity and his delightful speech. Brock had never been around many children, but he believed this one to be one of the brightest and most handsome he'd ever seen.

Abby had done a wonderful job of raising him. Jonathon was polite and confident, smart as a whip, naturally curious and outspoken. It was obvious he'd been guided with love and discipline, and Brock gave Abby due credit.

But the boy needed more than book knowledge and gentle guidance from a mother. He needed a man in his life, too, one to teach him how to train horses and hunt food and survive in this brutal land. The man Abby had eaten dinner with didn't fit the image of a father who would teach a boy those skills—not any boy, let alone Brock's *son*. The thought of Matthews taking over as Jonathon's father stuck in Brock's craw.

Horse in hand, Jonathon finally leaned back against the pillows, his eyelids heavy. He made a few halfhearted gallops across the covers before letting the carved animal fall still. His luminous blue gaze rose to Brock's in sleepy seriousness. "You won't leave, right?"

At the knowledge that the boy wanted him there, something in Brock's chest swelled almost painfully. "I won't leave," he promised, his voice choked.

"Even if I thleep."

"Even if you sleep. I'll wait right here."

Jonathon studied him, his eyelids drooping lower and lower, until finally they remained closed.

Brock took the opportunity to observe the delicate veins in his temples and the sprinkling of freckles across his nose. Jonathon's fair hair fell in a disheveled tumble over his forehead.

Brock raised his hand to brush the locks back from the child's brow, then stared in amazement at his trembling fingers. The moment seemed to extend unnaturally long. His hands never shook. He had stared down cold-blooded killers with total composure. His life had depended on nerves of steel for so long that any show of weakness had become intolerable.

Now here he was, shaking like a green kid in his first shoot-out, unsure of whatever threat this was that had a more frightening effect than all the outlaws he'd faced and conquered.

Tenderly, he combed the silky hair back, then stared at his blunt, dark-skinned fingers against the ivory skin of the boy's cheek. Jonathon's skin was softer than anything Brock had ever touched before—except maybe... He drew his hand away. This boy's mother. Her skin had been incredibly satinlike.

The image of Abby's fiancé rose in his mind. A handsome enough man, Brock supposed. Clean, well-dressed. A dandified city man through and through, and the world needed city men, it did. His own brother, Will, was a banker, and his profession took nothing away from his manliness. Brock couldn't fault Abby's intended for his job.

Neither did he want to imagine the man exploring the

satiny contours of her body, so he clamped his will down tight on that disgusting image and corralled his runaway thoughts.

Careful not to wake Jonathon, Brock slipped the horse from his small fingers, gathered the others and placed them all on the stand beside the bed. The Watsons didn't seem to be lacking anything. This room held heavy, well-made furniture, and the bed was more comfortable than the one Brock had been sleeping on at the ranch. Each time he'd seen Jonathon, the boy had been nicely dressed, and he owned a warm coat and boots. So far the only thing he didn't seem to have that he wanted was a horse. Obviously that wasn't because Abby couldn't afford one.

Hardware was a lucrative business, and this store was the only one of its kind for a hundred miles.

Footsteps sounded behind him, and Brock turned to see Abby crossing the room toward the bed. She pulled up the covers and smoothed Jonathon's hair back much as Brock had, but as a caress when performed by her. She had braided her hair, and the thick rope hung down her back. A crisp white apron had been tied over a plain, high-necked blue dress. The exotic scent of her hair filled the room.

"He needs his sleep," she said softly.

Brock nodded, then took a deep breath. "I promised I wouldn't leave."

She straightened and shot him a surprised look.

"He asked me not to leave, even if he fell asleep. I said I'd stay right here."

Her brows lowered in angry frustration. "You had no right to do that."

"It made him go to sleep."

She glanced around the room, avoiding his eyes. "And now what?"

"Don't worry about me. I'll just sit right here until he wakes up."

"He'll probably sleep for hours."

"I don't mind." Just then his stomach growled, reminding him he hadn't taken time to eat before he'd hurried away from the ranch.

Abby clasped and unclasped her hands. "You haven't eaten."

"I can go a long while without food."

She gave her head a small shake. "Not at my house you won't go without eating. That's foolish. The bread is still warm and I have ham to slice. I haven't eaten, either. Come into the kitchen."

After glancing at Jonathon's soundly sleeping form, Brock stood and followed her.

She gestured for him to sit at the table, and he did so, watching her set out two blue-patterned plates and checkered napkins.

Efficiently, she sliced fragrant bread and ham on a cutting board, then brought out a wedge of cheese and cut it into thick chunks.

Her kitchen even held a barrel-shaped, cast-iron ice box, from which she drew a pitcher of milk, pouring them each a cold glass. One convenience to living in town, he supposed, was ice delivery. The Kincaid ranch had a well cooler, which did the same job, but too often froze in winter. When it did, milk and butter were kept on the enclosed back porch.

She offered him bread, butter and ham, and he made a sandwich. "How did—" The words *your husband* wouldn't push past his lips. "How did Jed die?"

She seated herself across from him, as though resigned to his company. "Caught a fever two years back. He was a healthy man, but it took him in just a week."

*Did you love him?* The question burned in his gut.

Brock watched her make a sandwich and daintily slice it into quarters. "Was Jonathon attached to him?"

She looked up. "Jonathon believed Jed was his father. What do you think?"

"Well, I don't know. Some fathers and sons are close, others aren't."

"Jed was good to him." She sat holding a square of bread and meat, but not tasting it. "He was good to me. He gave us everything we needed."

*Did you love him?* Why did he even care? "You have nice things," Brock agreed, glancing around.

"I didn't marry Jed for his money," she said defiantly. "My father brought me here and told me this was what I was going to do. It just so happened Jed made a good living."

"And left it all to you."

"I was his wife. Don't act like I planned to marry him and inherit his money. I didn't kill him. I didn't want him to die."

"I never said you did."

"You should be glad that Jonathon has been well provided for."

Brock wouldn't deny that. "I am."

"I never asked your family for anything."

He ate solemnly, thinking about her words, mulling over her anger. Finally Abby bit into her meal and chewed.

"Abby," he said at last. "Everything you say to me is accusatory. As if I knew I had a son and abandoned him."

She swallowed and took a sip of her milk.

He pointed out, "I didn't know about Jonathon."

She blotted her upper lip on her napkin. "If you had known, would it have made a difference?"

He'd thought the question over a hundred times since his return. "I don't know," he answered honestly. He wiped his fingers and laced them above his plate. "Even if I had stayed, even if I had known about Jonathon, what about how you felt toward me? How you still feel toward me? You hated my guts, Abby, and you wouldn't have changed those feelings overnight. You haven't changed them in nearly eight years. If I hadn't run off like I did, can you say you'd have wanted to let me be a father to him?"

She blinked and looked down at her plate. "You could have stayed to find out."

"The only reason I'm here now is because you're afraid I'll spill the truth and embarrass you. Maybe make you lose your shot at marriage to the dandy."

Some of the color seemed to drain from her face.

"So don't constantly harangue me about my supposed desertion. You told me you hated me and I left. Simple."

Simple, he said. *Simple.* The word festered in Abby's head. Nothing about the two of them had ever been simple, least of all her feelings on or about the day he'd killed Guy. She had been mad about Brock, had worshipped him, would have done anything for him. Blindly, exclusively, desperately in love with him she'd been.

She'd excused his rowdy behavior, his drinking and carousing as the actions of a confused young man who'd lost his father and was coming to terms with his identity in his family. She'd overlooked any rash talk, and his greedy passion for their lovemaking had been flattering and euphoric. The killing capability had been there all along, and she'd been too stupid to recognize it.

Her brother had been gunned down in the street, his life's blood had ebbed into the dirt, and she had deluded herself into thinking she'd loved the man responsible. Perhaps she'd even played a part in allowing Brock to think he could do no wrong, to imagine that she'd forgive him no matter what foolishness or atrocity he performed. She'd overlooked every bad thing before.

Simple. Her every ideal and dream had been wrapped around the vulnerable heart she'd offered him.

She hadn't been able to tell her father about her and Brock. She was too ashamed, too hurt. Even if Brock had stayed, she couldn't have revealed her weakness to the world. *Look, this man planted a baby in me without intentions of marriage, and then he killed my brother. But I love him.* No.

What had happened wasn't simple. Much as she hated to admit the truth now, he'd forced her to acknowledge that her accusations where Jonathon was concerned were small-minded. She had shouted angry, hurtful things at Brock that day, perhaps helping to drive him away. But she wouldn't admit a mistake to him.

"Abby," he said softly, and her stomach fluttered at her name on his lips. "I see now that I didn't act like a gentleman back then."

She said nothing, thinking of how she'd craved his ungentlemanly behavior.

"It was wrong of me to take liberties when I hadn't considered getting married."

Heat spread up her cheeks. Was he admitting he'd never intended to marry her? Or only that he'd never thought that far ahead?

"I did a lot of things back then that I regret," he continued.

So he regretted "taking liberties" with her. Meaning he was sorry he'd gotten her with child, no doubt.

Abby stood and placed a kettle of water on the stove for tea. How was it he still had the power to create confusion and inflict pain? Why did she allow him to affect her this way? Emotion surged in her heart, pangs of hurt and guilt and piercing regret. She struggled against the tears of humiliation rising to flood her eyes.

Getting herself under control, she brewed tea, poured them each a cup and placed one before Brock. Remembering the pumpkin pie she'd bought, she cut him a slice and sat back down.

He took a drink of the tea and grimaced. Holding the cup aloft, he asked, "Does Matthews drink this stuff?"

"Tea? Yes."

He shook his head and set down the cup.

"There's cream. And sugar."

Finishing the dessert, he pushed the plate back and ignored the tea. "We might as well make a truce," he suggested.

"What do you mean?"

"I'm not going anywhere. I'll be visiting Jonathon and having him out to the ranch. You and I will be seeing a lot of each other."

"How am I supposed to explain that to Everett?" she asked sharply.

"That's not my problem," he replied.

The man was infuriating. Always thinking of only himself. "Nothing is ever your problem, is it?"

He leaned forward. "That's exactly the kind of talk I want you to cut."

She folded her napkin and set it aside. "Now you're going to tell me how to talk?"

"I'm going to tell you how *not* to talk, anyway. And you're going to stop talking as though I'm irresponsible."

"Aren't you?"

"You have no idea what I am or who I am."

"I'm sure you're right about that. I thought I knew once, but I was wrong then, too."

He tossed his napkin down in a heap. "Are you this hateful toward all the men in your life, or just me?"

The insult burned and she wanted to cut him to the quick. He made her feel hateful. He did this to her, and she resented him for turning her into someone she couldn't stand. She stood and picked up their plates, carrying them to the enamel pan. In a huff, she scraped off a curl of soap and poured the remaining hot water from the kettle over their soiled dishes.

"Thanks for the meal," he said from his seat behind her.

She plunged her hands into the sudsy water and scrubbed energetically.

"I'll just go sit beside Jonathon," he said.

"There's a rocking chair in the other room. You can take that in beside his bed." She didn't care whether or not he was comfortable, but her manners wouldn't allow her to not offer.

His boots sounded on the wooden floor, then muted on the carpet in the hallway. Abby washed and dried the dishes, giving herself time to calm down.

A tap sounded on the outside door, startling her. She opened it and discovered Everett.

He pushed past her and her heart thundered. What would happen when he discovered Brock here?

"I was surprised you missed church this morning."

"Jonathon had a cough. We stayed home so he could rest. Laine gave him something and he's sleeping. Here, let me take your coat."

He turned around and when he did, she ripped off her apron and threw it over Brock's wraps and gun belt, then turned back quickly to assist Everett in slipping off his coat. She hung it and draped the neck scarf that followed over another hook.

"Have you eaten?" she asked.

"Yes, thank you."

"Well, let's go into the sitting room then." She led the

way, keeping her body between him and Jonathon's room. As they passed, she made sure the curtain wasn't gaping open. *Please, Brock, stay in there and stay quiet!*

"I won't stay long," Everett said unnecessarily. He never stayed long, unwilling as he was to harm her reputation. "I just thought I'd see that you were all right."

"We're fine."

He seated himself on the divan, and Abby took a chair across from him.

"Would you care for tea?" she asked.

"No, thank you."

She folded her hands in her lap and they glanced at one another and away. Abby had tried unsuccessfully to imagine him living here with her. He had a room at Mrs. Harroun's boardinghouse, so they'd decided that he would move here until the time came that they were ready for their own house.

This had been Jed's home and these were his furnishings, and she'd added her own touches over the years. Jed had been satisfied living over his business, and Abby had acclimated herself to his life and his home. They'd been comfortable together, and Jonathon had filled out their family.

Everett's company wasn't comfortable. Prolonged silences screamed for someone to speak. She was always relieved for him to ramble on about local happenings and news he'd passed along the telegraph wires, for it took away the pressure for her to come up with small talk.

He chatted a bit, discussing a reported railroad heist to the west and the latest on Amos Carlton's sickly wife. "Sheriff Kincaid is keeping an eye on the man calling himself Linc Manley. He hasn't actually denied being Jack Spade, and that's keeping suspicion high. He seems to have no purpose in Whitehorn except to gamble nightly."

Sheriff Kincaid was James Kincaid, Brock's cousin. "Why doesn't the sheriff just ask him to leave before there's trouble?"

"The law can't just run off every stranger without sure cause. The man seems harmless enough."

"But what type of unsavory people is he likely to draw? I don't think we can be careful enough in protecting our town from his kind."

"He *is* good for commerce. The saloons have been full every night since he's been here."

"Commerce!" she scoffed. "Drinking and gambling aren't respectable businesses. Sounds like trouble waiting to happen, if you ask me." As soon as she said the words she remembered Brock's asking if she was hateful to all the men in her life, and she could have bitten her tongue. But facts were facts.

Everett changed the subject, and after a few more minutes, he stood and excused himself. Grateful, Abby hurried ahead of him to get his coat and hold it open. He turned his back to her and accepted her assistance. "Thank you. Have a pleasant evening."

"I shall do that." She closed the door behind him and wilted against the wood in relief. The last thing she needed was for him to see Brock here and get suspicious. Lord, what if someone saw Brock arrive or leave, and told Everett? Where was Brock's horse? she wondered belatedly.

"Jonathon's hungry," Brock said from the kitchen doorway.

Abby spun to face him. "Where is your horse?"

"At the livery. I walked." He rested a palm against the door frame. "I held Jonathon off until your guest left."

"Thank you."

"I'm not the ogre you think I am."

She yanked her apron from over his guns. "I'll heat some soup. Ask him if he'd like bread and cheese."

Brock left and returned a moment later. "He said yes, please."

Stirring soup in a pan on the stove, Abby nodded that she'd heard him.

"He's not your type."

She turned her head. "Excuse me?"

"Matthews. He doesn't seem like your type."

"And how would you know what my type is?"

"I don't know. Just seems to me that since you didn't have a choice with your last husband, you'd be particular with the next one."

"I am particular. In case you haven't noticed, he's a perfect gentleman."

"Oh, I've noticed."

His tone was mocking, and she didn't care for it. "And he doesn't have to wear guns to prove anything to anyone."

Brock crossed the kitchen and stepped close beside her. "What do you think I'm proving by wearing guns, Abby?"

His voice from so close unnerved her.

"You start these arguments, you know," he said.

"But you continue them without any effort whatsoever on my part."

"I'm just trying to figure out what you see in him."

"I'm sure that escapes you."

"Does your pulse beat faster when he stands this near?"

Abby's heart hammered against her rib cage. "That's none of your business."

"Does the smell of your hair make him want to lean close and fill his lungs with you?"

She dropped the wooden spoon into the pan and fished for the handle. "I'm sure I wouldn't know."

"He's never said so?"

"Certainly not."

"Of course not. Does your breath come hard and fast when he touches you?" Brock touched her neck with a featherlight caress, and she couldn't draw a breath.

"Do his kisses start a fire in your veins that spreads through your whole body?" His warm breath against her neck made gooseflesh rise along her shoulders. She closed her eyes and felt her nipples harden into tight buds. The pleasurable sensation washed over her, gripping her in its bone-deep intensity. Part of her realized how much she'd missed these feelings, but another part was shocked at her wanton response to Brock's aggressive behavior.

Fighting the mortifying hunger he aroused so easily, she gathered her composure and inched away, wrapping a towel around the handle and removing the broth from the stove. She carried the pan to the mug on the table with trembling hands.

"Here." He took the pan from her, brushing her fingers with his strong, callused ones in the process. Abby watched him perform the task with steady hands, feeling the heat from his body, recognizing the heady smell of his shaving soap and the fainter scent of horse and leather. He poured the savory-smelling beef broth into the mug without spilling a drop.

Her heart pounded so hard she could sense it thrumming in her ears, her fingertips, the very core of her woman's body. She couldn't look away from him now, her greedy gaze climbing from his strong hand, up the length of his cotton-clad arm to his broad chest...to his eyes, a sultry, hungry blue she remembered well...his mouth...and she could barely breathe at the remembered delights of those lips....

# Chapter Six

His hot gaze caressed her face, her mouth, and the blatant desire in his expression sapped her resolve, drew her instead, like a nail to a magnet. Abby didn't realize she'd moved, but in the space of a heartbeat she was in his arms, pressed against the hard, delicious length of his body. She met his mouth greedily, tasting the heady maleness of him, glorying in the sensual slide of heat and texture as their tongues met and melded in an enthusiastic dance.

Every place their bodies touched, she was fiercely aware of him—of the slight scrape of beard against her tender cheek, her breasts crushed against his hard chest, his biceps beneath her exploring palm, his arousal through layers of denim and cotton and crinoline. Abby raised a hand and thrust her fingers into the cool thickness of his hair, lifted her other palm to the front of his shirt and pressed against hard muscle in an explorative caress.

His chest and shoulders were broader, his arms more muscled, but she still fit against him perfectly.

Years fell away. Everything that had happened since their first physical encounter was seared into temporary oblivion by the explosive heat of this passion they shared. Abby pressed both hands to his cheeks and kissed him hard. She pulled away long enough to breathe, and their combined breaths sounded ragged and hot in the silent room. This was never enough with him. She craved more, needed more of the delightful indulgence she found in his embrace.

He pressed his hips against her rhythmically and her eyes fell shut. He turned his face and darted his tongue against her palm. Her entire body quivered and wept with pleasure. She ran her thumb over his lip, touched his teeth. He nipped the pad and released it.

Their lips met again, this time more tenderly, this time with a care for the artful finesse of the act. He kissed the corner of her mouth, caught her lower lip, a sensuous move that had never failed to elicit a moan, and didn't now.

He caught her cry with another kiss, tormenting her until her body trembled and her knees grew too weak to support her weight.

Abby wanted to drop back to the floor and pull him hard against her. Nothing would suffice now but to have more of him, feel more of him, relish the heat of his flesh, taste him, take him....

She took a moment to get her bearings, thinking of where they were, where they could go.... His lips nibbled the column of her neck in exquisite torture, but she opened her eyes.

Her kitchen came into focus. Yellow-and-white gingham curtains at the window. Brock's coat and hat hanging by the door, his gun belt slung over a hook beside them.

Reality crashed down on her like a wave of ice water.

She pushed at his shoulders. "Stop."

Brock's arms were a band of steel around her.

"Stop!" she said more forcefully, and pulled back.

His grip loosened. He studied her with passion-glazed eyes, and blinked as if trying to orient himself.

Abby disentangled her limbs and took two steps backward, reaching for the back of a chair for support. She thrust a hand into her hair and caught her breath. What kind of woman was she that she fell so easily into the same old trap of sensual ensnarement? Where had propriety and sensibility flown?

She wasn't a foolish young girl with unrealistic dreams. She was a mother, responsible for herself and her child, and she knew better than to think that anything more than momentary physical satisfaction—and perhaps even a baby—could result from her senseless lack of judgment.

Humiliation welled inside her and scorched her cheeks. She jerked her gaze up to his. *This* man! Not her kind and gentle husband! Not her respectful, amenable fiancé, but *this* man! This corrupt, irreverent traitor had the power to unleash these stunning feelings and make her greedy for more. She covered her face with a shaky hand.

"Mama? You bringin' me thoup?" Jonathon called.

She heard Brock pick up the tray she'd prepared and carry it toward the other room.

Abby stood, still gripping the chair, still hiding her face and still castigating herself for her loss of control. She *hated* that Brock knew her weakness. And he knew. Oh, he knew. She'd practically torn his clothes from him and straddled him on her kitchen floor! That picture brought another flash of heat, and to cast it aside she dipped a cloth in cool water and pressed it against her cheeks.

She'd never dreamed this could happen. She detested the man. She did. She hated what he stood for and what he'd done. Climbing all over the man who had killed her brother was more than disloyal, it was sick. She must be depraved to have let that happen. She should have let him go hungry. She should have let him sit there until he died of starvation, she thought irrationally.

Abby straightened her apron, smoothed her hair and

garnered all her courage to walk into that room and see to her son in the presence of that man.

Brock had tucked the curtain back over a hook, so Jonathon saw her approach. "Brock thaid you had to let the thoup cool a little bit. I like it."

She smiled weakly and seated herself on the opposite side of the bed from where Brock sat, helping Jonathon with the heavy mug.

"You okay, Mama?"

"Yes, of course."

"You look kinda funny. Maybe you got a fever, too."

Brock turned his head to look at her, but she ignored his gaze.

"No, I'm fine," she assured Jonathon. "The stove was hot, is all."

"Sit in the rocker and cool off, Abby," Brock said, his voice deliberately solicitous.

She moved to the rocking chair and watched her son eat his meal.

Brock enjoyed holding the mug for Jonathon, tearing off bits of bread and cheese and seeing him savor them. How many mealtimes had he missed? How many childhood sicknesses and sleepless nights and bedtime stories? "What's your favorite food?" he asked.

"Licorith," the boy answered immediately.

Brock chuckled. "How about your favorite food that your mama makes?"

"Mmm. I think prob'ly her fried chicken. Mama'th a real good cooker and maketh a lot of food I like."

"What's your favorite story?"

"The one where Jack Thpade trackth the bank robber through the mountainth an' hith horth dieth, an' he walkth all the way to Cheyenne with a bullet in hith leg. That prob'ly hurt."

Brock blinked. "There's a story about that?"

"Yup. Mr. Thpencer read it to me."

Brock glanced at Abby. Her lips were pursed in disapproval, but she held her silence. If she'd just found out about this, he'd bet Asa Spencer had an earful coming. "What do you think about your mama marrying Mr. Matthews?"

"Brock," Abby cautioned, finally looking at him.

"I'm just asking the boy his opinion. He can have one, can't he?"

She slanted a glance at Jonathon.

"Go ahead, Jonathon," Brock said. "What do you think of their wedding plans?"

Jonathon looked a little sheepish as he said, "Mama thaid I'd alwayth be her favorite." He handed Brock the empty mug. "Mither Matthewth don't like me very much."

Abby's brows furrowed in concern. "He likes you, dear."

Jonathon shrugged his narrow shoulders.

"Go ahead, Jonathon, speak your piece," Brock said, and cast Abby a look to silence her again.

"He only talkth to Mama," Jonathon continued, "but when he doeth talk to me, he tellth me how to thay wordth better."

"He corrects your speech?"

"Yeah. I mean yeth. Ye-*s-s*." He struggled to get out the correct sound.

Brock glanced at Abby. Looking displeased, she studied her hands in her lap. "But your mama doesn't tell you to say words better?"

"Nope. Well, I ain't th'poth to thay ain't. Uh-oh, I thaid it, din't I?" He glanced at his mother.

"That's okay," she said with an indulgent smile.

Brock had recognized the bond between mother and child from the very first, but every hour that passed pointed out how badly Everett Matthews fit in this picture. What did Abby see in him? Did she love him? How could she fall into Brock's arms and respond to him so quickly if she did? No, she didn't love Matthews.

After she took away the tray and Jonathon chattered for a while longer, Brock told him he was going to leave.

"Can you come back tomorrow?"

"I'll come back tomorrow," he promised. The wrenching desire to touch his child, to hug him close, left Brock feeling incomplete. He ruffled the boy's hair instead, but the gesture felt empty. He could hardly hug him or kiss him or Jonathon would wonder at his forwardness. This was a need Brock had never experienced. He walked away with a hollow ache in his gut.

In the kitchen, he buckled on his gun belt. "Will you keep him home from school tomorrow?"

"I don't know. I think he might need another day of rest."

"What will you do? Stay here with him?"

"I'm afraid I can't. I'd have to take him downstairs with me. I have to be in the store in the morning because Sam's been staying home with his wife until about ten."

"Sam works for you?"

She nodded. "Yes, but his wife's baby is due soon, and she's not feeling well. Her family are all back East. I could send for Laine, I suppose."

"I'll come," he said simply.

"You can't do that," she said, keeping her voice low.

"Why not? I did just fine today, didn't I?"

"As long as I was cooking and checking on him."

"I can heat up soup and slice bread," he assured her.

"It just wouldn't look right," she told him in an irritated whisper. "You can't keep coming here without people becoming suspicious."

"Matthews, you mean," he said, careful not to let the boy hear their conversation.

"Anyone!"

"Why are you marrying him?"

She blinked. "Everett?"

"Who else are you engaged to?"

"I don't owe you an explanation."

"I think you do. You're taking my son into a marriage with you, and I have a right to help decide what's best for him."

"No one knows he's your son," she whispered.

Brock tugged on his coat. Caleb had known, but had said nothing. Jonathon's hair and eyes were unmistakable clues that he was a Kincaid. Perhaps Abby was the only one fooled. He paused to look at her thoughtfully, but dared not shatter her illusion. She needed no fuel for her hatred. "*I* know."

"You can't order me around," she affirmed. "You rode out of my life and I got by the best I could. I don't want to be alone. I have a right to marry and be happy."

Brock took his hat down and curled the brim absently. "Nobody gave me any choices, Abby. I have rights, too. You do have a right to marry, I guess. But he's not going to make you happy."

"You can't say that."

"I said it." He leaned forward and emphasized the words. "He's not going to make you happy. My God, woman, you'd eat him alive."

She blinked, confusion apparent in her luminous green eyes. "What do you mean by that?"

"Think about it." He settled his hat on his head and went out, closing the door behind him.

It felt good to get away, to feel the crisp cold, to smell wood smoke and evergreen in the air. He inhaled deeply to clear his head. Turning left at the foot of the stairs, he trudged through the alley, instead of entering the street from beside the hardware store, making sure no one saw him leaving her place. It was almost surprising to find the snow around the hardware store hadn't been melted away by the heat they'd generated with those kisses. The frigid air cooled his heated face.

Since leaving all those years ago, Brock had tried to put Abby out of his mind. A man couldn't concentrate on the tasks at hand if he allowed the past to dull his senses. But she had been hard to forget. And all it had taken was seeing her again to bring it all back: the passion, the hunger, the confusion. All it had taken was to kiss her again to know that nothing had changed. The years hadn't taken away one degree of desire.

She was fooling herself about more than just believing no one knew about Jonathon's parentage. She was fooling herself to think for a moment that she'd be satisfied with a husband like Matthews. Abby needed a man to match her fire and her passion.

Being Sunday night, the saloons were closed up tight. All the talk about the man in black had Brock wondering if he shouldn't check out the situation, see who this fellow really was and what he was up to in Whitehorn. Brock decided to visit the establishments tomorrow night. He got his gray at the livery and rode for the ranch.

Abby read Jonathon a few of his storybooks before he drifted off to sleep. She was sure he was better, but one more day of rest was in order. She tidied his room, wiped the kitchen table and checked the fire in the hard-coal stove, finding tasks to keep her thoughts busy.

Finally, she went to her room and prepared for bed. She had avoided disturbing thoughts all evening, but once she'd changed into her cotton nightgown and extinguished the lamp, the troublesome memories besieged her. Sitting

on the edge of her bed, she hugged her elbows and remembered the hungry, unconstrained kisses she and Brock
had shared.

That's the way it had always been with him, sponta-
neous, natural…without the reserve she'd learned from
Jed—from Everett. She and Brock had shared a passion
without limits, one that couldn't be forgotten or dismissed.
With him lovemaking had come so very naturally, with
heat and abandon and the immeasurable joy of sweet indulgence. She couldn't forget the unbounded freedom.

Only days ago she'd reminded herself that stability was
better than passion. She'd also told herself that being older
and more mature had taken away the thrill, but she'd been
wrong. This evening had proved that. All he had to do
was touch her to make her go up in flames. His parting
words about Everett taunted her: *He's not going to make
you happy. My God, woman, you'd eat him alive.*

Brock had been talking about her physical appetites!
Hadn't he? Mortified, Abby flung herself back on her bed.
He may have meant her temperament. She'd thrown some
well-deserved, but caustic comments his way; perhaps he
didn't think Everett could hold his own in a battle of wits.
But she and Everett never argued.

They never made love, either. Never even came close.
Of course not; he was a gentleman. But shouldn't two
people preparing for marriage be eager for the physical
aspects of the union? Perhaps Everett tamped down his
eagerness for her sake. That's what she'd been assuring
herself all along. He would show more enthusiasm once
they were married.

*Does your pulse beat faster when he stands this near?*
Her heart had hammered mercilessly at her ribs at Brock's
mere presence behind her. *Does your breath come hard
and fast when he touches you?* Never. Only when Brock
touched her had she ever lost her ability to breathe evenly.

Abby's breasts tightened at the memory of his enticing words and his fiery touches. What was wrong with her that she physically desired a man she detested? *Do his kisses start a fire in your veins that spreads through your whole body?* Everett's kisses had never even set off a spark. Brock's kisses and his hard-edged lovemaking had always been a torture so sweet she craved more, craved it all. She placed her hands over her breasts and knew the only man she wanted to have touch her was the one she shouldn't want. She'd already made the mistake of letting her body rule her head where Brock was concerned.

Abby brought trembling fingers to her eyes as if she could hide from the truth. She could not make the same mistakes again. She would marry Everett and she would be content. Frustrated tears wet her fingertips. She knew the textures of Brock's strong, muscled body, had reveled in the heat of his kisses, knew the sensation of taking him deep inside her and riding out crests of intense pleasure.

Time had not erased her desire for him, for more of what they'd shared during the brief time in which her son had been conceived. The years had primed her ardor, refining it to a new degree. Her humiliation was sharp and complete. And he knew exactly what kind of effect he had on her, had used it to its fullest. He had bluntly pointed out everything that was missing between her and Everett.

At least Everett didn't make her hate herself for her lack of control. With him she retained command of her senses. She could use the discipline to her advantage. She would never make a fool of herself over her new husband.

It was none of Brock's business why she was marrying Everett. Whatever they were, her reasons were her own. She'd rationalized that Jonathon needed a man around, that she needed a companion, but if she really wanted to marry him because he didn't make her lose her head, that was her choice.

But Jonathon's words to Brock came to undermine her confidence and make her question her choices. Her son had never said anything to her about Everett not liking him...but then, she'd never asked. Brock had asked Jonathon what he was thinking and feeling, and her son had been forthright in sharing his doubts.

Brock had spent the entire afternoon and most of the evening at Jonathon's side, and he claimed he'd be back tomorrow. Everett, on the other hand, had come to see why Abby wasn't in church, and now that she thought about it, she couldn't remember him inquiring about Jonathon's health. She'd chosen him to be a father to her son, and now she questioned her choice.

Prospective brides always got the jitters, she assured herself. She would never sleep if she allowed her thoughts to run wild and these doubts to assail her, so she fought them down once again and thought about the orders she needed to place, until she fell asleep.

Brock passed Caleb's study on the way through the silent house. A light could be seen beneath the door, so he tapped softly.

"Come in."

Brock entered. "Ruth and the boys asleep?"

Caleb nodded from his seat behind his desk. "I had some papers to go over before tomorrow, and never had a chance during the day."

"Am I disturbing you?"

"Yes, thank goodness. Sit down." He got up and opened a cupboard, removing two glasses and a bottle of aged bourbon. After pouring a splash into each glass, he handed one to Brock and seated himself across from him near the glowing fireplace. "How's Jonathon?"

"He's better. Abby said her friend Laine treated his cough." He took a drink and continued, "Is the girl credible?"

"She has quite a following of believers," Caleb assured him. "The Chinese have healers like the Cheyenne. Ruth has the touch herself, you know. Let her know and she'd be glad to check on him."

Brock nodded. "He seems to be all right. Abby said he had a slight fever, but it's gone now. I'm going to go back tomorrow and stay with him."

Caleb swirled the amber liquid around in the bottom of his glass before speaking. "You're making things hard on Abby, you know."

"Are we going to have a heart-to-heart talk now?"

"Maybe. Abby made a life for herself," his brother said. "She's done the best she could raising a child alone and running a business."

"You sound just like her."

Caleb was silent for a long minute, and Brock thought of the situation his brother had been in when he had left nearly eight years ago. Caleb had married the woman he'd gotten with child, even though Marie had tricked him into bed. And he'd stuck it out, as miserable as he'd been. Brock, on the other hand, hadn't bothered to find out if he'd fathered a child or not.

"I don't want to see either one of them hurt," Caleb said at last.

"I'm not going to hurt them."

"Not deliberately. I don't want you to get hurt, either."

Brock nodded. "I know."

"What are you going to do?"

Brock finished his drink. "I'm going to look out for the boy. That's my responsibility. You understand responsibility." Zeke had been the outcome of that loveless union, but Caleb loved him with all his heart.

"At the expense of Abby's happiness?" Caleb asked, raising one brow.

"What do you want me to do? Pretend like I don't know? Deny that Jonathon is my son? I can't do that."

"I know that."

"Then what?"

"Then you're going to have to make it right."

"That's sounds about as easy as putting out a forest fire with a mouthful of spit."

"Family is family."

Brock stood and paced in front of the fire. "Even if she didn't hate the sight of me, I don't know that I'd want to marry the woman, if that's what you're thinking. She's as prickly as they come."

"You must have gotten past those prickles at one time."

"That was a long time ago. Things were different then."

"How?"

Brock shrugged.

"You loved her then?"

"I don't know. I don't think so."

"She loved you?"

Brock had never thought about Abby in terms of love, so he wasn't prepared for Caleb's provoking questions. Love had never had anything to do with what he and Abby had done together....

He didn't like to think about his life back then. He didn't like to remember the chaotic feelings and his unhappy home life and how restless he'd been and how drinking and gambling and fighting had become a purging of the anger and frustration. He wasn't proud of those times. And Abby had been part of them. A big part. But *love?*

"She seems like a woman who would have to love a man she gave herself to," Caleb said.

"What about Jed Watson?" Brock asked roughly. "Did she love him, too, then?"

"This country's hard on women," Caleb replied. "Sometimes they do what they have to do. I knew Irvin Franklin, and he was a good man, but a hard one. If he found out about Abby's condition, he wouldn't have given her a choice. I always figured he'd dragged her into town and watched until the ring was on her finger. Jed had admired Abby for some time, but he wasn't the kind of man to court a younger woman without some encouragement. Irvin knew his interest and used it to marry off his wayward daughter."

Which was exactly the way Abby had told him it had happened. If Brock accepted all that, if he believed for a moment that Abby had once loved him, then he had to accept responsibility—no, *blame*—for leaving her in that predicament.

"I don't know much about love," Brock muttered uncomfortably to his brother.

"Who does?" Caleb asked. "But I learned that you never really get your first love out of your system no matter how hard you try. Maybe there's something you need to admit to yourself."

"The voice of experience speaking?"

"Something like that. The important thing is that you're back now. And that you want to do the right thing."

Brock wished him a good night and carried a lamp to his room. The right thing had been a lot clearer when he was upholding the law or protecting someone's property. It was when the edges of right and wrong had blurred that he'd decided to cash in his chips while he was ahead and find his way home.

The right thing here was to take responsibility for the child he had fathered. He was sure of it. But how did he go about that when the child's mother wanted him to leave them alone? Caleb's disturbing talk about love had him thinking in directions he didn't want to go. Love was something stifling and manipulating, and he didn't want any part of it.

He'd asked Abby if she loved Everett. He'd wondered if she loved the man. If she'd loved her husband. Why would he care if he didn't place significance on it? Love wasn't scorching kisses and satiating sex.

Brock removed his holsters, rolled the belt and tucked it within reach beneath his bed. After undressing, he blew out the lamp and stretched out upon the mattress.

Thinking about the way he'd wanted to take care of Jonathon, the way he'd wished he could hold him, hug him, he decided that was probably more like love. That odd, tight feeling he got in his chest when he looked at the boy. He would do anything to protect his child. Brock thought back, assured of how carefully he'd burned his past and covered his tracks before returning.

Yes, he loved Jonathon. No weakness in admitting that.

He relaxed. It had been a long time since he'd spent more than a few nights in one room, since he'd taken off his guns and lain down without a revolver under his pillow. If he hadn't been absolutely certain he was not leading trouble to this place, he'd never have come back. The last thing he would ever do was bring danger to his brother's home, to the son he hadn't known about...to Abby.

But that man calling himself Linc Manley might have brought a problem to Whitehorn by not denying that he was Jack Spade. Jack Spade's reputation drew unsavory men like dung drew flies. Brock had to find out what the man was doing. He owed it to the people he loved.

* * *

Abby woke late with a splitting headache. She made herself a powder and drank it before padding back across frigid floors to her room with a pitcher of warm water.

The sound of horses and a wagon outside drew her to the window, where she peered down at the bulging delivery wagon. Tom Meeks and his sons had arrived with a load of supplies from Butte, where the railroad passed, and she would bet a warm bed that Sam was still at home with his wife, as he had been every morning of late. He was a conscientious husband, she gave him that.

Hammering up the window with the heel of her hand, she called into the freezing air, her breath puffing out in white clouds, "I'll be down in just a minute, Mr. Meeks!" then slammed the window shut and shivered.

She should have had the potbellied stove glowing and coffee made for the man.

A knock sounded on her outside door, and she cursed under her breath. "Of all the... Just a *minute!*"

She pulled her chemise and drawers on over her cold skin and leaned into her wardrobe for a skirt.

"It's cold in here," a familiar male voice said from the other room. *How had Brock gotten in?* She'd locked that door last night.

"Mama din't make the fire yet," her son replied. Jonathon was up.

"What's she doin'?"

"Dunno. I heard her yellin' a minute ago."

"Who's she yelling at now?" he asked, and his boots pounded along the floorboards of the hall. "You got someone in there, Abby?"

"Stay out of here!" she sputtered, snatching the first shirtwaist blouse that her fingers located. "I was calling down to the delivery man is all. I got up late."

Too late. The curtains were parted by a large hand and Brock took a step into the room.

# Chapter Seven

His gaze fell across her breasts beneath the thin cotton chemise, and to her horror, Abby felt the peaks tighten. His heated gaze darkened knowingly. She clutched her skirt over her scantily clad body and glared. "It's cold in here is all. How dare you walk into my home and into my bedroom without so much as a knock?"

A reckless grin creased his handsome features, and he said lightly, "I knocked. Jonathon let me in." He glanced at the door frame. "And there doesn't seem to be anywhere to knock here."

"March yourself back to the kitchen and wait for me. Make yourself useful and start a fire."

"Yes, ma'am." The curtain fell back into place, her heart resumed its pace and his retreating footsteps matched the heavy beat.

She scrambled into her clothing and took a clean apron from a drawer, dropping her hairbrush into its folds to use later when she had a few minutes.

Her awkward fingers fumbled over her stockings, but finally she got her shoes buttoned, and hurried out. "I have to get down to open the front door," she told Brock, and kissed Jonathon on the way past. She picked up a loaf of bread she'd wrapped in a towel. "I'll be back in a little while."

"Okay, Mama. Mithter Brock and me'll find our own breakfatht."

She turned back, chagrined that she hadn't seen to Jonathon's morning meal.

Brock waved her on. "Don't worry about us. We'll do just fine."

Abby hurried down to let Mr. Meeks and his strapping young sons into the store. Apologizing all the while, she started a fire and put on a pot of coffee. She sliced the boys bread and watched them slather it with apple butter and enjoy the treat.

"One of these days your boy will be eating like that," Tom Meeks said with a laugh. "I don't know where they put it all. Their mama fed us before we left."

"They're growing boys," Abby said.

"That's for sure. Can't keep 'em in coats and boots. But they earn their way. They're good, hardworking boys."

His sons proved him right by carrying in kegs and crates and spools without any seeming effort. Abby directed them where to stack items and, as she always did, paid them for the work. Having the Meeks boys unload and stack saved her and Sam a lot of hard work and muscle strain. "I've been saving a job for you!" she called.

Tom Jr. hurried to do her bidding, hoisting a cast-iron stove and carrying it to a new position. Abby marveled at his youthful strength and swept up the dust that had gathered beneath the stove.

When they were gone and her early customers had paid and loaded, she took the hairbrush from her pocket and loosened her disheveled hair, brushing it out and replaiting the heavy length. A few minutes later, Sam arrived. He threw off his fur-lined cap. "It's going to be any day now," he told Abby. "She hasn't slept much the last few nights."

Abby didn't want to tell him she'd been too uncomfortable to sleep well for nearly a month at the end before Jonathon was born. Haley Kincaid, Jesse's wife, had visited Sam's wife a few days ago, and she, too, thought that Mary had a few weeks left. Haley had worked for a doctor before coming to Whitehorn, so she was accepted as the local expert on birthing babies. "I'm sure it will be very soon," Abby agreed.

Sam took his wraps to the back room and returned.

"I'm going up to check on Jonathon," she told him.

"He's not at school?"

"No, he wasn't feeling well. He's better, but I thought he needed another day of rest."

"Abby, is he alone? I'm so sorry I was late again today."

She held up a hand. "No, no, don't worry. You need to be with Mary. I want you to be with her. Jonathon—isn't alone."

"Good." He picked up a wooden toolbox and carried it toward the front of the store. "Who's with him? Daisy?"

"You going to fix that door?" she asked, ignoring the question.

"Yep."

She hurried toward the back, leaving him to his work.

The remains of breakfast sat atop the stove and table, the scent of flapjacks lingering in the warm air. Brock's guns hung beside the door, she noted with grim appreciation.

She heard no sounds, so she walked curiously toward Jonathon's room. His bed was neatly made and his horses stood in a row on the night table, but no one occupied the room. Alarmed, she turned and hurried down the hall, glancing into her own room, and noting with amazement that her bed had been made, too.

Upon entering the sitting room, she brought her hand to her heart. There, a never anticipated, heart-stopping sight met her gaze. Brock lay stretched along the divan, his fair head on a brocade pillow, one booted foot hanging off the end, the other grounded securely on the carpeted floor. One hand lay on his gently rising and falling chest. The other arm was wrapped protectively around her sleeping son.

Jonathon lay with his head on Brock's chest, nestled in the curve of his arm, his face sweetly pink and slack in slumber. The similarity between the two was unmistakable. Anyone seeing them like this would know they were father and son.

Abby studied the two for a full minute, her heart fluttering crazily in her breast. She raised both hands and laced her fingers before her lips. The touching picture of serenity and trust brought tears to her eyes. Not wanting to intrude on the idyllic scene, she observed in awed silence.

What had she done? She'd created a child out of wedlock with this man. What could she have done differently once that had happened? Told her father the truth. Made him go after her baby's father. But she hadn't wanted Brock that way. And she hadn't wanted him because he'd killed Guy.

Sleeping peacefully, Brock didn't look like the murderer she'd believed him to be. Lying with their son in his embrace, he didn't seem at all like the man with whom she'd been so angry that day. If she truly believed him to be a cold-blooded killer, would she have allowed him in her home? The protective wall she'd constructed around her heart now had a crack, and that frightened her.

She wanted to hate him. She needed to hate him. For

if she didn't, what were the alternatives? For her son's benefit, could she let the world know the truth?

Jonathon breathed easily enough, no sign of a cough apparent. What was Brock's presence going to do to him? He craved the attention of a fatherly man, which Brock provided. Jonathan was loving this, eating up every minute. And why shouldn't he? Why should her son be deprived of the attention he so rightfully deserved?

But what if Brock left again? It would break the boy's heart.

As much as she'd wanted Brock gone, the prospect of him leaving again now was devastating.

Brock's eyes opened and he looked right at her. She realized she'd made a pathetic little sobbing sound, and placed her fingers over her lips. Had he actually been asleep?

She hadn't known she was standing so close until he reached out a long arm and caught her skirt, tugging her toward him.

She grasped the fabric. "Don't you dare hurt my son," she warned in a deadly quiet voice. Then she yanked the material from his grasp and hurried from the room.

Brock watched her go, a mixture of regret and anticipation chugging through his veins. He loved her.

He'd loved her from the beginning, when she'd been the only one who accepted him and showed him any concern. He'd loved her from the first time he'd looked into those green eyes and lost himself. He'd loved her since the night she'd eagerly surrendered herself, body and soul, to his touch.

He'd loved her all those years he'd spent trying to make up for disappointing her—by rooting out outlaws and risking his life and proving his merit.

He'd loved her the nights he'd bedded auburn-haired whores and found them sadly lacking. He'd loved her as he'd planned his return and cautiously disappeared from his previous life without a trace, spending months making certain no one followed or knew his true identity.

He'd loved her the day he'd seen her appear on the dock in an apron, a look of startled recognition on her lovely face. And he loved her now. Even though she couldn't stand the sight of him and he had to blackmail her into allowing him to know his son. Even though she wanted to marry another man. Even though she wished he'd never come back.

Jonathon was the icing on the cake. He smoothed the child's hair and inhaled his little-boy scent. Jonathon made it all worthwhile.

The sound of Abby washing dishes roused him from his musings. They'd made a game of cooking breakfast, and Jonathon had been dutifully impressed at Brock's flapjack skills. Then they'd set about righting his messy bedroom. While the child dressed himself, Brock had peeked into Abby's room.

Fascinated by the feminine sight of crocheted lace on the pillow slips and the delicate powdery scent in the air, he'd stepped in and absorbed that place where she slept and dressed and...he'd glanced at the mirrored dressing table scattered with pins and ribbons...and brushed out her hair.

Drawn to touch something of hers, he had reached down and straightened her pillow, pulled up the white linen sheets, and been struck anew by her soft, familiar lilac scent. It had suddenly seemed so intimate to be touching her bed, knowing she slept beneath these sheets and blankets. Alone.

But she hadn't always been alone here, he couldn't help thinking. She'd shared this bed with her husband. The knowledge pierced him cruelly.

Her words of explanation about how she'd come to be

here were vivid in his mind. She'd been afraid to tell her father about the baby growing inside her. *But when he knew I was getting sick in the mornings, he figured it out. He made all the arrangements, then he hauled me off to Whitehorn, watched Reverend McWhirter marry us, and rode back to the ranch without a backward glance.*

How terrifying that must have been for her. She'd been young and alone. And forced to marry a man she barely knew. She'd probably felt completely deserted—by her father—and by Brock himself. No wonder she hated him.

She had raised her lovely face and looked him straight in the eye to say, "I cooked and cleaned and learned about hardware, and I had a baby. There wasn't anywhere for me to run."

Brock had stared long and hard at that bed, thinking of her lying there with Jed Watson, hating the thought, hating his own part in putting her there. But right then he accepted the blame for placing her in that position, and he understood her resentment.

He would make it up to her. Whether she wanted him to or not. Easing Jonathon out of his hold and onto the divan, he stood and moved silently to the kitchen.

She stood at the sink, drying dishes.

He moved in behind her. "I was going to do that. Don't you have work to do?"

She dropped the plate and whirled, but with a lightning fast reaction, Brock caught it before it hit the floor. He handed the china to her.

Blinking, Abby took it and set it aside. "Yes, but I wanted to see how—how Jonathon was doing."

"You checked up on us, and I didn't let him starve or bleed or anything, did I?"

"It appears you did an adequate job." She turned away.

"He could go to school this afternoon. I'm glad to stay

the rest of the day, but he's getting bored and restless, and he didn't cough the whole time."

"And he's not warm or anything?"

"Not a bit."

She nodded. "Maybe that's a good idea. He can go after he has a bite to eat."

"I'll fix it and take him on my way out of town."

She shook her head. "No. You can't take him. Too many people will see you, and it won't look right."

"I'm not going anywhere," he told her. "Eventually everyone is going to see us. I don't care what they think."

"You never have cared what people thought. But think about me for a change. Think about what they'll say about me. And about Jonathon. I'm planning a wedding!"

Remembering his resolve to make things up to her, he bit back the remark on his tongue. "All right. I'll feed him and bring him down. You can walk with him, if he wants someone to go along."

She studied Brock skeptically, as if his abrupt change of attitude unnerved her. "Good." She pointed to the ice box. "Make certain he drinks milk."

He gave her a salute, and she headed for the hall door, looking at him over her shoulder. "In a little while then."

"A little while," he agreed.

Jonathon was happy at the news that he got to return to school. They ate, and Brock gathered their coats and hats and walked him downstairs.

Abby bundled up her son and stood on the dock while he walked down the street to the schoolhouse. Through the panes in the door, Brock observed her wave before she came back inside.

Sam was absorbed in a task in the back of the store, and Brock took a moment to pull on his coat and strap his gun belt around his hips. "Maybe you will have to get used to people wondering about Jonathon,'' he said quietly.

Sorting a box of screws, she shook her head against the possibility.

"Maybe more people suspect than you think."

She shot her gaze to his. "What makes you think that?"

"Caleb knew simply by observation. How difficult is it to have done the figuring when Jonathon was born? And the older he gets the more he looks like me, right?"

Abby's cheeks blazed. "I was married to Jed when Jonathon was born. He has a good name and a good inheritance."

"Then you'd better decide what lies you're going to tell to explain my interest in the boy. And think about what you're going to tell *him* when he's old enough to figure it out on his own. His inheritance doesn't change what he'll see in the mirror."

Abby looked absolutely stricken at his words, but she was going to have to face reality. Brock spoke the truth as kindly as he could, but facts were facts.

"Some kid who's overheard his parents talking might tell him if you don't," he added.

Those green eyes filled with horror.

"Think about it. Because I'm going to be around." He adjusted his hat on his head. "A lot."

And with that, he left the store, the bell clanging behind him.

Abby made a fist and brought it down on the counter, catching the edge of the box and sending screws flying in all directions. The man was infuriating, but more than that, she was beginning to fear he was right. Panic edged her consciousness, and she blinked to clear her vision.

Seeing the two of them together had thrust the truth into her heart like a rusty knife. The similarity between

Brock and Jonathon was unmistakable. She'd only been fooling herself to think no one would know. Maybe people had guessed all along. She'd been aware of Caleb's silent knowledge, but were there others? Laine hadn't figured it out, but then she'd never seen Brock until his return, never had a reason to suspect, because she hadn't heard the stories of Guy's death.

If people had known all along, and Abby hadn't realized it, then nothing had really changed—except that now she knew they knew. She had an obligation to go through with her promise to marry Everett. Calling it off now would only cause more speculation and gossip. She could still hold her head up. She'd done the very best she could.

Brock's question about Jonathon was the truly disturbing one. She would hate to admit she'd let him believe a lie his whole short life—that Jed hadn't been his father. What was in his best interest? For him to know? She had never allowed herself to consider that someone else might tell him, but now that very real possibility terrified her. How could she protect him?

"Need some help?"

Abby jumped at Sam's call from the doorway, but immediately busied herself with collecting the strewn screws. "Oh, no. I just tipped the box over. I'll get them."

She knelt and plucked more from the wooden floor. Obviously, she had a lot more to think about than she had ever admitted to herself. And ignoring the facts hadn't gotten her anywhere thus far. Abby was going to have to face the truth. And deal with it. Heaven help her.

Gribble and Warren Saloon was mostly deserted that evening. Brock nursed the lukewarm beer, chatted briefly with the bartender and glanced at the surroundings. Nothing had changed here in the last ten or fifteen years. The bar was more scarred, the floorboards more worn. The ceiling had more holes dotting the tin where bullets had pierced. The circuit judge still held court here, evidenced by a Bible and gavel on top of the dilapidated piano.

Tossing a coin on the bar, Brock nodded and left, making his way across the icy boardwalks toward another establishment. The Centennial Saloon featured boxing on Friday and Saturday nights, but this was Monday, so only the billiard players would be circling the tables.

He hadn't been in the Double Deuce since his return, since Caleb was now part owner, so he headed for the sounds of tinny music and laughter behind the closed double doors.

This was where the activity was tonight, he discovered, the bar lined with miners and ranch hands, the tables surrounded by those intent on card games. Thick smoke hung near the ceiling and made a gray haze around the throng of men and brightly dressed women. He found an open space and ordered a shot. The bartender, Cameron something, sounded vaguely familiar as he shared his knowledge of the most recent election in a nearby town.

Brock, ever alert and vigilant, studied the patrons, assessing each one. It had taken him all of thirty seconds to pick out the man who'd been the center of Whitehorn gossip and conveniently taken away much of the attention from Brock's return. Trying hard to look like a dime novel hero, the man referred to as Linc Manley sat at one of the poker tables, a slim cigar between the first and second fingers of his left hand. He wore black well, appearing sleek and ominous in the slim trousers, shirt and leather vest. Brock noted the curved handle of the Smith & Wesson Pocket .32, a light model esteemed by many gunfighters, that showed from his holster.

The man had noticed him, too. Though he showed no external sign, his recognition was there in the set of his shoulders, his seemingly relaxed but alert position on the chair. He had a planned vantage point, his back in a corner, his face to the door, a defensive station Brock knew well. What flawed the man's credibility was the blatant dress, the deliberate call for attention. Men like that were as dangerous because of their foolishness as were the more-chameleonlike predators who blended into their surroundings.

Brock recognized several men, who either nodded or raised a hand in greeting as he took stock of the customers. At another table, a familiar man sat with his back to Brock, and after a moment of nagging awareness, he identified Everett Matthews. George Lundburg, the butcher, beckoned to Brock. "We have a seat open. I'll buy you a drink."

Brock sauntered over and draped his coat on the back of the chair. "Thanks."

The expression on Matthews's face when he looked up and recognized Brock was worth sitting in on a game he didn't particularly want to join. He slid onto the chair, instinctively noting the players and those who sat at nearby tables.

"Everyone know Brock Kincaid?" George asked.

A couple of the men who introduced themselves were ranchers Brock had met at one time or another. The one named Alvin Waverly dealt Brock in.

"You related to the old fellow who occupies a chair at the hardware store?" Brock asked.

"My uncle," the man replied. "Hasn't had anything to do with my family for a dozen years. Some feud between him and my father."

A saloon girl in a low-cut red dress with a sagging feather in her upswept hair delivered a bottle and placed a spotted shot glass in front of Brock. George handed her a coin and she poured Brock's drink.

Thanking her, Brock studied his cards.

"What're you doing in Whitehorn, anyway?" Matthews asked, his tone deliberately probing.

Brock took stock of everything from the expression in his eyes to the way he held his cards.

"Brock is *from* Whitehorn," George said by way of explanation.

The others grew silent.

Everett leaned forward, elbows on the table. "Way I hear it, you hightailed it out of here a long time ago. What brings you back?"

"A man don't have to explain himself," George said.

"It's all right," Brock assured him. "Mr. Matthews is obviously quite concerned about my business. I don't mind setting him straight."

The silence at the table was palpable.

"My family's here," he said easily. "And my family's ranch. I have every reason to come home."

"Why now?" Matthews asked. "You killed Abby's brother and took off. Why come back now?"

His forwardness brought a quick intake of breath from the girl who stood beside Brock's chair.

Brock's gaze didn't waver. "I defended myself. If you know anything about that, then you know he came after me intent on murder. And if you knew me, you'd know I never wanted to kill him. A dozen witnesses can tell you it was self-defense."

"There weren't even charges against you? I guess it pays to have a rich, powerful family in Whitehorn."

Now an ever-widening circle of silence eddied across the smoky room.

If the fool drew a gun, he would never know what had hit him. He wasn't wearing one where it could be seen, but he could have one beneath his jacket. Brock couldn't let that happen. Kill Abby's brother and then her fiancé? No, the situation had to be diffused.

"I'll take your remarks as coming from a position of ignorance," Brock said calmly. "I would guess you've heard somewhere that Abby and I were friends before that happened, and now that I'm back, I suppose your confidence in her affections is shaky. I'd be a little nervous if I were in your place, too. So your manners are excusable."

Matthews face glowed as red as a beet. He sat with his lips clamped shut, his fingers white as he mangled the cards in his grip. "You can go to hell, you cocky son of a bitch," he managed to choke out.

Brock chuckled. "Thanks for your permission, but I don't think I needed it."

A few uncomfortable laughs erupted around the table.

The girl in the red dress sidled up against Brock's shoulder and rubbed his neck. "Win a hand with those cards and buy me a drink," she said, placing her red-painted lips near his ear. Her cheap perfume mixed with the cloying scent of cigar smoke, whiskey and fear.

"Do I know you?" he asked, averting his attention only when he was satisfied that Matthews wouldn't pull a gun.

"*Ruby*, darlin'," she said, gesturing with a hand flattened on her spilling white bosom.

Recognition dawned. She'd been all of fifteen or sixteen the first time he'd bought her a drink in this saloon. The years hadn't been particularly kind to her. "Of course," he said, with a smile just the same. "Ruby, darlin'. I'd love to buy you a drink."

She smiled gratefully.

The men around the table exchanged knowing glances, and the attention shifted away from Matthews.

Brock sat through several hands, Ruby at his shoulder, Matthews glaring. George called it a night for himself and the game broke up. Grabbing his coat, Brock let Ruby take his hand and lead him through the doorway to the back stairs.

Out of sight now, Brock pulled his hand from hers. She stood on the bottom step and gave him a curious frown. Brock took a gold coin from his pocket and placed it in her palm.

Skirts swishing, she turned and started up the stairs, then, realizing he wasn't following, stopped and faced him. "You coming?"

He shook his head. "Enjoy a night to yourself. On me. No offense intended."

She wrapped her fingers around the coin and blinked rapidly. "None taken."

"'Night, Ruby."

"Good night, Brock."

He left through the kitchen, the only one there to see him a Chinese woman washing glasses in a tin tub. He nodded a greeting and shrugged into his coat, quickly opening and closing the door as he let himself out into the frosty night air.

Lionel Briggs let him into the livery, and they exchanged a few comments about the weather before Brock saddled his horse and headed for the ranch. The snow glistened beneath the luminous white moon, and he gave the gray his head, sensing his restlessness and trusting his keen ability to retrace their earlier tracks.

Brock had defrayed the challenge from Matthews this time. The man didn't seem the type to actually draw a gun and have a face-off, but men who had their territory threatened never let up. Matthews seemed more the type to cause dissention in a less flagrant way. Especially if he knew he wasn't going to win in a straightforward confrontation. Brock needed to stay more alert than ever, especially watching his back. Matthews's attack might not be from a bullet.

## Chapter Eight

Holding an iron skillet with the corner of the white apron she wore over her beaded shirt and leather skirt, Ruth placed sausages on each man's plate. John Whitefeather thanked his sister with a nod and waited for Caleb to pass the pitcher of syrup.

Brock sipped strong black coffee and watched with amusement as baby Bart smeared his chubby hands in the pool of butter and syrup on his tray, then wiped it into his fair hair until the tufts stood up in spikes.

Ruth turned from setting the skillet on the stove to discover his latest antic. Placing her hands on her hips, she gave him a loving look that clearly showed her amusement as well as her frustration. "What am I going to do with you, little one? I have calls to make this morning, and now I will have to give you a bath."

"If you'd let me hire someone, you'd have help with the boys," Caleb said matter-of-factly, as though they'd had the discussion before.

"Your husband is wise," John told her. "A helper could share the chores and see to the children's needs."

"Once again you are siding with my husband, *hesta-tanemo*," she replied without offense.

John glanced at Brock. "My sister's healing skills are often needed at the reservation. Her pride makes her think she can do more than one thing at a time. And my nephew is a full-time job for one person."

Barton punctuated that statement by flipping a soggy chunk of flapjack from his finger to his father's sleeve. At Caleb's surprised look, he chortled with glee.

Caleb smothered a laugh, finished his coffee and glanced around. "Have you seen my pipe?"

"Perhaps you should hire someone to keep track of your pipe," Ruth replied in a teasing tone. "It's beside your chair over there."

Caleb retrieved his pipe and returned to give his wife a brief kiss. She touched his cheek tenderly and said something Brock couldn't hear. His brother's obvious joy and contentment with his family contrasted sharply with Brock's chaotic situation, but he couldn't have been happier for Caleb.

"Don't forget," Ruth said, including Brock and John in her admonition, "that Asa Spencer is giving his wife an anniversary party at the Carlton Hotel this Saturday night. We're all expected to attend."

"They don't want me there," John said.

"Daisy spoke with me and was very certain about wanting you there," she told him. "It will be a good chance to meet the available young women."

"I hardly think the fathers of Whitehorn want me dancing with their white daughters."

"I understand your feelings," Ruth said gently. "But Daisy would be hurt if we didn't attend."

"You can go."

"I am as much Cheyenne as you. This is her way of trying to make peace between the townspeople and ranchers, and show them that we are accepted."

"We will never be accepted, and you're fooling yourself if you think so."

"John," Caleb interrupted. "Your sister has suffered her share of rejection, but she's willing to make this gesture for the Spencers. Anyone who doesn't want to come because of the company has a right to stay home. But don't let it be you."

John took a drink of his coffee and grimaced. "I will go. But I won't stay long."

Ruth hugged him around the shoulders and poured him a fresh cup of coffee.

John reached across the table and ruffled Zeke's hair, and Brock wondered why the half-Cheyenne had never married. It had been a surprise to find him living at the ranch and working as foreman, though he and Caleb had been friends for many years. John wore his long black hair in a tail that hung down his broad back. Brock could only imagine how difficult it must be to find acceptance among two different peoples who were intolerant of one another.

John noticed Brock's look. "You riding with me today?"

Brock nodded. "East to look for wolves?"

"Yes. Yesterday I found an old bull elk that had been killed. I want to follow the tracks and check the herds. We should probably bring the first-time calvers in close."

There was still plenty of time before calving season, but the cows with their first calves needed to be protected and eventually brought into the corrals for help.

"Take this deer jerky in case you don't get back for dinner," Ruth said, handing Brock a cloth sack. She gave his arm a gentle squeeze and waved to her brother.

The three men bundled into their coats and walked outside, where feathered flakes lit on their hats and shoulders.

"I figured you'd take the hardware store run later in the week," Caleb said to Brock.

"Make a list," he replied.

Caleb's mouth inched into a grin.

John moved ahead toward the barn.

Caleb slowed and spoke. "Got a plan yet?"

Brock squinted toward the snow-capped mountains. "I'm gonna be a father to my boy. And I'm going to make up to Abby for taking off like I did."

"Interesting triangle you'll have goin' there."

"Yup. What d'you know about Matthews?"

"Spends a lot of time at the Double Deuce."

"I figured that." They reached Brock's horse, which was tethered at the corner of the corral. Brock untied the reins and rubbed the gray's forehead with his knuckles. "What else?"

"Not much to know. Lives alone. Likes cards. Courting Abby."

"She must see something in him," Brock mused aloud.

"What do you suppose that is?"

"Damned if I know."

Caleb puffed on the pipe he'd carried with him, and the smoke curled lazily into the morning air. "Face wouldn't curdle milk."

Reins still in one hand, Brock pulled on his gloves, using his teeth for the left one. "'Spose not."

"Proximity says a lot."

"Meaning what?"

"Meaning he was here and you weren't. Winters are long. Anyone would get lonely."

Brock gave a half nod. "And appearances mean a lot to her."

"Like most women," Caleb concurred.

"Seems she was holding tight to the belief that no one suspected Jonathon wasn't Jed's son."

"If people talked at first, it wasn't to me." Caleb stood aside as Brock mounted the gray. "How're you gonna make it up to her?"

He thought a moment. "Be there."

"Does Abby want you there?"

"She will." With a shouted, "H'yah!" he turned the gray's head and kicked the horse into a run after John, who was already riding eastward at a good pace.

Laine had offered to stay with Jonathon, though Abby had tried repeatedly to convince her to attend the party.

"You know how I feel about social gatherings," Laine told her again as she helped Abby curl and pin her hair. "Just because Daisy wants me there does not mean I would be comfortable with the stares and whispers."

"Well, it's not right," Abby complained.

"Perhaps not. But it is so. And my father would never approve." Laine wound bright green ribbons through Abby's curls.

"How will you find a husband?" Abby asked. "And I know you want one, so don't deny it."

"My ancestors will bring me one. If I ask them."

Abby smiled at her in the mirror. "Does that work?"

"Most definitely."

Standing, Abby presented her back. "Now pull the laces tighter."

"I will never understand this torture garment you insist on wearing."

"My waist is not as tiny as—yours. I need all the h-help I can get. Oh!"

Laine tied the laces and studied her friend's image in the mirror. "How does a woman do this alone?"

"She doesn't. Proper ladies have maids, I understand."

"Yes, I read about them in the stories from the library." Laine took up Abby's emerald-green, satin dress and helped her into the yards of rustling fabric. "You look like a fairy-tale princess."

"I wouldn't go that far. I'm a little too muscled from work," Abby mused, studying her arms and waist, "and my hands are neither soft nor white." She examined both sides of the offending appendages before plunging them into a pair of long white gloves. "My feet are a nice ladylike size, however." Extending a stockinged foot, she wiggled delicate toes.

"I am sure Mr. Matthews will lend all his attention to your feet this evening," Laine replied with a raised eyebrow.

They laughed, and Abby pulled on satin slippers, lamenting that she'd have to wear boots over them.

"Mama, Mi*s*ter Matthew*s* i*s* here," Jonathon said from the doorway, emphasizing his *S*s.

"Thank you, darling. I'll be right out."

"You look beautiful," he said, his blue eyes lit with adoration.

Abby kissed his fair head. "Thank you. Now you be a good boy for Laine."

"I will."

"I know you will. And don't let him convince you that I said he could stay up past nine-thirty," she said to her friend.

"Oh, no," Laine replied, then winked at Jonathon, who giggled.

Abby grabbed her cloak and hurried out to where Everett waited.

"That's a lovely color for you," he said, taking her wrap and helping her into it.

Abby perched on a kitchen chair and pulled boots on over her fancy slippers.

The Carlton Hotel's dining room had been decorated with bright streamers, the tables and chairs arranged around the perimeter of the space, leaving a platformed area for the band, and a larger one for dancing.

Guests had begun to arrive, and Asa and Daisy greeted each at the door. Abby knew nearly everyone, ranchers and their wives, bankers and businessmen alike, as almost everyone had been to the hardware store at some time or another in the last seven years. These occasions were always a pleasant diversion from the winter isolation and a rare chance for the citizens of Whitehorn to dress in their finery and catch up with friends and acquaintances.

Abby greeted Haley and Jesse Kincaid. "It's so nice to see you."

"And such a happy occasion," Haley agreed.

"Asa and Daisy are a blessing to me," Abby told them. "They are good company, living so close and always eager to help with Jonathon."

Jesse nodded. "It's good to see Daisy contented." He wore an introspective expression, but smiled at Abby's curious gaze. "She and my father were…friends before my father died."

"I didn't know that," Abby replied.

When Jesse walked away to find the punch, the two women discussed the approaching birth of Mary Rowland's child.

A hush fell over the crowd, and Abby glanced up as Caleb and Ruth Kincaid entered the dining room. Daisy embraced each of them, as well as Ruth's brother, his ebony mane of hair in a tail that divided his broad back. John Whitefeather, obviously uncomfortable with the hug and the situation, trailed his sister to a table. Many scrutinizing pairs of eyes followed his journey.

Abby's attention riveted upon Brock, however, as he accompanied his family across the room. He wore a dark suit and white shirt, a tie knotted at his tanned throat. The clothing contrasted with his fair hair, making him breathtakingly handsome. She realized she was holding her breath, a painful act inside the restricting corset, so she quickly released it.

Haley looked at her oddly, and Everett returned with two plates, each holding a few sandwich squares. He set them on the table. "He's got a lot of nerve coming here," he said, holding Abby's chair.

She sat, her heart fluttering nervously. "Brock?"

"No, the half-breed."

"The Spencers invited him."

"I'm sure they didn't think he would attend."

"They wouldn't have invited him if they hadn't wanted him to come. They invited Laine, too."

"At least she had the sense to stay away."

Abby blinked at that remark. "What do you mean?"

Everett sat beside her, speaking softly. "Only that it's wiser to stay with one's own kind. I didn't mean anything else. It's Caleb Kincaid's business who he married, but he must know his wife and her family are not the same ilk as these folks."

An uncomfortable warning rang in Abby's head at those words. What she recognized as anger made her purse her lips and study Everett's profile, wondering if she knew him as well as she thought she had. Surely he meant no harm. Some people were conditioned by experience and frightening stories to fear Indians, no matter their bands or actual character as individuals. It was a common bigotry, but one she hoped could be diminished with education and tolerance.

"The Kincaids are nice people, Everett," she said softly. "Ruth does a lot of kind things for neighbors and is always willing to call on the sick. John Whitefeather has always been a prefect gentleman whenever he's in the store."

"Why are you sticking up for the Kincaids all of a sudden?"

"I'm not sticking up for the Kincaids."

"Yes, you are."

"Well, if I am, I guess it's because you're attacking them."

"And you feel some need to defend them?"

"I would defend anyone who was unjustly criticized."

"Oh, really?"

"Really."

"How about that murdering brother? You wanna stick up for him again now, too?"

Abby looked down at her plate, resentment and defensiveness warring in her breast.

The band struck up a tune just then and people moved onto the floor to dance. Hazel Wright, a widow with a dressmaking shop, approached them. "Hello, dear," she said to Abby. "Mr. Matthews, you handsome devil."

"Mrs. Wright," Everett replied, politely scrambling to his feet.

"I haven't seen you for quite some time," Abby told her.

"I haven't been out much this winter. My hip is bothering me and I don't trust myself on the ice. One of Big Mike's boys comes and takes my grocery order and shops for me."

"Well, if there's anything you need from the hardware store, you send him to me," Abby instructed her. "And if you need help, I'll be glad to come—or I can send Sam."

"That baby come yet?"

"Not yet."

"You're not dancing with this beautiful young thing?" Widow Wright asked Everett pointedly.

"Not just yet."

"Well, music shouldn't be wasted." She extended her arm and Everett took it. "Bear with an old woman's clumsiness."

He led her to the dance floor. Abby nibbled her food and observed with an amused smile. Everett pulled a face over Widow Wright's shoulder.

"Where is our son tonight?"

The question as well as the voice snapped Abby's heart into a rapid flutter. Her first reaction was to check for anyone who may have overheard.

"No one's listening," Brock said, standing over her.

"Have a care for propriety, will you?" she whispered indignantly.

He seated himself on the chair next to hers and spoke softly. "Where is Jonathon?"

"He's at home. Laine is with him."

"He might have come out to the ranch to play with Zeke. Ruth's young niece is with the boys."

"He might have," she said in agreement. She had no problem with Jonathon playing with Zeke or visiting at the Kincaid ranch. It was good for him to have friends and experience something other than his mother's narrow life.

"Next time I'll remember and make arrangements."

"All right."

"We agreed on something," he said, amusement lacing his tone.

She allowed him a brief glance, noting his freshly shaved jaw and the glimmer of his blue eyes, before glancing down to discover the absence of guns tethered to his thighs, then quickly looked toward the dancers. "Where are your guns?"

"Checked them at the door, like everyone else."

"What if someone crosses you and you've no

weapon?'' Her remark was meant to be cutting, since the conversation had turned uncomfortably friendly.

''I didn't say I didn't have a weapon.''

Her gaze shot back to his face, and he gave her an insolent, one-sided grin. Unconsciously, her attention dropped to the front of his dark jacket, and she couldn't help wondering whether or not he concealed a deadly weapon beneath the elegantly tailored garment.

Surreptitiously, Brock leaned toward her, his gaze focused elsewhere, and slowly opened the front of his jacket, revealing only cranberry-colored satin lining and the crisp white fabric of his shirt. No gun lurked against his ribs or protruded from the inside pocket.

The dress shirt covering a chest she knew to be hard and warm struck Abby as the most teasingly masculine sight she'd ever seen, and her insides turned to liquid. Against her will, her gaze slid from his shirt to the impeccable black trousers covering his muscled thighs.

He turned his head slowly, and she brought her eyes to his, working to keep her breathing even. He had made that move deliberately, knowing the heated effect he had on her, and she had fallen into his sensual snare like a mindless strumpet.

In a graceful motion, he stood and reached a hand to her. ''May I have this dance?''

''Don't do this,'' she begged softly.

He only waited, his hand extended.

An embarrassed glance proved that several pairs of curious eyes were on them. She had no choice but to force a friendly smile and take his hand.

The minute she did so, warmth shot up her arm, the contact, even through her gloves, a fatal mistake. He guided her to the dancing area, and without giving her time to balk, placed a hand at her waist and drew her smoothly into step.

For these few glorious moments, she was not the widowed proprietor of a hardware store. She became a genteel, sought after young woman in the embrace of a handsome admirer. Brock's part in the fantasy was no stretch of the imagination, for he was unquestionably the best looking man in the room. Her slippered feet glided effortlessly in time to the music.

Abby's senses were besieged by the masculine scents of starch and leather that enfolded her. Through her gloves and his jacket, she knew the strength of the arm and shoulder that she touched, however innocently. She knew what his skin felt like, sleek heat over corded muscle; possessed keen recall of the erotic sensations their bodies created pressed together in passion; could close her eyes and hear the sounds of pleasure coming from his throat.

Perspiration formed beneath Abby's corset, heat spiraled from the inside out and she felt as though she were trapped in a drugged spell. Her eyes had drifted shut and she forced them open, focused her gaze on the dancers around them. She had control over her own reactions, and she refused to lose her head over this man again.

"You're a beautiful woman, Abby." His voice held admiration and perhaps a touch of regret.

She refused to look up. She didn't reply, but turned her head aside as if interested in something she'd seen.

"You don't really want Matthews," he said.

She glanced up then. "Don't presume to tell me what I want."

His deep blue gaze studied her features, rested on her mouth and then met her eyes. "He cheats at cards."

His words took a minute to register. "How do you know?"

"And he doesn't even do it well."

"You've played cards with Everett?"

"That says something about a man, Abby."

She wanted to laugh, but she would have much preferred to stomp on his foot and scream in frustration. Instead, her fingers tightened on his arm. "What do you care?"

"You're planning to marry him," he said, carefully keeping his voice low. "He's the man you've chosen to replace me as Jonathon's father."

"Replace you? Replace would mean that you'd been his father first. And you weren't. Jed was Jonathon's father."

"In whose opinion?"

"Jonathon believed he was his father."

A muscle ticked in Brock's jaw. "He has a true father. It's unfair of you to deny him."

"Me? I'm not the one who denied him a father."

"You are now, Abby."

She glanced around, making certain their conversation wasn't picked up. "I am giving him a father by marrying Everett," she whispered. "I was going on with my life quite nicely before you came back."

"And I told you. You don't really want him."

"And I told you…" She stopped, took a breath and changed gears. "You would say anything to get what you want. I'm not sure what it is you want, but I'm not a pawn. Neither is Jonathon."

"I think you should smile."

"What?"

"Smile. People are starting to look concerned."

Somehow, she turned up the corners of her lips. "I think you're a selfish, egotistical slug, and I regret the day I met you."

Brock returned her smile. "Oh, really? Why is it then that I could pull up your skirts and bury myself inside you at any time and you would welcome it?"

Abby's skin burned with humiliation. "I hate you."

"So you've said."

The music ended and she pulled from his easy embrace and marched across the floor, her chin high, the smile plastered to her scorching face. Everett stood near the table where she'd been sitting earlier, a frown creasing his features. He handed her a cup of punch, which she accepted and drank thirstily.

"You two seemed quite friendly," he said.

"Simply a dance," she replied. To her extreme displeasure, she realized Brock had been walking behind her.

"Thank you for the dance, Mrs. Watson," he said, with a polite nod.

"You're welcome."

"Save me another, if your fiancé doesn't monopolize all your time."

"Why she'd want to dance with you, I can't guess," Everett said.

"I think it's my suave execution of those tricky steps." Brock's grin was evidence of his refusal to be baited.

Abby sank onto the seat of a chair, and noticed Brock's brother Will and his young wife approaching. "Good evening, Will. Lizzie."

Brock turned to greet his brother and sister-in-law. Lizzie took a seat beside Abby and brushed a lock of curly blond hair away from her face. "I've been looking forward to this evening. Winter can get so dreary, can't it?"

She engaged Abby in conversation, and the men took a few steps away. Abby paid scant attention to Lizzie's dialogue, while half listening to make sure Everett wasn't causing a scene. He simply stood in their midst as the brothers were joined by Matt Darby and Bart Baxter, and the subject of seeking a new town doctor came up. She relaxed.

"When is the wedding?" Lizzie asked.

"What wedding?"

"Your wedding, of course!"

"Oh!" Abby clapped her hand to her cheek and gave an embarrassed laugh. "March."

"You'll let me know what I can do to help?"

"I will, Lizzie. Thank you."

A hush ran through the crowd and Abby followed Lizzie's blue-eyed gaze. A lean, dark-haired man dressed in black, with silver spurs and a silver conch at his throat, had arrived with a young woman on his arm.

"Who is that?" Lizzie asked.

"I think it's the man some say is Jack Spade."

"Whatever is he doing here?"

Abby shook her head. "I can't imagine Asa or Daisy inviting him," Abby replied. "Sylvia Banning must have asked him as her escort."

Daisy had been friends with the widowed Sylvia for several years. Some said she was a former saloon girl. Daisy had never been one to hold people's past or heritage against them, so Abby wouldn't be surprised if it were so.

"It's glaringly obvious that none of the ladies from the Benevolence Society accepted this invitation," Lizzie said with amusement.

The gathering was a rather odd mixture of types, Abby realized. She couldn't help but take note of Everett's frown as the newly arrived couple were greeted by the hosts and shown to the table of refreshments.

Everett at last asked Abby to dance, and she spent the time during several musical selections working hard not to compare his effect on her with Brock's. Brock made her angry, and that's why her heart raced when she was with him. She had made up her mind about this joining, and she and Everett had long ago announced their engagement. If Brock hadn't returned to Whitehorn, she would never have questioned her decision. Darn the man for placing doubts in her head. In her heart, she knew marrying a reliable man like Everett was the right thing to do for her son.

The evening grew late, and Abby became weary. She'd worked the better part of the day, reserving only minimal time to run up and bathe and dress. "I'm tired," she told her fiancé a little before ten. "May we leave now?"

Everett glanced around the gathering and pulled out his gold pocket watch. He flipped the cover closed with a snap. "Whatever you'd like. I'll get our wraps."

Several others had thanked Asa and Daisy and were making their way toward the door as Everett helped Abby into her coat. They followed the crowd through the open double doorway, and Everett turned back to pull the door shut.

A shot rang out, and the wood above Everett's head splintered. Women screamed and Everett ducked to a crouch. In a moment of confusion, men and women scrambled and cried out. Abby glanced around at the chaos, caught in a rapidly unfolding scene that seemed like a dream.

From out of nowhere, a heavy weight launched itself against her, and she found herself flattened into the crusty snow, an enormous body pressing her down.

# Chapter Nine

Abby tried to see what was happening. "What the—"

Another shot rang out.

"Keep your head down," Brock cautioned, and pressed her cheek into the snow. Abby sputtered, but lay still, her heart thundering. From the corner of one eye, she could make out the enormous barrel of the gun Brock held at the ready in his bare hand. Panic welled up in her chest and her body began to tremble with cold and fear.

"A rider heading west, fast. Between the buildings over there." Caleb's voice.

Brock's weight lifted immediately. He lunged toward a horse standing at the post and vaulted into the saddle. "Tell Darby I have his bay. Someone get James," he called, referring to his cousin, the sheriff.

"I'll go." John Dillard pushed his wife, Tess, toward Will and ran toward the sheriff's office.

Brock hesitated, glancing back at Abby, then at Will. "Will?"

"I'll make sure Abby's looked after," Brock's brother assured him.

Without another word, Brock kicked the horse into a run.

Will guided Lizzie and Tess back into the hotel, pausing briefly to wait for Everett to move away from the door, then he came back for Abby. "You all right?"

"My cheek is frozen," she said, rubbing warmth into it with her gloved hand.

Everett stepped between them and brushed snow from Abby's coat and hair. "I can take care of her."

"See that you do." Will gave him a steely-eyed, warning glance before joining his wife and Tess Dillard inside.

"This is the last time we join an event attended by this class of people," Everett declared when they were alone.

Abby stared at him. "How can you blame the people here?"

"Look at the guest list, Abby," he scoffed. "What did the Spencers expect? Someone probably came gunning for the half-breed or that gunslinger. Because of them everyone here is in danger. Let their enemies pick them off somewhere else, I say. Spare civilized people."

Abby pulled from his grasp in disgust. "I'm going home."

"You need to come inside with the others until it's safe."

"Whoever it was is long gone, and Brock and the sheriff have ridden after him."

"Come back immediately, Abby."

She turned and stared at him. "Don't order me about as though you have a right. I want to go home, and I will."

"This is unbecoming behavior." Everett moved forward and took her coat sleeve. "Do as I say until we're certain the streets are safe."

"Go back inside if you wish. I'm going home." She pulled her arm away and hurried along the snow-packed path, muttering to herself. "Do as I say...humph!"

\* \* \*

Brock followed the tracks as best he could in the light of the half-moon. It didn't help that it hadn't snowed off and on for a few days and that a myriad of tracks led every which direction in and out of town.

James met up with him at the base of a narrow gully overgrown with scrub and drifted with snow. There they discovered a campsite that had been used for several days, but was now deserted.

"Man'd have to be crazy to stay out here in the weather when there's a hotel and a boardinghouse within an hour's ride," James commented.

Brock had seen many a night when he'd preferred the elements to the possibility of being spotted in a populated area, but said, "He'd have to be crazy to take shots at half the town when they were gathered with their womenfolk, too, but someone did."

Together they examined the campsite, discovering a few buried remains of meals. Brock was no tracker; he would ask John Whitefeather to accompany him to this spot tomorrow and see what the Cheyenne could decipher about the man and the horse.

Riding back toward town, Brock felt a sick worry settled like a rock in his belly. He'd been so careful. He was sure no one had been able to follow him. The shooter, whoever he was, was probably after Linc Manley, and the fact that Brock had been there was merely a coincidence. But until he was sure, he wasn't taking any chances with Abby or Jonathon's safety.

It wouldn't do to place Caleb and Ruth in any additional danger, either, so he'd stay in town for a few days.

It would be more difficult for a stranger to go unnoticed in town, and after tonight the population would be wary.

After discussing with James his plans to engage John Whitefeather's help, he located Matt Darby and returned his horse.

Making a furtive inspection of the saloons, Brock found them for the most part quiet and sparsely populated. Matthews occupied his usual seat at the Double Deuce, which meant Abby was alone. Without making his presence known, he stood at the bar and observed the game for a moment. A girl in a tight yellow dress with black beads twined around her neck and wrists carried a foamy pitcher of beer to Matthews. He tucked a bill into her powdered cleavage and hooked her around the waist to pull her onto his knee.

Disgust boiled in Brock's chest. With a woman like Abby, a man had no need of the crude attentions of these girls. Matthews's behavior cheapened what he could have with Abby, and Brock was embarrassed for her, even though she was unaware. He would love to tell her what kind of man Matthews was, about his lack of commitment, but Brock was no saint himself. He'd taken his pleasure with any number of nameless women over the past several years, but since his return, just the thought brought a sense of regret. Anyway, she'd only think he was making it up to bully her.

After leaving the Double Deuce, he turned into the alleyway across from the hardware store and observed the building and the street for several minutes. The structure was dark, except for a light in an upper window he knew to be Abby's room. Crossing the street, he ducked into the alley, watched and listened, making certain no one followed or had seen him, then he bounded silently up the stairs and gave a light tap.

Moments later, the door opened a crack, exposing the yellow glow of a lantern and Abby's shiny auburn braid as she peeked out.

"You should have asked who it was," he said, and pushed the door open wider to enter. "Don't open the door unless you know who it is.'' He closed the door behind him and locked it.

''What are you doing here?'' She clutched the neck of the simple white cotton nightdress with one hand and held the lamp in the other. Dainty bare toes peeked beneath the voluminous hem.

''I'm staying tonight.'' He removed his coat and hung it on a peg, then pulled out a chair and sat to remove his wet boots.

''What? You—what are you doing? You're not staying here.''

''I'm staying to make sure you and Jonathon are safe, and that's that.''

''What did you find when you rode after that man? And why would we be in danger?''

''All we found was a campsite. He could be anywhere, could be gone for all I know. I thought about taking you to the ranch, but it's more isolated. It's safer here.''

''Safer from what? I don't have any enemies. Jonathon and I have been alone for two years. We don't need your concern now.''

''You don't even own a gun,'' he told her, standing and placing his boots on spread newspaper near hers.

''And I never will,'' she replied.

''Go on to bed.'' He motioned for her to precede him into the hallway.

''You can't stay here!'' she insisted, refusing to move.

''Abby.''

''What?''

''Shut up.''

She blinked. Her mouth opened and closed. Her skin appeared pinker than usual in the lantern light. Finally, she seemed to find her voice again, and when she did it was laced with indignation. ''Put on your coat and boots and leave my property at once. I have no need for your protection.''

Brock moved into the hallway and checked the door that led downstairs to make sure it was locked. Satisfied, he paused to peek in on Jonathon, but couldn't see anything until Abby came up behind him with the lamp. The child slept peacefully on his side, his knees curled up beneath the blankets, his fair hair tousled. Brock had missed a lot of bedtimes. A good many evenings and mornings and all the simple pleasures, like just watching his son sleep.

He glanced back and discovered Abby's expression gentled as she, too, observed their son's serene slumber. Her gaze lifted to his and questions troubled her brow in concerned lines, but she remained silent.

At last he moved past her toward the sitting room.

She padded behind, shadows bobbing and weaving upon the walls. ''I don't understand,'' she said finally.

''I know.'' He took the lamp from her and placed it on a mahogany table. ''Just trust me that I know what's best. Get some sleep.''

She didn't move. Her bare feet had to be freezing, because his were cold in his wool stockings. ''No one saw me,'' he assured her. ''I'll leave at first light and be careful not to be seen.''

He stepped over to the hard-coal heater and added fuel.

She turned and walked into her room, then returned with several blankets and a pillow, which he accepted. The memory of dancing with her was vivid in his mind, and her alluring scent played havoc with his senses. Her skin had a pearly glow in the golden light, and fire danced in her incredible hair. If he touched her, she'd turn to liquid heat in his arms. If he kissed her, she would respond with an angry intake of breath and then return the kiss with enough energy and passion to bring him to his knees.

She had no idea how much power she held over him. Wouldn't she just laugh if she knew? "Go to bed, Abby."

She walked as far as her doorway and paused to look back. "I hated dancing with you."

"I know."

The moment stretched out, with Brock's senses tuned to a painful pitch. The floor beneath his feet was cold, the blaze from the heater a contrasting blast against his back. The wind made the roof creak overhead, while a clock ticked rhythmically from a nearby shelf. Abby shifted her weight and the shape of her knee became visible through the thin cotton nightdress. Brock's imagination filled in the rest of her shapely leg, the flare of her hip and the breasts she hid behind her forearms. He imagined them fuller, softer, more womanly now.

He could cross the space separating them and watch her eyes widen and hear her catch her breath. He could kiss her, and after an obligatory struggle, she would take him to her lilac-scented bed. He wanted that more than he'd wanted anything except anonymity and peace for a long time. And afterward she would hate him more than she did now. And she would hate herself, too. That wasn't what he wanted to happen. "Go to bed, Abby."

She turned and fled into her room.

Abby tucked her feet into the covers and rubbed them together for warmth. The dim light from the other room was extinguished, and she listened intently for the sounds of his presence—oddly reassuring when she had convinced herself she didn't want him there. After a few rustles, the black night grew still.

She'd been sitting at her dressing table when she'd heard his knock. Somehow, she'd known it was Brock; he needn't have been angry that she'd opened the door without asking. She'd opened it quickly so he wouldn't

pound and let the sound echo in the alley, perhaps to alert
the Spencers.

His arrogance was infuriating. Telling her she shouldn't
be marrying Everett…! Even if he had a right to say anything, how did he know what was best for her? She had
a mind of her own and a right to choose. He'd thought
that being Jonathon's father would stand in his favor, but
he was wrong. That and his lack of caution in speaking
out in public were enough to fuel her hostility for a good
long time.

At least they should have been.

Abby worked to relax her body and close her eyes.
Against her will, images and sensations floated in her
mind and memory. She remembered the way he'd touched
her while dancing tonight—proper for all appearance, but
with an igniting fire that never failed to race through her
veins and seduce her. Any touch from Brock, the most
innocent of grazes, could set her skin to tingling and cause
her blood to run fast and hot.

And he knew it, damn his hide.

Her reactions were illogical. She wanted solidity. Security. Stability. All the things that Everett represented.
But could she truly bear a passionless marriage—again?
Memories of her youthful adoration made Brock seem
larger than life. She'd been foolish with him, and he'd
been happy to take advantage of her. With Everett she
was using caution, and he was exercising respect and patience. A gentleman was willing to wait for marriage.

Brock wouldn't show the same restraint.

That troubling thought graphic in her tired mind, she
dozed, sleeping lightly and encountering disjointed
dreams. After a particularly disturbing and sensual one,
she came fully awake and lay listening to the night. Some
maternal instinct forced her out of the relative warmth of
her bed and into her son's chilly room to check on him.

He slept soundly, though he was huddled into the covers for warmth.

Their quarters were uncommonly cold, and she padded silently out to add more fuel to the heater. Her bare toe came in contact with an object near the end of the divan, and Brock sprang from his prone position and knocked her to the floor, where she bumped her elbow and immediately cradled it against her ribs. In the meager light from the heater, she made out the long barrel of his revolver pointed at her head. Her heart stopped beating before thumping madly in a panicked rhythm.

The speed and agility with which he'd leaped from his position to throw her to the floor held her in amazement. What kind of man reacted that way? "Either shoot me or get that thing out of my face," she said through clenched teeth.

He cursed and leaned forward to lift her to her feet.

Abby pulled her throbbing arm away from his hold, disturbed by whatever force had impelled him to do such a thing.

Brock lit the lamp on the table, bringing an illuminating glow to the room. The blankets lay strewn from the divan, and she recognized his boot as the object she'd tripped over. His boots had been by the back door when she'd last seen them. He still wore the elegant black trousers and white shirt, but they were wrinkled now, and his fair hair fell over his forehead.

He slid the revolver under the pillow. "I heard that whack," he said, turning to survey the arm she cradled with her other hand. She allowed him to push her cotton sleeve up and examine her elbow. "Sit while I get some snow."

She didn't bother to protest as he pulled on his boots and disappeared into the kitchen. A few minutes later, he returned with a crockery bowl full of snow, and a towel.

He guided her to the divan, then knelt on the carpet in front of her.

Letting him nestle her battered elbow into the freezing coldness, Abby winced.

"What were you doing sneaking around in the dark?" he asked irritably.

"How very like you to blame me," she retorted. "I am attacked in my own home and you find me responsible." It simply wasn't common for a man to come awake with such a ferocious instinct. On one hand his reaction frightened her, while on the other it reassured her that she and Jonathon would come to no harm in his presence. He'd proved that earlier in the evening when he'd immediately pushed her down and covered her with his own body at the first sign of danger.

She met his eyes, but couldn't hold the intense look there, so averted her gaze. That was a mistake, too, because attending her as he was, the long fingers of one hand were wrapped gently around the flesh of her upper arm. Her elbow had gone numb from the cold, and she shivered. "That's enough," she said softly.

He set the bowl aside, dried her arm with the towel and leaned to retrieve a blanket and wrap it around her shoulders. "Can you move your arm?"

She flexed it to show him she could.

"Good. I'll take care of these and be right back." He carried the bowl and towel to the kitchen and returned. "Is Jonathon warm enough, do you think?"

"I was on my way to add some coal and get a brick for him when I tripped over your boot."

"I can do that." He proceeded to add coal to the stove, waited until he was sure the bricks on top were good and warm, and slipped one into one of the wool sleeves Abby indicated. He carried it to Jonathon's room and returned.

"Did you tuck it under the covers by his feet?" she asked.

"Yes." He went back to the heater and prepared another. "For your bed."

She took it from him, the heat radiating through her fingers.

"Jonathon should have had a brother," he said.

She had started to rise, but stopped to glance at him.

"Someone to sleep with. Keep each other warm at night."

"Not everyone has someone to sleep with," she said, but she'd thought the same thing many times. She should have had more children. It had never happened with Jed, but she would have more children with Everett. Somehow the thought didn't fill her with hope and happiness as it should have.

"Still think Matthews is the one you want warming your bed?" Brock asked, as though he knew her private thoughts.

"That's none of your business." She stood and padded toward her curtained doorway.

"Isn't it?" He had followed and stood behind her as she paused with one hand on the wooden frame, the other holding the hot brick.

"No, it's not. And we've been over the subject before." She called his bluff by turning toward him, placing him on the receiving end of the intimidation for once. "Would you like to explain what gives you the right to think you need to be here in the first place? Why do you feel Jonathon and I need protection? Why did you draw a gun on me in my own home? Are you in trouble? Hiding from the law?"

He gave a half laugh. "Curb your girlish fantasies. I'm not hiding from the law. I'm related to the law in this town. I wouldn't come here to hide."

"Sounds perfectly logical to me. Family would protect you."

"If I was an outlaw, James would arrest me, anyhow. Wrong is wrong. I got paid to protect others. I've worked on the side of the law, remember?"

"Maybe someone has a grudge against you."

His posture changed fractionally. "I would never endanger you or Jonathon or anyone in my family if I believed that."

"But it's a possibility. I can tell I've come pretty close to the truth by the way you're acting."

One side of his mouth inched up mockingly. "I suppose the Pinkertons will be coming to you for advice now."

"You're so smug."

He ran a long-fingered hand through his already mussed hair and rubbed the back of his neck in a weary motion. "Don't you get tired of this?"

"What?"

"This constant battle between us. You'd think if you let down your hair a fraction, the world would come to an end."

Maybe it would. Her world as she knew it, anyway. This was safe. Agreement on anything wasn't. "I am who I am," she told him. "And if you don't like it, consider yourself mostly to blame."

She turned and swept passed the curtains, dived into the bed and placed the brick at her feet. Immediately the delicious warmth spread across her toes. Solidity, she told herself again. Security. Stability. Those were the things worth having. She was just stubborn and hardheaded enough to get what she wanted.

But, she wondered some time later, as dawn tinged her lacy curtains with pink, was she doubly determined to do this thing she'd planned simply because of her stubbornness—because Brock had told her not to?

"Abby?" His voice seemed to be coming from a distant dream, but she realized it was only from the doorway, and that she had finally fallen asleep.

"Yes?"

"I'm leaving. Lock the door behind me."

She did as he instructed, sleepily closing the door after him and caressing the wood with her fingertips as though she were touching him.

The talk in church that morning was centered on various suppositions about the shots fired at the front of the hotel the night before. Being a frontier town, Whitehorn had seen its share of shootings and chases, but the last fifteen or so years had brought law and order to the forefront, and now this type of happening wasn't normal or acceptable.

Everett sat beside Abby during the service, his presence not as comforting as she thought it might have been. He was handsome, hardworking, respected among the local residents, and a regular churchgoer. What more could Abby have sought in a mate? It was Brock Kincaid who had her head in a spin, and she needed to put a stop to his interference once and for all.

Perhaps she could move her marriage to Everett forward. Saying "I do" and bringing him to live in her quarters over the store would be a deterrent. While Reverend McWhirter was making an announcement about a drive for the Ladies' Benevolence Society, Abby leaned sideways and whispered, "What would you think about moving our wedding date forward?"

Everett turned and looked at her with a raised brow. "Why?"

"I just thought that—well, that perhaps we shouldn't wait so long."

His eyes raked her face and warmth bloomed in her

cheeks. Let him think she couldn't wait to be intimate with him. Let him think whatever it took to discourage Brock.

"It would appear to everyone as though we'd engaged in improprieties and were trying to quickly set things right," he replied in a choked whisper. "I couldn't damage your reputation like that."

"I—I don't care what people think," she said, and knew it was a lie straight from the pits of hell. She fully expected lightning to pierce the roof and set her ablaze in the pew. Of course she cared what people thought! That was why she'd worked so hard to keep up appearances and why she couldn't admit to anyone except Laine what Brock had really been to her—and what he was to Jonathon.

"Well, I care what they think of you," he replied. "I'm marrying a respectable woman, and respectable you'll stay."

Folding her gloved hands in her lap and glancing down at Jonathon, who was frowning on her other side, she forced a smile and patted her son's leg reassuringly.

Respectable. For the first time she thought about Everett's reasons for courting and proposing to her. He hadn't professed undying love, true, but she'd fancied he'd admired her for more qualities than her respectability. Ashamed, she remembered the things she'd ticked off about why she was marrying him, and knew respectability had been important.

From a nagging corner of her mind, the thought of the hardware store and the ranch she owned mocked her. She'd always seen Everett as well-dressed and securely employed, but he probably wasn't getting rich from his telegraph job. Did he see her as a financial asset? Any man she married would benefit from her prosperity, though, so she couldn't accuse him of gold digging without good reason.

Somehow he should think more tenderly toward her. He should find her charming and enjoy her company. She needed to change his thinking. And she needed to prove Brock wrong about her marriage plans.

# Chapter Ten

Brock returned to the ranch with John in time to join the hands for the noon meal. All of them had heard about the shots fired the night before, and those who didn't resent John or shy away from him were curious to hear any news. Brock had learned from him that day that he was working for Caleb to repay money Caleb had loaned him to buy land for his tribe and spare them being sent to the reservation.

Floyd Cobb stabbed a chicken breast from the platter and asked, "You able to tell anything from the tracks, John?"

"Only that the man was alone and that he wasn't a hunter or a trapper." He glanced at Brock.

"He ate from tins," Brock explained, helping himself to a piece of corn bread.

"The horse was well shod and well fed," the Cheyenne added.

"Maybe he got it from the livery," Bluey Muir suggested.

"That's possible. Same pattern to the shoes," John replied. "But then Briggs shoes a good many horses in these parts."

"You could check the horses he rents."

"Briggs doesn't think much of me," John replied. "I don't think he'd be big on letting me look at his stock."

"How 'bout we get you into the stable without 'im knowing?" Floyd asked.

"Even if I could identify the horse and we found out who'd rented it, do you think anyone would take my word for it?" he asked.

"James would," Brock said.

John merely shook his head. Brock understood, as Caleb surely did, that John had the responsibility of his entire tribe on his shoulders, and involvement with something like this would bring him trouble he didn't need.

A silence fell over the men, and they continued their meal, glancing from time to time at the hands who sat at the other end of the table to avoid John.

Brock thanked John, carried his tin plate to the tub of sudsy water and followed Caleb outside. "Been thinking about something."

Caleb withdrew his pipe and a drawstring bag, from which he pinched tobacco and poked it into the bowl. "What's that?"

"Maybe it's time I used my share of land. Built a house, started a spread of my own."

Caleb nodded. "The land is there. You just have to choose which sections you want." He lit his pipe and puffed until fragrant smoke filled the crisp air. "This have anything to do with Abby and Jonathon?"

The insightful question amused Brock. "Couldn't hurt to have a place of my own, could it?"

"Nope. Would confirm to anyone that you meant to stay." He gazed off toward the purple-hazed mountains. "Shows *me* you're staying."

"I'm staying," Brock confirmed, warmed by the fact

that his brother had been glad to have him back and truly wanted him here.

"We can get out the maps and go over the details tonight. You'll want good water and natural windbreaks for the house site. John helped me bring the maps up to date a year or so ago. There's something else, Brock."

"What's that?"

"There's a small case of our mother's jewelry in the safe. I've taken a couple of pieces for Ruth, and Will wanted a pair of earrings for Lizzie, but there's more. We didn't want to divide it all without you."

"Thanks." The fact that his brothers had waited for him to share their mother's keepsakes meant a lot. Brock agreed they'd meet after supper, and joined the men on their way back to their duties.

A week later he had a handle on exactly which sections were his and how he wanted the buildings laid out. He spent a couple of days in Butte, ordering supplies and contracting help for the project, which he planned to start after the weather cleared in the spring. An old settler's cabin and barn that had weathered many a season and sat far above where spring thaws would flood had been chosen as a central location from which to work.

Brock walked the gray around the log structure and the still-adequate barn, then halted and studied the winter-white landscape. A sound like thunder echoed in the distance, and he recognized the noise as an avalanche in a high canyon. A startled rabbit leaped from the underbrush several yards away and bounded toward a concealing thicket.

Brock had been too young and too headstrong to appreciate the legacy his father had left him here on the rugged Montana frontier. This land provided everything needed to sustain a man and his family: fresh water, abun-

dant game, virgin timber and good soil. It wasn't too late
to start over. Not here, anyway.

And he'd see to it that it wasn't too late to start over
with Abby and his son, too.

On Friday night the Double Deuce was filled with cow-
hands restless from the winter isolation and impatiently
waiting for calving season. Brock sat in a poker game
with Will and John. Linc Manley, Harry Talbert and a
hand from Matt Darby's ranch filled out the table. The
hand, who went by the name of Ajax, dealt the cards, then
leaned his chair back on two legs, watching the others
with a tick in his whiskered cheek. He'd been nursing a
bottle of cheap whiskey for the last hour.

Brock had been on a winning streak, having reaped a
stack of coins and as much paper money. He had another
good hand this time and only took one card, which filled
a queen high straight. He tossed five coins in the pot.

Ajax gave a menacing scowl when the bid came to him,
and used his thumb to still the twitch in his cheek while
he considered his bid. Only two coins still lay on the green
cloth at his right hand. "I got a horse to bet," he said in
a gravelly tone.

It always disturbed Brock to see a man so desperate for
a winning hand that he'd bet his last dollar or his property,
and this time was no different. He almost wished he'd
stayed home and played checkers with Caleb.

"Okay by me," Harry said with a shrug.

Murmurs of agreement went around the table. A bad
feeling rose in Brock's chest.

Final bids were made, John and Harry folded, and the
other men revealed their hands. Ajax laid down his full
house, a cocky grin on his lips, and waited expectantly.

Brock spread his hand on the table.

The man sprang from his chair, knocking it backward

with a clatter. "You cheated! Nobody's that damned lucky!"

"You dealt those cards, partner," Brock said, raising both hands above the table. He would not kill this man over a game of poker.

"Sit down and cool off," Will said calmly.

"The son of a bitch cheated," Ajax declared, swinging his arm in an arc that knocked glasses and cards and coins flying. He reached for the Colt at his hip.

Brock's lightning fast reaction was instinctive. Half a dozen guns cleared holsters and were aimed at the man, but their appearance came precious seconds after Brock had drawn.

The disgruntled cowboy glared wildly, first at Brock, then at Linc Manley, one of those with a revolver drawn, and finally at Will. The tick in the man's cheek had started to involve the corner of his eye.

"Put the gun down," Brock said in a calm tone.

The cowboy knew he'd made a mistake. He would either shoot to save face now or he'd back down, and Brock was betting he'd rather back down than take several slugs at close range. The odds were stacked against him. Wisely, he lowered the Colt to the table.

Will reached over to secure it. A collective breath was released in the room. "Somebody go get James," Will said.

John holstered his gun. "I'll go." He picked up his money and donned his coat before heading out into the cold.

Ajax made an awkward break for the door, knocking into a chair, bumping one of the saloon girls with his shoulder. Brock and Will were right behind him; Brock caught his arm and stopped his momentum, spinning him around. Will closed in just as Ajax fell, and jammed his foot in his back. Brock caught a length of rope that Cam tossed from behind the bar, and together they tied the struggling man's wrists and ankles.

Brock stood and met Linc Manley's intense stare. No one else had seemed to make too much of Brock's speedy draw; he'd always been faster than his brothers, faster than James or any of his youthful friends. But the man who apparently fancied himself a gambler and a gunfighter appeared affected by the scene—or the knowledge he'd just ingested. Brock looked away and gathered his things.

An hour later, he sat in James's tidy office, sipping strong coffee. Ajax had been locked in a cell, and James, after remembering he'd seen a paper with a drawing that looked like this cowboy, had sent a wire to Butte.

Irritated at being called away from his game to send the message and wait for the reply, Matthews flung the jail door open and slapped a paper on James's desk.

"You were right. Man who looks like him is wanted for horse stealing and various other crimes. Any more messages can wait until morning." He gave Brock a sideways glare and left as quickly as he'd entered.

"Looks like the horse you won may be stolen," James said.

"I don't want the damned horse," Brock replied.

"Why don't you look it over for a brand?" James straightened the papers on his desk. "Stayed as fast as ever with those guns, did you?" he asked, referring to the reports about what had occurred in the saloon.

Did James suspect anything? Brock shrugged. As youngsters they'd practiced on apples from Daniel Pratt's orchard, which they'd lined up along the top of the fence. Brock, James and Daniel had all three received a licking with a switch when their fathers had to replace a twelve-foot section of the Pratts' fence. Brock had always been the quickest, the most accurate shot. It had been something he'd done well, and the only thing that gained him much attention after his mother's death. "Stayed alive," he said finally.

"You think Linc Manley is this Jack Spade fellow?" James asked. "Seems Spade hasn't been seen anywhere else since the man got here."

"He acts the part," Brock replied noncommittally.

"Maybe. But what would he be doing here? We don't have any range wars or need for a marshal. S'pose he's followed someone here for bounty?"

"This Spade fellow's a bounty hunter, too? Where's he find time to change his drawers?"

"Granted, the dime novels probably have him drawn a little larger than life," James said with a wry grin.

"You've read them?"

"Hasn't everybody?"

"I haven't."

James opened a drawer and shuffled through until he found what he wanted. Handing a dog-eared, softcover book to his cousin, he grinned. "It's winter, you know?"

Brock studied the drawing of the mustached gunfighter, garbed in black, captured in a lethal-looking stance with a blazing revolver in each hand. He raised a finger to rub his bare upper lip thoughtfully. Slipping the book into his coat pocket, he headed for the door. If James did have real questions, he was keeping them to himself. "I'll check out that horse for you."

Lionel Briggs was eager to talk to someone who'd witnessed the excitement firsthand. Brock gave him a quick explanation and asked to see the horse belonging to the cowboy.

The superbly proportioned gelding, a chestnut with a white blaze and white stockings, was healthy, with good teeth. It bore a clearly altered brand. "This is the stolen baby,'' Brock told him. ''I'll let James know and someone will come for him.''

''I don't mind the horse,'' Briggs assured him. ''Horses are my business, but I ain't takin' care of that mangy mutt.''

''What mutt?''

''The one came in with that fella. I let it rest in a stall back there and gave it water, but I ain't no vet. Hasn't gone farther than a few feet. Don't think it can, really. Somebody ought ta put a bullet in its head.''

In the stall indicated, Brock discovered the animal, a yellowish, long-haired breed of some sort, with a well-shaped head and muzzle. The poor thing was half-starved, its hair matted, and a raw wound glistened on one shoulder.

The creature raised its head in a weak greeting when Brock entered the stall and bent down on his haunches to look it over. The mutt wagged his sweeping tail a few sluggish times.

Brock reached out a hand to let him sniff. The dog licked his fingers with a warm dry tongue, a display of needy affection and desperate trust that injected Brock with instant sympathy. ''What happened to you, boy?''

Dark eyes showed flickering interest.

''What're you going to do with him?'' he asked the livery man.

''Put 'im out of his misery, I reckon,'' Briggs replied.

''Think he belongs to someone?''

''Couldn't say. He showed up when that Ajax feller rode in.''

''Can't leave him here to suffer,'' Brock murmured, thinking aloud.

''Can't leave 'im here period.''

Brock touched the dog's bony head, petted his silky

long ear. "Got a bucket and water I can use to wash his cuts?"

"Buckets are in the tack room. Horse tank out back's had the ice busted off. You can heat it on the stove back there."

"Thanks." Brock strode off to heat water.

It was nearly midnight by the time he'd washed the dog's cuts and gotten him to drink. He needed food and something for the wounds, but Brock couldn't see making him endure a ride, even if he carried him carefully to the ranch. He could take him to Will's or James's, he supposed, but at this hour their wives wouldn't appreciate an intrusion from their troublesome Kincaid in-law.

There was always Abby's place, he surmised. He'd intruded on her so much already that another time probably wouldn't make a difference in her opinion of him. She couldn't get any angrier than she already was. Anyway, it would just be a couple of days until the dog was able to travel farther.

Borrowing a horse blanket, he wrapped the animal and let Lionel know he was taking the dog. Keeping an eye out for anyone observing, Brock carried him through the alley, around the corner of the building and up the flight of stairs. He waited, cringing inwardly at imagining her reaction, but feeling rather clever at having thought of another means to wile his way into her place.

Sitting at the kitchen table with a ledger and a lamp, Abby was startled by a light knock at the door. Her heart lifted in an odd little tug. No one had ever come to her door late until Brock's return.

She stepped close to the wooden barrier. "Who is it?"

"Brock. Let me in."

"It's late."

"I know it's late. Open the door."

"You told me to ask who it was before I opened the

door. Since I know it's you, I don't want to open the door.''

"Open the door or I'll cause a scene.''

She considered his threat. A heartbeat later, before he had a chance to fulfil it, she opened the door. He stood silhouetted against the dark sky, his hat pulled low over his forehead, a covered bundle in his arms. He pushed past her impatiently. "Got an old blanket?''

"What is that?''

He moved toward the other room and the heater.

She followed.

"Please bring me an old blanket,'' he asked almost civilly, so she did his bidding. "Leave it folded some for padding and spread it out here on the floor.''

Once she'd done that, he lowered his burden to the pile. The blanket made a sound and moved, startling her.

Brock pulled the cover away to reveal a pathetic-looking mongrel. A rather large one. The beast barely moved, only beseeched Brock with doleful eyes and then cast pitiful dark eyes on Abby. What had the man been thinking to bring this near-dead animal to her home? What was she to do with it?

Her attention was drawn to a nasty gash in his golden fur. "Oh, he's hurt!''

"Do you have anything? Ointment maybe?''

"I think so.'' She hurried to the kitchen, wondering what she was doing, answering Brock's beck and call in the middle of the night, and returned with a tin Laine had given her for an infected cut on her wrist. She handed him the salve. "Why have you brought this dog here?''

"Didn't know what else to do with him. Briggs was gonna shoot him.''

Warily, Abby studied the dog's sad expression and warm eyes. The pathetic thing was so thin that perhaps shooting him would have been the kindest thing to do. "And you couldn't let him do that?"

"Let him sniff your hand," Brock said.

She looked from the dog to him and back again. Something drew her to tentatively extend her hand.

The mutt raised his head enough to lick her fingers. At the pleading touch, Abby's heart went out to the poor thing, even though she knew caring would be a mistake. "What if he dies?"

Brock hunkered down on one knee, his wrist dangling over the other one. "Then I tried."

She let herself rub the bony head. "But what if he lives long enough for Jonathon to get attached, and then dies?"

Brock looked up with a worried frown, as if the thought had never occurred to him. "I won't let him die."

Gazing into Brock's impassioned blue eyes, she wondered what it would be like to have such confidence in oneself, to believe you held the power over life and death just by the strength of your will. Oddly enough, when he spoke the vow, she believed it, too. He was a man who got what he wanted.

Together they doctored wounds, bandaging the largest one so the dog couldn't lick off the medicine. Abby warmed some broth and offered it, watching while the animal used what little strength he had to lap it up. All through those tasks she kept thinking about Brock getting what he wanted, and wondering exactly what it was he wanted from her.

He wanted to be a part of Jonathon's life. Fighting him was futile. But she didn't have to let him hurt her again. She couldn't. One time of having her dreams dashed and her heart severed into tiny bleeding pieces had been enough pain for a lifetime. And he hadn't changed.

Except physically. His face was that of a man—leaner, harder, with weathered wrinkles at his eyes and across his forehead. His hands were corded and strong, and fair hair dusted his wrists. He was taller and broader than the young man she remembered. Her appreciative gaze couldn't miss the added span of his wide shoulders beneath the wrinkled chambray shirt or the flex of thigh muscle beneath his trouser legs as he bent and moved.

But there, tethered to those strong legs, were the guns she hated and feared. Those weapons represented everything that had gone bad between them, still held a sickening connotation in her heart and mind. She bent to pick up the empty bowl, but her trembling fingers lost their grip and it clattered to the floor, hitting the corner of the heater with a clang.

Brock bent to retrieve it, pointed to a chip. "I'll buy you a new one."

"No, it's old. It doesn't matter." She took the bowl from him.

"Mama? What wath that?" Jonathon scuffed out barefoot and rubbed his eyes sleepily. "Mithter Brock? Whatcha doin' here?"

"I needed your mom's help," Brock replied.

Jonathon caught sight of the dog and bounded forward. "A dog? Where'd we get a dog?"

"He's not our dog," Abby cautioned.

"I found him sick and hurt, and I brought him here for your mom to help me take care of him."

"Bad hurt?" the boy asked, and he knelt cautiously.

"Not too bad," Brock replied. "But his cuts haven't been tended and he looks like he hasn't eaten for a long time."

"What happened to him?"

"I don't know. Maybe a fight with an animal. Maybe...maybe, I don't know."

Abby was grateful he hadn't suggested that a person might have done that harm. She hoped Jonathon had a lot of time left before he had to learn the cruel reality of this world.

Brock didn't have to suggest that Jonathon let the dog smell him. The child patted his furry head and the animal immediately turned his face to lavishly lick his hand. Jonathon laughed delightedly. "He liketh me! Look, Mama!"

"I see."

Situating himself more comfortably on the floor, Brock explained the dog's injuries and how they were going to help him get better and stronger. Jonathon wore the same excited expression he'd worn on Christmas morning, his innocent delight and enthusiasm tugging at Abby's heart. She prayed the dog would survive.

The canine fell into exhausted sleep and Jonathon covered him with the blanket, continuing to stroke his head.

"Time for you to go back to your bed," Abby told him.

"Do I have to?"

She nodded. "Yes, darling. It's late and you're a growing boy."

"Can Mithter Brock tuck me in?"

Both sets of blue eyes appealed to her. She nodded her assent. Brock held out his hand. "Come on, partner." Together they strolled into the bedroom.

Abby added fuel to the heater. Rather than put up a futile struggle, she scurried to her room for blankets and a pillow, and placed them on the divan. Brock returned at the same time. "He fell right to sleep," he reported.

"You're staying to watch over the dog, I suppose."

He leaned back from the waist, stretching his spine and emphasizing his imposing size, and nodded. Unable to pry her hungry gaze from him, she watched as he carried the basin, towel and tin to the kitchen, and listened as he apparently washed at her sink.

He returned, carrying his shirt, his chest bare, droplets

glistening in the golden hairs. Abby swallowed. His hair looked as though he'd run his fingers through it; his powerful arms were sleek and solid. "Do you have a shirt?" he asked. "Mine smells like a wet dog."

She managed a nod and found one of Jed's flannel shirts in the back of a drawer. Brock accepted the folded garment and laid it on the back of the divan, before he sat and removed his boots. Abby came to life and arranged the blankets and pillows, making him stand aside.

She finished and stood back.

"Thank you," he said finally.

"That must have hurt," she said, referring to the words she couldn't remember hearing him speak before.

"I did say please about the blanket," he said with a smirk. "I'm really a very polite person."

"Yes, and I'm your fairy godmother."

He chuckled—a rusty sound that surprised and pleased her. She softened a little more than she knew was wise, and found herself thinking about his needs and comfort. "Have you eaten?"

"Hours ago."

"Would you like something? And perhaps a cup of coffee?"

"Now I know you're right."

"About what?"

"You *are* my fairy godmother."

She turned toward the kitchen. "If I was, I'd turn you into a toad and let the dog eat you."

"I think you're mixed up," he said from behind her. "Fairy godmothers grant wishes, they don't turn men into toads."

"You're right. Men do that on their own."

He pulled out a chair and stood behind it, shrugging into the shirt, which wouldn't close over his chest. The cuffs rode halfway up his forearms.

She placed a slice of pie on the table and sized him up with a frown. "Forget the shirt." She glided behind him and grasped the collar, peeling the garment over his bare back and down his arms. "I'll wash yours, and if I hang it near the heater, it will be dry by morning."

"It's late, Abby—"

"Eat your pie." She tested the coffeepot, found it hot and poured him a cup. "Sugar?"

He nodded.

Washing the shirt gave her something to do other than stare at his naked torso while he ate and drank. She wrung the water from his garment, rolled it in toweling and then draped it over the back of a chair she pulled near the heater.

"Thank you," he said, placing his plate and cup in the enamel pan.

"That's twice."

"Told you I'm polite." He caught her wrist, where the fabric was wet from the chores, and turned her toward him. "Mind my manners, say please and thank you."

There was nowhere for her gaze to go except the broad expanse of smooth, hair-dusted skin or his mobile lips. Her gaze fluttered from one to the other.

"May I please kiss you?" he asked.

Her heart jerked against her ribs. At that moment, his mouth was the most appealing sight she'd known, and she'd love nothing more than to feel it against hers. "You've never asked for a kiss in your life."

"Sure I have." He lazily grazed her wrist bone and his eyelids lowered to a slumberous slant.

She concentrated on breathing. "When?"

"Just now." One hand went behind her waist and edged her closer. Oh, but he smelled good. Familiar.

She raised a hand to protest, but realized it would come

in contact with his flesh, so let it flutter. ''That doesn't count.''

''Why not?'' Heat spread from his fingers to her tingling skin beneath her dress.

She was losing track of the conversation and didn't know if she wanted to reply, anyway. She moved her hand again, and this time allowed herself to touch him. His warm skin flinched beneath her fingertips. Surrendering to her own craving, she flattened her palm on his chest. Beneath her hand his heart beat steadily. He was so warm, so alive....

He closed his eyes and cursed under his breath, but she heard it.

''That was *not* polite,'' she said, her voice more breathless than she'd intended.

He leaned toward her, each inch heart-stoppingly slow, and inclined his face to touch his nose to her hair. ''What wasn't polite?''

''That word.'' Daringly, she ran her palm from his chest downward and caressed his hard belly for her own pleasure, slid her hand to his ribs.

With a groan he said another coarse word, pressed his face to her temple and inhaled.

They stood that way, hearts beating erratically, breath escaping in shallow pants, for an eternity. He released her wrist to bring his hand up and cup her jaw, turning her face to his. He spread his hand beneath her ear and worshiped her with his eyes.

''Yes,'' she said with a sigh.

''Yes what?''

''Yes, you may kiss me.''

That spectacular mouth turned up in a self-satisfied grin. ''Maybe I never said please before...'' He inched so close, the warmth from his lips teased hers. ''...but you never said no, either.''

At that moment, he could have said anything and she wouldn't have cared, so attuned was she to the sensual onslaught of his dizzying nearness. She slid both hands to his back and pulled him closer.

## Chapter Eleven

He hauled her against him as roughly as she grasped him in return, an explosive clash of bodies that pressed the buckle of his holster into her belly. With one arm around her back, pulling her forward, and the other hand at her nape, he kissed her with surprising restraint, his lips warm, pliant, insatiable.

Abby ran her hands over his back, relishing the glorious feel of him, lost in the magic of his deep-drawn kiss. No one had ever kissed her as thoroughly and splendidly as this. No one had ever turned her insides to liquid heat and created this delicious eagerness in her body. Dimly, she thought of Jonathon, of the possibility that he could awaken and stumble back out.

Brock must have considered that, too, because he broke the kiss, released her, but kept hold of her hand, and leaned to extinguish the lamp on the table.

Abby's pulse beat all through her awakened body as the darkness enfolded them.

When he tugged her toward her room, she resisted.

"We don't have to do anything you don't want to do," he whispered, still coaxing with a gentle pull.

That was the problem. She wanted to.

"Just a few kisses if that's all you want," he said. "In here where Jonathon wouldn't see us if he woke up."

Against her better judgment, she went. Eagerly. Wantonly.

Brock sat at the foot of her bed and pulled her between widespread knees to frame her hips through her skirts and tip his face up to her throat.

She skimmed her palms over his shoulders, kneaded his neck.

"You don't know what heaven it is when you touch me," he said, his voice gruff.

If it was half what she felt when he touched her, she knew.

He moved back, coaxing her forward to straddle his lap. "I have my shoes on," she objected.

He set her away, raised one foot at a time to his thigh and unbuttoned her shoes, dropping them to the floor, then guided her back.

"You know I hate those guns," she said, when her knee bumped one holster and startled her.

Obliging, he leaned back to unbuckle the belt and remove the revolvers, hanging them over the bedpost.

"Is that everything?" he asked teasingly in the dark. "Anything else you'd like one of us to take off?"

"You don't have much left," she replied, stroking the skin of his shoulders and upper arms.

"Feeling left out?" He brought his hands up her rib cage. "We can even things up."

She leaned against him, bringing her breasts under his chin. "You're much to bold for someone who should be far more repentant."

"What do you want me to do? Beg your forgiveness on my knees?"

She thought about it, and couldn't picture him doing so in a million years. She shook her head, not caring whether or not he could see. His hair beneath her chin was cool and silky. She speared two handfuls and pulled his head back so their faces were close, but tauntingly kept her lips from touching his.

He lowered his hands to cup her bottom through layers of skirts and petticoats, an intimacy all the same.

She nuzzled his forehead and temple, inhaling his erotic scent. They hadn't kissed since they'd come in here, but her body thrummed as though they'd never stopped. He arched his hips up against that place where she pulsed for him.

"Remember how it was with us, Abby?" he breathed against her cheek.

"I remember." How could she ever forget?

"You were a little scared that first time, but so beautiful in your eagerness."

His words seduced, but still she kept her mouth a hair's breadth from his. "I believed in fairy godmothers back then, too."

He ignored that. "Your breasts were always so sensitive to my touch. I remember their perfect shape and—"

"I don't have a young girl's body anymore," she interrupted.

"Knowing that has kept me awake at night for weeks," he replied, then darted out his tongue so that it reached her lower lip.

Startled, she sucked in a breath, lost track of her thoughts and gave herself over to the sensation of his mouth, kissing him hungrily, controlling the pressure by her grasp of his hair.

Never passive, Brock explored her bunched skirts to find the hem and glide his hands up her calves, beneath her drawers and over her knees to the tops of her stockings, where he found her skin and tickled enticingly with his fingertips. When the fabric restricted further exploration, he flattened his palms on her thighs through the cotton and rubbed upward.

He created a rapturous suspense in her body, one she knew too well he could kindle and feed until both of them were sated and replete. One thumb found the placket in her drawers, and tentatively, enticingly, he stroked over the folds of her femininity and found her moist readiness.

Abby sucked her breath in, squeezing her eyes shut in expectation, releasing her hold on his hair until her wrists draped over his shoulders.

"Abby," he said, kissing her throat, her neck beneath her ear. "Abby." Each vocal caress of her name paralleled his stroking thumb.

She shuddered uncontrollably under the focused assault, shamelessly indulging in the pleasure he gave. She wanted this in her life. She wanted passion and fire and anticipation and the intense perfection of lovemaking she'd only ever shared with Brock.

His scent was in her nostrils; her blood pounded in her ears, her every sense compromised by his inflaming assault.

She found his mouth with hers, tasted him impatiently. He drew his hand away, and she almost wept.

He found the buttons at her throat and made quick work of opening her dress. Her head cleared enough to know it was time to make a decision. If she didn't stop this now, there would be no turning back. He kissed the skin of her chest, bared above her chemise. "No corset."

The kisses sent tingles across her shoulders and down to tighten her breasts. "I don't wear one to work."

Finding the ribbons that held her chemise closed, he pulled them loose and spread the fabric, letting the cool air wash over her fevered skin. He buried his face between her breasts, and she hugged him close, tears coming to her eyes at the vividness of feeling. She didn't want to end this experience. She wanted to revel in it.

Brock stood her up to remove her dress. Untying her petticoats, he helped her kick them off, then peeled down her stockings and drawers. He ran his hands over her hips and along her thighs, worshipfully, then guided her to the bed, where she hastily peeled back the coverlet and sheets and reclined while he made quick work of the rest of his clothing.

"Have we ever made love in a bed?" he asked, leaning over her, his hard body sliding against her sensitized skin from her breasts to her thighs.

"I—I don't think so."

He closed a hand over her breast, and she bit her lip against a lusty groan. Drawing her other nipple into his mouth, he tortured it with his tongue and lips until she wanted to scream.

Her powerful responses awakened a realization that her memories and fantasies had not blown Brock Kincaid's effect on her out of proportion. This tantalizing rediscovery was no dream.

Beneath Brock's hands, her sweet body trembled and tensed, twined and pressed. He remembered the combination of fragility and strength that had always made Abby unique and desirable. The energetic passion that had always matched his was still as fierce as ever.

He explored leisurely, giving lavish attention to each place that caught his fancy or stole her breath, all the while gauging her arousal, yet prolonging the enjoyment for both of them, honing the inevitable to a fever pitch. Her breasts were fuller than he remembered, her hips more curvy—womanly changes that made him crazy with wanting her.

She returned the caresses until he caught her wrists, stroked her damp shoulders and slowed her down. He

pushed to his knees and pulled her to a sitting position in
the V of his thighs, facing away from him. She snuggled
backward, eliciting an unrestrained groan from him. He
caught her disheveled braid, ran his hand to the end and
fumbled to unfasten the tie.

Using his fingers as a comb, he loosened her hair from
the ends to her scalp. Once the tresses were free and flowing over her back, he caressed her through the silky cool-
ness, leaned into her and inhaled her mind-numbing es-
sence.

Arousal pounding now, he pulled her back, weighed her
breasts in his palms, flicked the nipples with his thumbs
until she drew up her knees and whimpered.

Brock guided her to lie down, then stretched over her
and took pleasure in the way she opened her silken body
to him, eagerly drawing him close. Pressing into her, he
captured her cry with his kiss, groaned against her mouth
and held himself perfectly still lest he end the ecstasy as
soon as it started.

The tide abated and he moved. Abby caught his face
with one palm, and her chest jerked with a sob. At her
cry, his heart dipped. "Are you all right?"

"Yes. Yes, don't stop."

"I just want it to be good for you," he said, meaning
it with all his being. "This is for you, beautiful lady."

"You know I'll hate you now," she said, her breathy
voice lacking conviction.

"You hated me already," he replied, hearing the sadness with which he said the words.

"Not like this," she whispered. "Not like this."

"Oh, Abby," he said, and slowed his movements.

"If you stop now, I will get one of those guns and shoot
you in your black heart," she threatened.

Despite the sadness in his heart, he smiled at her spirit,

admired her never-flagging gumption. And thrust them both over the edge.

She hadn't been imagining how it had been between them. The years hadn't blown their explosive attraction out of proportion in the least. If she'd been testing that, she had an answer. And how.

Brock had pulled the covers over both of them, but she had drawn away, torn between wanting to hold him close so badly that her arms ached, and needing to distance herself so she could think.

They were too different, and the past had built too many hindrances to conceive of any kind of compromise. She had accepted part of the responsibility for his leaving, but how could she forgive him his part? True, he hadn't known she was going to have a baby, but if he'd cared in the least, he would have stayed to find out.

That thought jolted her into awareness and her head buzzed for a full minute while she collected her thoughts. What if she'd gotten herself with child again? Abby clutched the edge of the covers and squeezed her eyes shut. It was highly unlikely that this one time had created a baby. She was a little more knowledgeable than she'd been back then, and she knew the number of times they'd been intimate in the past had increased the likelihood. This was one time, and she'd just finished her menses. The time between cycles made a difference, too, she'd read.

Besides, fate couldn't be that cruel twice—not that Jonathon was a mistake. She had never regretted her child a day of his precious life. And she never would.

"Abby," Brock said from beside her.

"Don't say anything," she ordered, and pushed herself to a sitting position, taking the sheet with her. "You'll only make it worse."

"Worse than what? What just happened couldn't have been any better."

"For you. You have no responsibilities. No concern for tomorrow. If things don't go your way, you simply leave and don't look back."

"You're being unfair. And cruel."

She got up and found her robe on a hook. "I told you not to talk."

He sat; she heard the movement and saw his outline in the darkness.

"Just go," she said, turning her back.

"I'm not leaving."

She'd known that. But she didn't have to condone his presence in her bed.

Behind her, movements indicated he was pulling on his trousers, picking up his guns, preparing to leave the room.

"I have something for you," he said. "It's in my coat. I'll be right back."

"I don't want anything from you." But he was gone. He returned a few minutes later, carrying an oil lamp.

The light embarrassed her, and she tightened her robe around herself, refusing to look at him.

He came to where she sat at the edge of the bed, and extended a tiny velvet pouch.

She glanced at it and away.

Brock set the lamp on her bureau and slipped something from the pouch to show her. A lovely opal-and-diamond brooch twinkled in the lamplight.

His offering cheapened what had happened even more, and a sick feeling cramped in her belly. "You don't have to pay," she choked out.

Anger flickered in his eyes. "I'm offering you a gift."

"I can't accept it."

"It was my mother's," he said curtly.

Caught completely off guard by that announcement, she

looked at the pin again. Why would he give her a piece of his mother's jewelry when he felt nothing for her? Why did he imagine she would accept it? Did he think to appease her somehow?

Brock held the brooch out to her, suddenly feeling as vulnerable as he did when he went without his revolvers. He'd thought of Abby the moment he'd seen it among the heirlooms he and his brothers had divided. And he'd known there would never be another woman who meant what Abby meant to him. This was hers.

"I don't want it."

Her rejection bit deeply. With her scent still on his skin and the acute memory of what they'd just shared filling his mind, he absorbed the affront with stoic resolve. "Save it for Jonathon, then."

Brock jerked her hand from the front of her robe and pried her fingers open, placing the jeweled pin in her palm. "He should have something that belonged to his grandmother. Maybe it will mean something to him someday, even though it means nothing to you. He can give it to the woman he—" Brock stumbled over the word that almost fell from his lips. She would take any declaration of love or affection and turn it against him. "Marries," he finished, and stalked from the room.

A night on her divan gave him a crick in his neck, and he woke constantly. Occasionally, he checked on the dog or fed the heater. By the time morning arrived he'd gone over every detail of their explosive joining the night before. She had warned him. He couldn't fault her for not being honest. She hated him more than ever.

But did she truly? Or was it her lack of control that she detested? If he'd made any progress in his quest to prove his sincerity and win her trust, it surely wasn't apparent.

Seduction hadn't been in his plan. Desire just erupted between the two of them as naturally as fire consumed dry tinder. And since last night had proved that she was still as crazy for him as he was for her, he was assured he was on the right track.

He folded the bedding and left before Jonathon awoke and found him there, but returned as the two of them were eating breakfast.

"Hey, Mithter Brock," his son said with a welcoming smile. "We got more oatmeal in the pan—enough for you."

"Why thanks, partner," he replied, and, after hanging up his coat and holster, seated himself at the table.

Abby, a clean white apron over her church dress, spooned globs of cereal into a bowl and placed it before him without ever meeting his eyes.

"Thought I'd stay with the dog while you go to church," Brock said.

"Mama thaid we could give him more broth when we wath done here," Jonathon told him. "He'th prob'ly real hungry."

Abby didn't sit back down, though her bowl was only half-empty. She took some broth from the ice box and heated it in a pan.

"Do you go to the Epithcopal church?" the boy asked. "I didn't ever thee you at our church."

Abby still hadn't looked at him. "I—uh, haven't gone to church for a long time," Brock replied.

"You din't?" Jonathon said, eyes wide in his innocence. "You could come with me an' Mama."

"I have to take care of the dog," he replied.

Abby set a bowl on the table with a thud.

"I'm done, Mama." Jonathon pushed his own bowl away and stood. "I'll feed the dog." He took the dish and carried it carefully toward the other room.

"Got a lot to repent of this morning?" Brock asked when they were alone.

"You keep your gloating to yourself," she told him, pointing a spoon. "You'd be sorry, too, if you had a decent bone in your body."

"I'm not a bit sorry," he replied.

"I'm so surprised."

"And you've been reacquainted with every bone in my body, so you'd know what's there and what's not."

With a sputter, she threw the spoon, missing his head, but hitting a cupboard.

He couldn't hold back a chuckle. Her skin was pink and glowing, her green eyes ablaze with an internal fire. It seemed the night had done her a world of good. "Glad you haven't lost your pluck."

"Anything I ever lost, you took," she said hotly.

"Oh, no," he disagreed. "You gave it all up willingly."

Turning away, her shoulders tight, her spine stiff, she rested her hands on the counter and let her head fall back. "I hate you."

He got up and carried his empty bowl to the pan of water and dropped it in before pausing behind her. He studied the nape of her delicate neck, where her auburn hair had been pulled up and fashioned into a knot. He remembered kissing that very spot and the way she'd shivered and melted against him.

"You just keep telling yourself that," he said, and saw his breath flutter the fine hairs. He strode away to join his son.

He couldn't spend all of his nights at Abby's. He did care about her reputation, no matter what she believed. The dog improved enough so that Brock came in the morning to carry the mutt down the outside stairs and stand with him in the alley while he did his business. He returned at night to do the same.

On one of those return trips in the middle of the week, Abby had a late customer, so Brock joined Jonathon in the back room. The child jubilantly showed him that the dog could get up and take a few shaky steps to retrieve a rubber ball. The boy scratched the animal's fur and let him lick his cheek. "He liketh playin' ball, don'tcha, Dilly?"

"Dilly?"

"That'th hith name."

"I see. How'd he get that name?"

"Well, I wath eatin' one o' Mama'th pickleth, and he kept lickin' the juithe off my hand. He'd liketh pickleth."

"Dilly. Well, that's as good of a name as any. Do you think he's well enough to move now?"

Jonathon's face fell. He looked at the pet with yearning in his luminous eyes. "Where ya gonna take 'im to?"

"The ranch. I just had to make sure he could travel."

"Doeth he have to go, Brock? Couldn't you leave 'im here? I can take good care of 'im. I'll feed 'im and take 'im out to the alley an' everything. He won't be no trouble."

"Well…" Brock rubbed his chin and considered the boy's sincere wish. "That would be fine with me, but your mama is the one who would have to decide."

"Can we athk her?"

Brock nodded. Jonathon leaped up and flung himself against Brock's chest in an enthusiastic display. Brock's heart opened completely to this child he'd grown to love more than he'd ever dreamed possible. He placed his hand on his son's hair and stroked it, a knot forming in his throat.

The curtain moved and Abby appeared in the doorway. Her expression flashed from tenderness to indifference like quicksilver.

"Mama?" Jonathon asked excitedly. "Brock thaid I

can keep Dilly. Can I? I'll take care of him and you won't even know he'th here. I'll feed 'im and let 'im out...." He went through his list of promises, while Abby held her face impassive. "Can I plee-ez keep him?"

She let her gaze touch Brock for the first time all week, but returned it rapidly to Jonathon and the dog. "I guess it couldn't hurt to have a watchdog for the store," she said finally.

*"Yes!"* Jonathon jumped up and down and did a little jig around Dilly, who thumped his tail and yipped a couple of times, as if celebrating his good fortune.

Jonathon stopped and ran to his mother. "Thank you, Mama." He hugged her around the waist.

She returned the hug as best she could from her position above him. "Don't thank me. Mr. Brock brought him to you. He's the one responsible."

"Thank you, Brock." The "mister" that he'd recently dropped when addressing Brock was blatantly noticeable.

"You're welcome, Son."

The word had slipped out, natural-like. Jonathon thought nothing of it, enamored as he was with his new pet. He gave Brock another hug and knelt to scratch Dilly's ears.

Abby had noticed, however. Her shoulders stiffened and tears came to her eyes. She blinked them back and turned away to remove her apron.

Brock would feel better with a dog here to alert them to anyone who might approach the place during the night. This twist of events had turned out better than if he had planned it, he thought, mollified. Good old Dilly had provided a night of passion with Abby, a couple of hugs from his son, and now would look after them when Brock couldn't be here.

After a trip to the alley, Brock carried the mutt up the stairs and got him settled.

"Can you thtay and play checkerth with me while Mama maketh dinner?" Jonathon asked. "Mama, can he?"

She had washed up and tied on a fresh apron. Brock had begun to realize how hard Abby worked, morning to evening in the store, and then taking care of Jonathon and their quarters.

"Why don't I go buy us supper from the hotel?" he suggested. He would have asked her to go to the hotel for a meal, but knew she'd never agree to be seen with him.

Abby seemed hesitant to accept the offer, though he knew the idea had to be appealing. "I'm going," he said. "You two play checkers till I get back."

Abby watched him go, her emotions ragged after the last few days of constant self-reproach, and his insistence on showing up morning and night. Saying the dog was Jonathon's should take the responsibility away from Brock now. The more he ingratiated himself into Jonathon's graces, the harder it was to discourage him.

They had played three games before Brock returned with their meal. "I had to make a deposit for their lousy plates, can you believe it?" he asked.

"I'll return them," Abby assured him.

He had selected huge cuts of beef, fresh cooked vegetables and spicy fried potatoes. Abby enjoyed the treat tremendously, and managed to thank him when they were finished.

"Shall I carry Dilly down one more time?" Brock asked Jonathon. The boy agreed, and the two of them bundled up to take the dog out. Upon their return, Brock gathered his hat and guns and wished them a good night.

"I really like Brock, Mama," Jonathon told her as he put his checkers away.

She didn't know how to reply, so simply nodded. She remembered the way Brock had called him "Son." It had sounded more like an endearment than just a casual term, and maybe that's because she was sensitive to everything the man said and did, as though trying to find an underlying motive. As though she needed to preserve his true nature in her mind, so she wouldn't be caught off guard.

Jonathon took out his schoolbooks and went to work on a paper. Abby used the extra time she had gained by not cooking to wash out a few of her underclothes and stockings. She hung them on a rope she stretched across the kitchen. Some time later, there was a knock at the door.

Abby's heart leaped nervously, and Jonathon scurried out of his chair to answer it.

# *Chapter Twelve*

"**O**h, hi."

"Where's your mother?" Everett moved past Jonathon to step into the kitchen and close the door. "Hello, Abby."

"Guess what I got?" Jonathon asked.

He glanced down. "I came to speak with your mother."

"I got a dog. Hith name'th Dilly. Wanna thee him?"

"Hi*z* name i*z* Dilly," Everett corrected, enunciating the *s*s. "Do I want to *s-s*ee him? Not particularly." He glanced around and spotted the line of damp clothing. "You do your own laundry?"

Defensive anger had welled up in Abby's breast. "Why don't we step into the other room and let Jonathon do his schoolwork?" she suggested.

Everett followed her to the sitting room, where the dog raised his head from his mat and wagged his tail.

"Good God, where did that pathetic-looking mongrel come from?"

"Jonathon's been nursing him to health. He's done a fine job of it, too."

"Why you'd allow the creature in your home is more than I can understand," her fiancé said.

"Everett, please don't correct Jonathon's speech again," she said plainly.

"He's seven years old and still talks like a baby."

"He'll grow out of it if we don't make him self-conscious. He's just a child."

"Very well," he said. "I'll respect your wishes."

"Thank you."

"I haven't had a chance to leave work the last few days, and I wanted to ask you to have dinner with me Friday evening."

"Yes, of course."

"You'll find someone to stay with the boy."

"Yes," she replied, then realized he never involved Jonathon in their time together.

"Do you want to sit?" she asked.

He glanced at the divan, then brushed his hands across his black coat. "Thank you, no."

"I'll take your coat."

"No, I'll be going now." He walked back though the kitchen. "Until Friday."

"Good night." She slipped the lock into place and turned to study her son.

He glanced up from his figures on the paper. "He don't like dog*z*, I gue*s-s*."

"Some people don't."

"We won't have to get rid of Dilly when you marry him, will we?"

"No," she promised. "Dilly's yours to keep. I give my word." Just as she'd given her word to marry Everett.


She avoided Brock the rest of the week, assuring him by Friday that Dilly was strong enough to travel the stairs on his own. Daisy and Asa were happy to have Jonathon for the evening, so Abby bathed and dressed in blessed quiet. When Everett came for her, she donned her boots and coat and accompanied him to the hotel.

They shared a pleasant meal, and she was able to forget his behavior around Jonathon for an hour or so.

To her chagrin, Brock and John Whitefeather showed up and were shown to a nearby table.

She looked the other direction, but felt Brock's gaze boring into her as if she was an insect pinned to a display board.

"I'm appalled at the riffraff they allow in this establishment," Everett complained.

She attempted to change the subject. A few minutes later, a bottle of wine was delivered to their table.

"From the gentleman over there," the waitress said, nodding.

Brock gave them a sardonic salute.

Abby fumed.

Everett examined the bottle. "Excellent choice. Thank the man for us."

Abby stared at him.

The waitress moved away, and Everett uncorked the bottle and filled their glasses.

"I don't care for any, thank you," she said stiffly.

"A virtuous woman never touches spirits," he said with an appreciative note in his voice.

If Brock hadn't been watching them, she would have been tempted to snatch the bottle from Everett's hand and crack him over the head with it. The mental picture alone was satisfying.

Everett took a blissful sip.

Brock raised a brow at Abby.

She looked away. "Might we visit your place tonight?"

Everett's eyebrows rose. "I live at the boardinghouse, as you well know. Any fraternizing with guests of the opposite sex is prohibited."

"Couldn't you get me in without anyone seeing?"

"I wouldn't even attempt it, and I'm shocked that you would ask."

"It just seems our time together is so brief," she replied.

"That will change once we're married," he said.

That's what she'd hoped about everything. He drank another glass of wine, then instructed the waitress to cork it and wrap it so he could take it home.

He walked her toward the hardware store, and Abby pulled her collar up against the cold. Once inside, Dilly met them. Abby closed the door and locked it. "Would you like coffee?"

"Tea perhaps." Everett avoided the dog by stepping away.

"Sit in the other room while I prepare us a pot."

He moved away, Dilly sniffing after him and emitting low growls.

Abby shushed him before boiling water and steeping tea, then carried a tray into the sitting room. She spooned sugar into her fiancé's cup and handed the hot drink to him on a saucer.

"Thank you."

She took her own cup and sat beside him.

After a lengthy silence, she asked, "Where do you usually take your supper?"

"Mrs. Harroun provides breakfast and supper for her boarders," he replied.

"I've heard she's a good cook."

"Adequate."

"Do you visit with the other boarders of an evening?"

He sipped and lowered the cup. "Occasionally."

"Surely you don't stay in your room alone every night."

"I'm not much for mixing with the other boarders."

Abby set her tea down. "I'm curious about something. Before you were—interested in my company, did you have someone else in mind to court?"

"Why do you ask?"

"I don't know. I guess I thought a handsome bachelor like yourself would be more interested in someone younger. Someone who'd never been married before."

"You're not that old," he replied.

He wouldn't kill her with gushing compliments anytime soon. "Seems I recall you were seeing one of the Cooper girls some time back."

"She married a rancher from up north."

"Women aren't plentiful out here," Abby said. "I guess I was a prospect just because I was a female."

He gave her an odd look.

She shrugged in resignation.

"You're insinuating I'm not discriminating, which I assure you is not the case."

"Good. Glad to know that not just anyone would do."

"You're behaving rather strangely, Abby."

"Am I? A woman wants to be assured that the man she's going to marry finds her desirable."

He thrust his chin out above his collar in a gesture of discomfort.

"Do you find me desirable, Everett?"

"Without question."

"I don't just mean as marriage material. I mean as a partner...you know."

His ears turned red. "I don't think this is an appropriate conversation."

"Between two people who are engaged? Why ever not?"

"Ladies don't talk about such things."

"I see." She took his cup and placed it on the low

serving table. "Will you kiss me a few times, then—without us talking about it, of course?"

He turned toward her, his expression wary, and lifted an arm to the back of the divan. His gaze explored her face and rested on her lips. He swallowed.

If she didn't know better, she would swear he was afraid. But what did he have to fear? Perhaps men were nervous about a woman's acceptance of them. That was it. She could assure him. In the back of her mind a faint taunt rang: *My God, Abby, you'd eat him alive.* She blocked it out.

Seconds ticked past as she waited for him to lean forward or take her in his arms. Beginning to feel as nervous as he looked, she touched her hair at her neck and gave him a weak smile.

Finally, he leaned forward. She was so grateful that he'd taken the initiative that she met him and their noses collided. Not discouraged, she fitted her lips to his and herself to the kiss. His lips were warm and soft, not objectionable. But he remained like that, not seeming to breathe or move, until she opened her eyes and dared a peek.

His eyes were shut.

Abby raised her hand and placed it along his collar.

He brought a hand to her waist.

Still their lips were fused, but unmoving.

Maybe he hadn't had much practice, she thought with a start. She allowed herself to breathe and lean into him, turning her head slightly, changing the alignment of their mouths.

He took the encouragement, wrapped his other arm around her and intensified the kiss by holding her tighter.

Abby felt no rush of sensation, no liquid fire chug through her veins. But that was what she'd wanted, wasn't it? To stay in control of herself? To have a tight rein on her passions? He was making it easy. Just as she'd never experienced fire and loss of restraint with Jed, she wouldn't have to fear it with Everett.

All of Brock's gibes rose up to take bites of her confidence. *You don't really want Matthews.* She snuggled all the tighter against the man she planned to marry. She would prove Brock Kincaid wrong if it killed her.

Perhaps Everett just needed a little more warming up to turn the effect upon her. She ran her hands inside his coat jacket and touched him through his shirt, finding him warm and solid, if not as broad or muscled as Brock.

His breathing picked up pace, and he spread a hand around her waist. This was more like it.

*Jonathon has a real father, and you're denying him.*

She wasn't denying anyone anything by making a sound marriage choice. She touched Everett's hair, not as long, not as silky as Brock's. He pulled his lips away to kiss her neck. The sensation wasn't unpleasant, but no tremors ran through her body.

Boldly, she took his hand and placed it over her breast through her layers of clothing. His whole arm grew rigid and he didn't move his hand. She kissed him again, waiting for the pleasure to begin, waiting for him to make a move that set her on fire. She hated Brock's overconfident demeanor, his lack of care, his manipulative purpose and the coarse words.

*This* was the kind of man she wanted.

Everett pulled his hand back and released Abby as though she was a red-hot iron. She felt nothing. No regret, no shame, no desire. Nothing.

If he found her desirable, he hadn't showed it. Perhaps that was the difference between a gentleman and gunslinger.

"This wasn't wise," he said, adjusting his collar and his jacket.

It certainly hadn't been. She'd set out to prove something to herself—to prove Brock wrong.

And instead she'd proved him right.

A spring blizzard whipped itself into a fury during the night. Drifts against the front of the building prevented Abby from seeing out.

"There's nothing out there!" Jonathon cried. "Mama, where'd the town go?"

"The town's still there," she replied. "We just can't see out our windows because of the snow."

Jonathon ran toward the door and she shouted, "No! Don't open the door!"

"Why not?"

"Because the snow's as deep against it as against the windows and it might fall right inside."

"What're we gonna do?"

"We're going to bundle up good and go out though our upstairs door, down to the street and shovel our way to the front to get it cleared. We had to do this when you were a baby," she told him.

"You mean, you and my papa?"

The word drew her up short. Jonathon knew nothing different. Jed had been his "papa." "Yes, me and your papa. Now, let's go get our wraps on."

The chore was a lark to Jonathon. He cheerfully donned his sweaters and coat and hat and mittens and extra socks, and tied his boots, then, with Dilly on his heels, plowed his way down the stairs and plunged into a snowdrift. Laughing, Abby pulled him out and handed him a shovel, wondering how long he'd be able to lift the heavy tool and the wet snow.

Together, they made a path through the snow, which in some places rose over their heads. The dog tired of watching and bounded away to sniff to his heart's content. Perspiring from the exertion, Abby peeled back her neck scarf and took in lungfuls of frigid air that burned in her chest.

Jonathon soon tired of shoveling and played in a pile of snow. From around the corner of the building, Abby heard him talking to someone. "Who's there?" she called.

Mr. Waverly appeared, using Jonathon's shovel as a cane, and made his feeble way along the path Abby had dug. "Jest me," he said. "Come to give ya a hand."

"Well, bless your heart, Mr. Waverly," she said, grateful to her cold toes that anyone should be so kind as to offer help. The sounds of other storekeepers working on their buildings had reached her while she labored, and she knew Sam would be late, as usual. It would never occur to Everett that she might need help, but then he had his duties at the telegraph office.

The old man bent to dip the shovel into the snow, caught his balance, raised the tool and somehow tossed snow on the pile near his shoulder. Abby watched another painstaking dip and toss, and then returned to her task. They'd made their way across the dock to within a few feet of the door when a call echoed across the snow.

"Abby! Abby!"

Dilly answered the call with a bark.

Abby straightened, her aching back catching painfully, and peered about. Sam Rowland romped over a drift and burst into their cleared path, spilling snow. Out of breath, he panted, "It's time. You have to come. I sent Lionel's boy to go get Haley, but no telling how long she will be."

"Wouldn't you just know it? Baby has to choose a day like this to come into the world." Abby glanced around. Jonathon had come to see what the commotion was about. "I'll go get Laine," she decided aloud.

''I'll keep an eye on the store for you,'' Mr. Waverly offered.

It was unlikely that there'd be very many customers, anyway. ''Just keep a tally and I'll add purchases to people's bills later—if anyone stops by,'' Abby instructed him.

She glanced at Jonathon. Mary's baby could come immediately or it could take hours yet. The school bell hadn't rung that morning, so Kate Kincaid must not have made her way to the schoolhouse yet. ''If the bell rings, you go on to school,'' she told her son. ''If it doesn't, run on up and knock on Daisy's door. She'll dry you off and feed you. You just tell her where I went.''

''Okay, Mama.''

Abby propped her shovel against the storefront and followed behind Sam as he blazed a path to Laine's. Her friend lived with her father and brother, but they were off on another enterprising trip and had been gone for nearly a week. ''Where are they?'' Abby asked.

''I think they have taken a patent for a new trap to the capital,'' she explained.

The silence wrought by their absence was always noticed by the townspeople. Normally, several times a week, the sound of icy rivers being dynamited to bring fish to the surface echoed across the landscape.

''Mary Rowland is having her baby,'' Abby explained. ''I'd feel a whole lot better if you were there with me.''

''She approves of my coming?'' Laine asked uncertainly.

Sam was waiting outside. ''I think she'll be grateful to have us both there,'' Abby told her.

Laine put on her coat and boots and, slipping and sliding, their breath creating white clouds in the air, the trio marched toward the street, where Sam owned a small house.

Sam ushered them in, and after removing their wraps, the two women found Mary Rowlands in her bed, her face pale and dotted with perspiration. "Oh, thank goodness," she said breathlessly. "I thought I was going to have this baby alone!"

"We wouldn't let that happen," Abby assured her.

"I had no idea," Mary said, her blue eyes open wide with fright. "I had no idea it would hurt this bad."

"The good thing is you'll forget all about it once you have that little one to hold," Abby told her, but she and Laine exchanged a look.

"I don't know...." Mary bit her lip and tensed her body.

"What shall I do?" Sam asked.

"Bring hot water, soap, towels and clean sheets," Laine told him.

He hurried off to do her bidding.

Mary had turned to her side and groaned.

"How long have you been having these pains?" Abby asked.

"Off and on during the night. I thought I just had a backache again, but it got worse and worse until I didn't think I could bear it."

"Did you lose any fluid?" Laine asked.

Mary's eyes widened. "No."

Laine exchanged another look with Abby. It could be a good long while yet. "May I check to see how far down the baby is?"

Mary looked at Abby and Abby nodded.

"Let's wash," Laine said to Abby. They joined Sam in the kitchen to wash their hands, then Laine examined Mary.

"The head is not down very far yet. It is possible Haley might make it before it is time."

"Have you done this before?" Mary asked.

"A few times," Laine replied.

"Well, can't you hurry it up?" she asked, her brow furrowed.

"Nothing I can do. You could get up and walk a bit."

"Walk? It feels like I'm being ripped apart, and you want me to walk?"

"Possible it will bring the baby down," Laine replied.

By afternoon, Mary's pains had become regular and hard. Abby sent Sam to check on the store and see how Jonathon was doing. He came back to report everything was under control. Kate Kincaid had held school that afternoon and Jonathon had gone.

"Is it still snowing?" Abby asked.

"Not right now, but the sky looks ready to drop another load at any time."

"Will you please go back and see if Jonathon can go to the ranch with Zeke when John or Caleb comes into town?" she asked. "Stay until someone comes for them."

Sam returned again with the news that Brock had come for Zeke and had been pleased to take Jonathon back to the Kincaid ranch.

"Mr. Waverly was gone, so I locked up the store," Sam told her.

"Thanks." Abby gave him five minutes to visit with his wife and then asked him to fix them something to eat.

Haley Kincaid showed up at dusk, having left Jesse and the boys prepared to spend the night at the hotel while she delivered a baby. She efficiently took over, relieving Abby and Laine of duties they were glad to relinquish. They remained close by to assist.

Two hours later, Haley took them aside and whispered, "That's not the baby's head you see there. I'm afraid he's breech. I'm going to have to help her a lot to get this child out. She needs you to keep her focused, and hold her down if you have to. And whatever you do, don't let that man in here again.''

Abby and Laine exchanged frightened looks, but Haley's calm instructions kept them centered on the tasks at hand.

Forty-five minutes later, four women cried their eyes out at the beautiful tiny boy that nestled at Mary's breast. Together they bathed infant and mother, bundled soiled sheets and towels, and dressed Mary in a clean cotton gown. When all evidence of the struggle had been whisked away, Abby allowed Sam in to meet his new son.

Sitting at the small table in the kitchen, she and Haley watched Laine brew a mixture of tea to help the new mother produce milk and heal quickly.

Abby's entire body ached from that morning's shoveling and the day's anxiety.

Laine poured a cup of tea and cast them a cryptic glance. "The more times I see that, the less I think I ever wish to experience it.''

"It's not always so difficult," Haley told her.

Abby couldn't seem to disagree at the moment, though she'd always known she wanted more children. Haley had assisted her at Jonathon's birth, and she'd always been grateful for her care.

"You two have put in a full day," Haley said. "Go on home. I'll stay the night. Jesse doesn't expect me to join him at the hotel until morning.''

"You will rest?'' Laine asked.

"I'll have Sam make me a place on the sofa.''

They said their good-nights and stepped out into the cold darkness. "You okay being by yourself?'' Abby asked.

"I like it,'' Laine replied. "No one to cook for.''

"Thank you for coming with me.''

"I was pleased to help.''

Abby hugged her and they went their separate directions on the snow drifted streets. Pulling her coat tight, she made her way toward her store. The sounds of a tinny piano and laughter echoed down the way from the nearest saloon. Abby never traversed the streets alone at night, the only place she usually went being the hotel with Everett, so it seemed surreal to be out here by herself.

As she passed the Double Deuce, she remained on the other side of the street, but surveyed the well-lit building curiously. Two men in coats and hats exited the double doors, momentarily exposing the interior to her view and raising the level of noise. Men and gaily dressed woman sat at round tables, where smoke curled up toward a gray cloud that hung beneath the ceiling.

Abby wrinkled her nose, imagining the horrible smell.

Before the doors swung shut, she glimpsed a man who reminded her of Everett—same clipped hair, same shirt, vest and tie.

Abby blinked into the darkness and continued her journey. A lot of men kept their hair short and wore suits. But probably not a lot of men wore clothes like that to visit a saloon.

Something Brock had said about Everett cheating at cards came to mind. At the time, she had given it no thought, but how would he know that unless he'd been in a card game with him?

Nothing wrong with a friendly game of cards now and then, she assured herself as she arrived at her store.

She used her key to enter, barring the door behind her, and lit the lantern on the wall, as well as another on the counter. The potbellied stove had been left to go cold, so she worked at building a fire. It was easier to keep it banked at night than to start it anew and try to heat a huge area that had been left to the winter cold.

Mr. Waverly had made himself coffee, so she carried

the cold pot on her way to the back rooms. She paused by the counter where she kept her ledgers, and discovered notes the old man had scribbled for her on a scrap of brown paper. She could barely make out the items, but she smiled at his thoughtfulness.

Carrying the enamel pot into the back, she tripped over something and caught herself before she fell. The pot clanged to the floor. Abby reached down and, in the darkness, made out a shoe and a pant leg. Scrambling for a match, she lit another lantern and held it above the prone body on her storeroom floor.

# Chapter Thirteen

Horror prickled her scalp when she recognized Mr. Waverly. "Oh, my goodness! Mr. Waverly! Mr. Waverly, can you hear me?"

His crinkled eyelids fluttered. "I was…just nappin'."

"I thought you'd gone home!" She knelt beside him.

"Heaven?" he asked. "I…didn't make it that far. Unless you're…an angel."

"No, I meant…well, can you get up?"

He pursed his lips a couple of times. "Maybe in the mornin'."

She looked him over. "Are you hurt anywhere?"

"Don't think so."

She would feel terrible if his shoveling that morning had been too much of a strain on his heart. She felt terrible already that he had collapsed in her store and lain here for who knew how long. "Let me help you. There's a cot over here where Jonathon naps."

"Can you reach me my cane?" he asked, coming to a sitting position with her help.

She dragged the cane over and handed it to him. "Oh, I wish there was a doctor in town. I can send for Laine."

"I don't want that China girl doctorin' me."

"Well, we don't have a real doctor." Abby helped him to the cot. "Ruth Kincaid, perhaps? Would you let her look at you?"

"That Cheyenne woman? That's more like it."

Abby rolled her eyes. Ruth probably did know more about elderly people than Laine, since she treated so many on the reservation. "Okay, you stay right here."

Abby grabbed her coat and made her way, slipping and sliding, to the sheriff's office, only to find it closed for the night. James's cottage sat behind the jailhouse, so she followed the narrow path to the door. James promised to send for Ruth, and Abby went back to sit with the old man.

It was eleven by the time Ruth arrived, accompanied by Caleb. She thought perhaps Mr. Waverly'd had a weak spell because of his aging heart, and suggested he rest for a few days. They fashioned a travois out of the cot and, with Caleb's help, carried him to the boardinghouse, rather than to his room at the livery, so that Old Lady Harroun could look out for him.

Caleb, who had waited for Ruth in the foyer, spoke to Abby as the two women came toward him. "Jonathon is just fine with us," he assured her. "You can ride back to the ranch with us if you'd like."

"Thank you, both of you, but I don't have a worry about him while he's at your place. And I'll be fine here. I suppose Brock is with the boys now?"

"Brock and John," Ruth told her. They stepped outside. "The little boys are all fast asleep and the big boys are probably still in a standoff at the checkerboard, waiting for us to get there."

"We'll bring Zeke and Jonathon to school in the morning," Caleb told her.

He untied the reins tethering two horses to the hitching post.

"You didn't bring a wagon?" Abby asked.

"Not in this snow," he replied. "And the dark. Letting the horses have their heads is the safest travel."

"Good night, then," Abby told them. "Thank you for your help."

They rode behind her until she reached the store and let herself in. The exhausting day had taken its toll on her mind and body. She extinguished the lamps and wearily climbed the stairs.

How much more chaotic could things get? Thank goodness Jonathon had gone to the Kincaids', where he had a friend and someone to feed him a hot supper. Abby wouldn't have been up to it. She'd eaten only a few bites of the charred flapjacks and sausage Sam had prepared at lunchtime. Now she forced herself to eat some cheese with a chunk of bread, and washed it down with warm broth.

She hadn't seen Dilly that evening, so she assumed he'd gone to the ranch with Jonathon. She double-checked all the rooms and opened the back door to look out over the alley just to make sure.

She barely got out of her clothes before her head hit the pillow and she slept.

The following morning, she'd pulled herself from bed and was staring at her tangled hair in the mirror when a knock sounded on the outside door.

She pulled on her wrapper and padded to the kitchen. "Who is it?"

"Me, Mama!"

Abby threw open the door. Dilly bounded in ahead of Jonathon, snow clinging to his fur. Zeke followed Jonathon, giving her a shy smile, and Brock brought up the rear. He had his arms filled with a wooden crate, which he set on the table.

Abby hugged Jonathon and grabbed a towel for the floor.

"I've come to help you today," Brock told her.

She blinked up from the pile of slush she was mopping. "Help me what?"

"Whatever you need. There's breakfast in there." He pointed to the crate. "I'll heat water so you can have a bath."

Even though the thought of a hot bath was delightful, the idea of him preparing it seemed all wrong.

"I'll go down and get the stove hot, open the store, do whatever Sam usually does, while you take some time to yourself. The boys will come with me, and I'll send them off to school."

She stood and clutched the front of her wrapper. "I couldn't possibly let you do all that."

She remembered her disheveled hair and raised a hand self-consciously. Knowing how she looked and remembering what had happened the last time they'd been together, hot embarrassment rose in her chest.

"Well, you're going to have to let me, because I don't see how you'll stop me without causing a scene in front of the boys."

The children he referred to had tromped into Jonathon's bedroom and were emitting horse noises.

"It's so...so wrong," she managed to say.

"For someone to offer a hand? The way I hear it, you spent the whole day helping Mary Rowland yesterday, and half the night taking care of Mr. Waverly—"

"I didn't take care of him, really."

"You're tired and need a little time to yourself. Everyone can use a hand sometimes, Abby. It's no disgrace. I'm going to heat water while you eat this food."

He placed covered dishes on the table.

"Ruth sent this?"

He nodded and held out a chair.

Abby acquiesced and took a seat. The potatoes and some kind of meat casserole were barely warm, but delicious, and she indulged her appetite.

The whole time Brock filled her tin tub, she imagined him thinking of her bathing in it, and couldn't meet his eyes. Finally, he had it filled and called to the boys.

"Don't come down until you're rested," he told her. "I don't care if it takes all day."

"How will you know how to run the store?" she asked.

"I'll figure it out. Come on, boys."

"Bye, Mama." Jonathon kissed her cheek and followed Brock into the hallway. Their boots thudded down the inside stairs.

Abby locked both doors, removed her nightgown and got into the steamy tub of water. It felt wonderful to her aching body. She never filled it this full herself, because filling and emptying it was such a chore.

An hour later, she sat before the heater, drying her hair, feeling drowsy and pampered. How positively indulgent to sit here like this when the store was open below. She'd never before had the luxury. Intending to merely rest her eyes, she woke an hour later, sat up on the divan and stretched. How many customers had seen Brock working in her store by now?

Dressed in a fresh dress and apron, her clean hair neatly braided, she descended the stairs. The floor had been swept, she noticed right off, and the strong smell of coffee wafted through the building.

Following the sound of men's voices, she discovered Brock and Harry Talbert in a discussion near the stove. One foot on a chair, leaning forward with his elbow on his knee, Brock held a cup and gestured with the other hand.

Her steps alerted them, and Harry turned first. "Held the store down for ya, Mizz Abby."

Brock turned an appreciative gaze, and she hoped her blush wasn't visible. "Thank you."

"It's thawing," Harry told her.

Abby glanced at the front windows, where the sun shone weakly. "What have you heard?"

"It's a Chinook," Brock told her. "Thaw and rain in the forests in the high country."

"Should we sandbag?" she asked with a worried frown.

"River is brown and muddy, but not overfull," he replied. "I think we'll have another snow before the week's out. We won't have a real thaw until April." He stood and emptied his mug, then hung it on a peg. "Sam will be back to work tomorrow."

She had sorely missed Sam's help, but she knew Mary didn't have family.

"Mary's going to have someone in to help her for several hours each day," Brock said, as if reading her thoughts.

"Really?" Abby asked curiously.

"Brock's sister-in-law found a girl from the reservation," Harry told her.

Abby studied Brock's placid expression, but if he'd had a part in finding help for the Rowlands, he said nothing. He met her gaze evenly. Disturbingly sensual thoughts came to Abby, and she looked away.

Harry got up from his chair. "Need a couple of bolts while I'm here." He hitched up his trousers and ambled off toward the back of the store.

"The boys got off to school just fine," Brock told her.

"Thanks." She didn't know what to say to him. "And thank you for watching the store while I rested. I do appreciate the thought."

"I'll be going if you think you'll get by for the rest of the day."

"Yes, of course. You've done plenty. More than I would have expected."

He settled his hat on his head and shrugged into his coat. "I'm going to dump your bathwater, and then I'll be gone."

She nodded and watched him stride toward the back. She just hadn't had the energy to be angry with him that day.


Brock had been right. By the end of the week another snowfall had covered the landscape. The air turned bitterly cold once again, and as luck would have it, calving began. The first-timers had been kept in the corrals, and they got them over first, whisking the newborns out of the cold into the barns by wheelbarrow before their ears could freeze. There, their ears would be bandaged prior to sending them back out to their mothers.

They were coming about twenty a day, giving the ranch hands barely time to rest and handle the other chores in between, so for another week, Brock didn't make it back to town. He would have loved for Jonathon to see this.

Brock watched one slippery young calf come into the world, steam rising into the cold air, and thought how his son would have reacted. Helping the cow clean her baby quickly, he bundled the calf for a ride to the barn. The miracles of nature never failed to humble and amaze him, and his thoughts quite naturally turned to Abby, helping Sam's wife give birth. Not for the first time, he regretted not knowing about his son, not being there for the miracle of his tiny life as it came into the world.

Who had helped Abby? Had it been a long labor? A difficult or easy birth? Had Jed been at her side? An ache consumed Brock at the thought. Had she thought of him? Cursed him, no doubt.

Brock tied a bandanna around the cow's right front leg so he could identify her when he returned the calf, and pushed the wheelbarrow across the rutted, frozen earth to the barn.

That night he sat at the table in the bunkhouse, the oil lamps lit against the night, and listened to the snores of the sleepers and the weary talk of those eating in shifts. This was a good life, a life he could tuck into and enjoy if, like Caleb, he had a warm bed and a wife to go home to at night.

How could Abby proceed with her plans to marry Matthews? Brock hadn't planned what had happened between them to make her change her mind, but it should have. Lord, it should have. How could she deny the pull between them? How could she shrug it off as a mistake or a physical act that meant nothing? He'd thought of it every day. And every night. Along with every other confusing thing about Abby.

Belatedly, he chastised himself for getting carried away with his desire for her. The last thing he needed was to plant a baby inside her and have her marry another man again—this time right in front of him. How could he have been so reckless? A tiny, nagging voice told him a baby would trap her, would make her his, but he knew better.

Even if she chose to tell him, which she quite likely would not, that didn't mean she would suddenly change her mind about him. And even if she did, he didn't want her that way.

He wanted her, but he wanted her to come to him because she cared for him.

What more could he do? Maybe drastic measures were called for. Finishing his meal and taking a turn on a narrow cot for a few winks, he let his plans take shape.

* * *

It had been nearly two weeks since Abby had seen Brock. Everett had come over for dinner twice, but he'd never mentioned the kissing incident. The whole time she was with him, she strained not to compare him to Brock. When she was alone, thinking and planning, she could make this impending marriage seem more plausible, because Everett was just an idea then; but when she spent time in his company, a growing uneasiness invaded her peace of mind and her confidence. She would remember the kiss, and his reaction and her reaction, and her stomach would tighten.

Since it was Saturday, and fairly nice weather, she had a steady stream of customers. By late afternoon business dropped off, and Sam swept the floor. Through the panes of glass, Abby watched Jonathon build a snowman on the corner of the dock.

A gray horse and rider appeared, leading a black horse with a rope, and Abby recognized Brock immediately.

Even wearing his long coat, he dismounted in a fluid motion and tied the reins to the post at the corner of the dock below Jonathon. Her son waddled over in his layers of winter clothing. Brock tipped his hat to the back of his head and looked up.

He gestured to the horse in tow.

Jonathon jumped up and down and nearly fell off the edge of the wooden structure. Brock steadied him and then lowered him to the ground. A minute later, he lifted the boy to the saddle on the horse's back and grinned up.

Abby got a bad feeling in the pit of her belly. What was going on? Grabbing an old coat, she slipped into it and stepped outside, wary of her footing on the icy dock.

Jonathon saw her approach. "Mama! Look! Brock gave me a horse! A horse of my very own! I can even name him! Ain't he purdy?"

The fact that the word *horse* had come from her son's lips without a lisp surprised her more than the manipulative deed Brock had executed.

"Where will you keep this horse of yours?" she asked, careful not to say he couldn't have it and therefore alienate him.

"He can stay at Brock's ranch and I can thee him there! Ain't that grand?"

"That's just grand," she replied without enthusiasm.

"Can I ride him now?" Jonathon asked.

"Have you ridden alone before?" Brock asked.

"No, but I can do it. I know I can."

"You need a little practice first," Brock told him. "Just for safety. I'll walk you down the street."

Jonathon's expression fell.

Brock took the reins and led the sad-faced boy on the shiny black gelding away from the store.

The wind bit into Abby's cheeks and made her eyes water, but she watched until they returned.

"Brock thays I can come to the ranch for the night. Can I, Mama? Please?"

"Why don't you join us for the evening?" Brock's tone sounded deceptively innocent. "You'd probably like some time away for a change, right? We can pop some corn by the fireplace."

Jonathon's expression pleaded for her to concede.

"Do you have a wagon?" she asked, fearing she knew the answer.

He shook his head. "You haven't forgotten how to ride, have you?" he asked. "You and Jonathon can ride together."

"Thay yes, Mama! Thay yes!"

"I have a few things to do before I can close the store." She gestured lamely behind her.

"We'll help." Brock reached for Jonathon and placed

him back on the dock before tying the horse beside his and sprinting around to the stairs to meet them at the door. ''That's a fine-looking snowman you made there, partner.''

Delegating the tasks, and running upstairs to change and get extra warm clothing, Abby delved deep inside herself, desperately seeking the anger that she needed to get her through this.

This horse was another ploy by Brock to worm his way into Jonathon's life, and maybe even into hers. Denying a boy his father would be wrong, she had started to realize, but before she could sort anything out in her head, the man was always coming up with something else. There was no way Brock could acknowledge Jonathon as his son and she could save face at the same time.

Her hurt and her anger had served her well in reinforcing the protective shell she'd drawn around herself and her son. She'd fended the man off with torrents of nasty words and scathing looks and disapproval—the one exception being that solitary physical encounter, which had set her on her ear emotionally.

Perhaps she was just plain weary of the animosity. Maybe he'd beaten down her defenses until nothing remained but resignation. Otherwise, why would she be going with him? She had used her brother as an excuse for so long that she hadn't faced the truth of her real reasons for holding a grudge. Guy had been the obvious excuse. Brock's desertion had been the true cause of her resentment, and now she could admit she'd played a part in his leaving.

Sam went home and Abby locked the store. Brock steadied the horse, while she and Jonathon mounted from the dock, Jonathon in front of her in the saddle. She pulled a blanket around them, covered her face with her scarf, checked Jonathon's wraps and nudged the horse after Brock's.

"She's a fine horse, ain't she, Mama?"

"She's a he," Brock told him.

"He is a dandy horse," Abby replied.

She couldn't remember the last time she'd ridden. After growing up on a ranch, she found the rhythm came back quite naturally. She had forgotten how much she enjoyed the experience.

Brock guided them toward his family home. "How's Mr. Waverly?" he asked.

"He seems just fine. He was at the store most of this morning. Told me his nephew actually came and visited him while he was in bed at the boardinghouse."

"Heard there was a family feud of some sort there," Brock replied.

"Look at all them baby cowth!" Jonathon cried, pointing with a mittened hand.

"Those are calves," Brock said. His collar was pulled up over the lower half of his face, but his eyes sparkled with amusement.

"But they're baby cowth, ain't they?" Jonathon asked.

"Yes," Abby explained, "but they're called calves."

"How come thome of 'em have tape on their ears?"

"Those are the newest ones," Brock told him. "The wrap is to keep their ears from freezing and disfiguring them."

"My ears won't freeth, will they?"

"That's why I tell you to wear your cap and scarf," Abby told him. "Ears and fingers and toes can get frostbite."

"Noses and cheeks, too," Brock added. He proceeded to tell Jonathon about the calving season that had just passed, sharing the experience in such a way that even Abby found it fascinating, and she'd grown up with it.

The discussion continued as they neared the house, where steady streams of welcoming smoke spiraled from the chimneys. A ripple of apprehension waffled through Abby's stomach. What would Caleb and Ruth think of her coming to the ranch with Brock?

"You can head into the kitchen and get warm, while I put up the horses," he told her.

"Couldn't we—um—help you with the horses?" she asked.

"Sure." He led the way to one of the barns, where he did most of the work, while Abby and Jonathon stood by. A ranch hand showed up and offered to finish the task, and after thanking him, Brock guided them to the house.

Ruth turned from the stove and spotted Jonathon first. "Zeke will be pleased to see you! He's been asking me all afternoon to put together a puzzle with him, and I've been baking."

She peeled a checkered cloth back from a golden-crusted pie. "Do you like apple?"

"I love apple pie!" Jonathon assured her, shrugging out of his coat.

"Abby!" Ruth dropped the cloth into place and wiped her hands on her apron. "What a nice surprise! Have you come for supper, I hope?"

"Abby came for a change of scenery," Brock told her with good humor in his voice. "She's here in time for supper, too." He took her coat and Jonathon's and hung them up.

A metal clang echoed through the room, and Abby glanced around to spot baby Barton sitting before a cupboard, a sea of enamel pans surrounding him.

"It keeps him out of mischief for a short while," Ruth explained.

"Entertaining Jonathon safely in the store was a challenge at that age,'' Abby remarked. ''Jed built a gate at both ends of a counter, so I could corral him.''

Ruth smiled.

Abby realized suddenly that Brock had grown unnaturally still at her mention of Jed, but when she glanced at him, his stoic expression revealed nothing.

''Where's Zeke?'' Jonathon asked, saying his name correctly.

''Probably working on that puzzle in the other room,'' Ruth replied. ''Go look for him.''

Jonathon sprinted from the kitchen.

''Can I help with anything?'' Abby asked.

''How are you at peeling potatoes?''

''My specialty,'' she replied, and accepted a knife.

''I'll give the men a hand with chores,'' Brock said, and left.

Abby needn't have worried about Ruth's reaction to her arrival; the woman was friendly and accepting as always, chatting with her about this thing and that as they finished putting a meal together.

The enormous kitchen and the long table were adequate to seat all of them when Brock, Caleb and John arrived. The boys joined them, and Ruth plopped Barton in his wooden chair.

Caleb and Brock wore their guns to the dinner table, John displayed an enormous knife in a leather sheath on his thigh, and Ruth didn't blink an eye. Her obvious acceptance of their weapons eased Abby's discomfort. She had begun to realize that her fear of guns had come from her brother's careless use of them. He had constantly fired off shots at anything that moved or angered him.

The casual chitchat and friendly banter around the table were a welcome change to Abby, and she knew why Jonathon enjoyed his visits to the ranch so well. While she and her son were happy together, this family atmosphere warmed a person's heart clear through.

"Did I smell an apple pie?" Caleb asked, touching his wife's waist as she removed his empty plate.

"You did," she replied, flashing him a smile.

Abby observed their underlying exchange, and the obvious love in their eyes was almost painful to watch. She had a most embarrassing thought cross her mind, wondering about their intimacy, and whether or not Caleb made Ruth lose her head when he looked at her like that, touched her, made love to her.

She observed Brock, who glanced away from his brother and sister-in-law at the same time, and their gazes collided. Caleb was stable and responsible, but somehow Abby didn't think those had been the deciding factors in Ruth's decision to marry him. Heat rose in Abby's cheeks, as if Brock knew what she was thinking. She tore her gaze from his and stood to help Ruth.

After dinner, Ruth shooed her into the other room with the men and boys, where Caleb and John promptly set up a checkerboard, and Caleb puffed on a fragrant pipe.

Jonathon and Zeke created a ranch from a set of blocks and miniature horses, and Abby entertained Bart, so he didn't destroy their play world. Brock played with the boys, his long form stretched out in front of the hearth.

When Ruth came to take Bart to bed, Abby gave him up reluctantly, then watched the boys. Brock retired from the make-believe ranch to sit with Abby, and the boys moved back to their puzzle.

Some time later, Caleb knocked the tobacco from his pipe into the fire. "Think I'll join my wife," he said, and wished them a good night.

John helped the boys place a few puzzle pieces, and then excused himself to head upstairs.

Jonathon's yawns had grown in frequency, and finally,

he came to lay his head on Abby's lap. She stroked his silky hair and watched his eyelids grow heavy. Abby looked up to find Brock's deep blue gaze tender.

"Can Jonathon come sleep in my room?" Zeke asked.

Brock questioned Abby with a raised brow.

She nodded. It was too late and too cold to carry him home now.

"Come with us," Brock told her, so she followed, surprised to learn that Brock adeptly observed their preparations for bed and made sure they cleaned their teeth.

Ruth came to check on the ritual, giving both boys a hug and leaving Brock to tuck them into matching narrow beds.

"Read us a story, Uncle Brock," Zeke begged.

Brock took a book from a shelf and flipped through until he found something he liked. The story, of a boy on an adventure into a forest after a lost colt, took on life when read with his melodious deep voice. This was a side of the man Abby had never seen, and while she sat across the room and listened, her gaze moved from one boy's sleepy face to the next, to Brock's marvelous mouth as he formed the words, then to the guns he wore.

Only at Abby's home did he remove them—an act of respect for her wishes. Here, they were a part of him, like his voice or his smile. No one seemed to mind, and she realized that the presence of his revolvers no longer bothered her as it once had.

The children slept long before the story ended, and Abby experienced a pang of disappointment when Brock closed the book. He extinguished the lamp and led Abby from the room and down the stairs.

He showed her to the sofa and seated himself a respectable two feet away. "Thanks for letting him stay."

"It was best for him. He was too tired to ride home."

"I would have hitched a team and a wagon."

That sounded like a lot of work, and she still had to go home herself.

"I want you to stay tonight, too," he told her, his voice gruff, but somehow vulnerable.

Abby's heart dipped at the request that she couldn't admit she'd wanted to hear.

# Chapter Fourteen

"I have something I want to show you tomorrow," he said.

"There's church tomorrow." A shallow objection. Her heart fluttered erratically.

"We can get up early. Or you can miss one time. It's important."

She was tired, and a cold ride home in the dark did not appeal. "Where would I sleep?"

"You can have my room. I can go to the bunkhouse."

"I wouldn't want to put you out."

"I've slept a lot worse places than a warm bunkhouse, believe me. It's settled. You're staying."

She shrugged. "Ruth and Caleb won't mind?"

He grinned. "She already put out a few things for you and instructed me to bring you water." He got up to tend the flame, and Abby watched the play of golden light on his strong profile and shiny hair. He hunkered before the fire, one knee drawn up. "Tell me things, Abby," he said. "I need to hear."

"What kind of things?"

"Things like what you told Ruth tonight about Jonathon as a baby. I want to know about the day he was born,

and when he first walked, and his first day of school...."
His voice sounded oddly thick and choked, and the sound
gave Abby a ponderous ache in her breast.

The need to tell him rose up in her like a restlessness
that had never been satisfied. Through the years, Brock
had been there, in the back of her mind. Like the missing
piece to an unfinished puzzle that, if she at last told him
about the events of her life, would be complete.

Not better. Just complete. The facts, nothing more. He
didn't need to know how he'd hurt her and how she had
silently cried for him. "It was a day in late spring," she
began. "We'd had flooding that year, and the rivers were
brown and muddy and overflowing their banks. A train
was washed off the tracks near Butte and we lost a ship-
ment. Most of the men from town went to help with the
cleanup. Jed, too, to save what he could of our supplies.

"I was hurting all day that day, thinking like many
women do that it was another backache. But this one
didn't let up, and got worse and worse. I was alone at the
store, so I closed and went upstairs, stopping for Daisy's
opinion. She came and sat with me while I slept, but I
woke with stronger pains, so she sent for Haley.

"By then I knew it was time, and I prepared myself,
though it's nothing you can prepare for." She laughed a
little at her foolish thoughts and memories. "It seemed an
eternity before Haley got there."

"What about Jed?" Brock asked, moving to sit at her
feet. "Was he still gone?"

"He came home sometime that night. I didn't know
when, really. The night became a blur. I thought once
Haley got there everything would suddenly be better."
She managed a wry smile. Just like Mary Rowland had
imagined, she thought to herself. "Haley's presence was
comforting, but Jed insisted on Dr. Leland being there,

too. Somehow I got through it, and had a beautiful baby boy to hold and take away the pain.''

''What did he look like?''

''He was pink all over…just amazing, really. He had a lusty cry…and a fringe of dark hair.''

''Dark, Abby?''

She nodded. ''It grew out lighter as he got older.''

Brock's chest ached so badly, he could have cried with the cold, empty pressure. Imagining the tiny infant taking his first breaths, crying that beautiful first cry, he found tears welling in his throat for all he'd missed. How he would have loved to have held him, to have smelled his newborn skin and to have touched his feathery hair.

''Jed had a cradle built for him,'' she went on. ''He was afraid to hold him at first, because he'd never been around an infant, but eventually he held him and played with him. He ordered toys and enjoyed giving gifts to him.''

Brock let himself picture the gruff-looking man he remembered as being a parent to a new baby. He must have been a kind and accepting man. What a surprise it must have been when Jonathon's hair turned from dark to light. What had Jed thought? What had Abby thought? ''What did you think?'' he asked. ''Did you think he looked like me? Even back then?''

''Babies look pretty much the same when they're tiny,'' she said. ''At least that's what I told myself. And as he got older, well, I saw what I wanted to see.''

''Did Jed know he was mine?''

''We never discussed it,'' she replied simply. ''I don't know what he thought. He accepted him, loved him, and that was all that mattered.''

The layers of resentment that Brock had harbored since he'd learned of Jed peeled away to reveal a grudging appreciation. He'd taken Abby for his wife and embraced as his own a child who belonged to another man. Brock had to wonder if he would feel as favorable toward Jed today if he were still alive. Since the man was no longer a hindrance between him and Abby, Brock could afford to be gracious now. Being honest with himself wasn't pretty.

Abby talked about Jonathon getting teeth, learning to walk, taking spills and bumps, weathering childhood diseases and saying his first words.

Brock listened to her as though she held the mysteries of the universe, hanging on her every word, asking for details and picturing the scenes and days in his mind's eye. He sat deep in thought, wondering what he'd been doing those weeks and months and years, and how his life would have been different if only…if only it had. Regret was a waste of time. Each day was a chance to start over. And he had. In some ways.

He'd left behind his old life and come here to begin again, but once he'd learned about Jonathon…and Abby…he'd taken up his old tactics to get what he wanted. He had used Abby's fear of exposure to give him an edge. Now he recognized how wrong that was. He didn't want either one of them because they had no other choice.

He realized she'd stopped talking some time ago, and had been sitting in silence, studying him. He had planned to make it up to her for the way she'd been forced to marry a man she didn't love, forced to live an unfamiliar life, but how could he do that? He had to put his past behind him if he was ever to know a measure of peace, but Abby was a part of his past that he didn't want to bury.

What kind of man did he want to be? The kind of man Abby could love and respect. The kind of man who could respect himself. The kind of man a boy would be proud to call father.

He stood and reached a hand down to her. "Thank you, Abby."

Hesitantly, she took his hand and stood, somehow instinctively understanding his need to hear all about the child he'd fathered and had never known about. It was plain to see his feelings for Jonathon were genuine. But would they keep him from leaving again when things got rough?

He banked the fire and extinguished all but one lamp, which he handed to her, instructing her to head upstairs while he drew her water. Carrying a pitcher, he found her waiting in the hallway, the lamplight flickering across the roses on the wallpaper.

"This one." He ushered her into a room at the far end of the hall. Tentatively, she perused the heavy wood furnishings and the wide bed covered with a multicolored quilt. A crackling fire burned in the brick fireplace. Brock poured water into the bowl on the washstand and set the pitcher aside.

Ruth had laid out a plain cotton nightgown, a wrapper and wool socks, as well as towels and a bar of fragrant soap.

"Anything else you need?" he asked.

Abby shook her head. She was too weary to desire anything but the comfort of the bed.

Stepping close, Brock touched her cheek with a gentle caress. "I've made a lot of mistakes in my life," he said hoarsely. "You're not one of them. Neither is Jonathon."

Unbidden tears sprang to her eyes and burned her nose at his words. She'd never believed her son was a mistake, either, and to hear Brock say so with such assurance sealed her own feelings.

"The mistake I made was not staying and facing your

anger, not dealing with the situation and the consequences. A man prides himself on not being afraid,'' he said. ''But I was a coward when it came to seeing how you'd been hurt, and avoiding how you would react. I ran.''

He'd never even come close to admitting his fault, and his confession took her by surprise. In all the years she'd lived with the secret of what they'd meant to each other and how he'd left and broken her heart, she had never cried. Not since those first emotional days when she'd learned of the baby she carried, and her father had discovered the truth, had she allowed herself to break apart under the hurt and betrayal.

She'd girded up her defenses of anger and mistrust, gritted her teeth and made a life for her son.

''I accept the blame,'' Brock told her gently now, ''for your fear, and the years of living with a man you didn't want to marry. I understand your anger and all the things you hold against me.''

Abby squeezed her eyes shut and spun away from him, her chest wrenching with the unexpressed grief. She clamped a hand over her mouth and held her other arm to her aching middle.

This was what had hurt—not the tragedy of Guy's death—and she experienced a flood of guilt over the admission. Brock's leaving—even though she'd played a part in forcing him away—had broken her heart, not her brother's death. Guy had been a hothead, looking for an opportunity to use his guns. Brock had been caught in the middle of a bad situation, with no way out. And she had helped place him there.

Relentlessly, Brock smoothed his palms over her shoulders and pressed his hard length comfortingly along her back. With his face buried in her hair, he whispered, ''Go ahead. Cry, Abby.''

Guiding her to the bed, he turned her and pulled her to him as the tide within her broke and tears poured out in a torrent of release. Brock pulled the quilt around her, muffled her sobs against his chest and stroked her hair, wiped her tears, kissed her temple.

A great emotional dam exploded, and Abby was in no condition to turn back the flood. She cried until her chest hurt, until her throat was sore, until no more tears came, until her eyes felt dry and hot and she grew weak with exhaustion. Years of penned-up resentment and suffering burst from her like nails from a dropped keg. Abby wept until she was weak from the emotional drain. Brock leaving her was worse than her own brother's death. Guy was the excuse she could admit to the world, but the thing that had really ripped her apart was her own responsibility.

Quite naturally, when Brock released her to remove her shoes and stockings, Abby complied. Without question or forethought or embarrassment, she allowed him to unbutton her dress and untie her petticoats, and she watched him hang them neatly on hooks beside his jackets and hats.

He picked up the cotton nightgown and held it out with a question in his eyes. She removed her chemise, seeing the way her action changed his expression, and raised her arms for him to drape the gown over her head. She adjusted the garment, pulling it down, and stood to remove her drawers and fold them with her chemise.

Brock had pulled back the sheet for her, considerately offering her his bed as he had his broad shoulders to cry on. Abby slid between the sheets, growing alarmed at the possibility of his leaving her alone now. She'd never been this defenseless, and she couldn't bear to be by herself. As he smoothed the covers over her, she caught his hand and pulled it to her cheek.

Leaning over her, he gently caressed her skin with the back of his knuckles.

"Don't go," she said simply.

He opened and closed his mouth once before finding his voice. "You know what would happen. I can't stay and not touch you the way I want to touch you."

"Stay and touch me," she said, daring him, arousing him with the words.

"But you hate me," he said, and she thought she heard a thread of vulnerability in that statement.

She had certainly told him enough times that she hated him. She'd been quite sure that she had, in fact. But she didn't have enough energy left to hate. "I can't hate you tonight," she told him. "Not now."

"What about tomorrow?" he asked, wisely thinking ahead to the consequences that would follow a moment's weakness. "I won't give you more reasons to be mad at me."

She didn't hate him anymore. She never had. She had hated her own weakness—her weakness for him. "I'm done being angry," she told him sincerely. "I need you to hold me. Kiss me."

Brock pulled his hand away to cross the room, and for a moment she feared he intended to leave. But he turned the key in the lock, returned and sat on the bed to remove his boots.

He stood and unbuckled the holster, rolled it and tucked it under the edge of the bed. After removing his shirt, he washed his face and hands in the basin of water, brought a damp cloth forward and bathed Abby's face, kissing her eyelids, which she knew must be swollen and red.

He'd grown from a handsome youth to a beautiful man, and she was still wicked enough to appreciate the arousing sight of his hard-carved body in the lantern light. From the very first, desiring him had been her weakness, and that hadn't changed.

He hung the cloth over the bowl's edge and blew out the lamp, plunging the room into darkness. The sound of him removing his dungarees was loud in the sudden stillness. "Where is Caleb and Ruth's room?" she thought to ask.

"At the other end of the hall, by Zeke's. John is a safe distance away, too. There's an empty room between us and anyone else."

She opened the covers to welcome him, and he wrapped her in his strong embrace. Abby gratefully snuggled into the warmth and comfort of his arms, pressed herself against his hard limbs and sleek skin and sighed with pleasure. She felt safe here…secure.

When she sought his lips in the darkness, he complied by kissing her mouth and drawing her tongue into his. When she needed air, he sensed it and kissed her neck, nipped her chin and her shoulder. When she craved his hands on her body, he satisfied her every wish by plucking her nipples teasingly, then flattening his rough palms over her breasts and intensifying the sensation.

Abby didn't have a need that Brock didn't anticipate and cater to. Once she even thought she need only imagine her desire and it became hers beneath his skillful attention.

He gritted his teeth and withstood her intimate explorative caresses, tensing and releasing quick breaths. The touches he returned had her clinging to him and holding her breath in sweet expectation.

He pulled her beneath him, entered her and rode her pleasure to its quivering climax, then jerked away and spilled himself on her belly. Reaching for the cloth, he gently wiped her clean and kissed her tenderly. The interruption was unexpected, forcing her to remember their situation. The last time, neither one of them had thought about the chance they were taking. This time he had protected her. He might have planted his seed in her to force her to his will, but he hadn't. He had thought more carefully than she. And in doing so, he had changed.

It was then, in the darkness, with the air cooling her damp skin, that she remembered Everett.


Brock cradled her for hours, touching her hair, kissing her temple, her shoulder, and she slept. When he tiptoed from the room in the early morning darkness, she awoke at the loss of warmth. His remembered tenderness, his scent and the gentle loving cocooned her and she slept again.

When she came fully awake, the sun streamed through the part in the drapes and created a beam of light on the carpeted floor. Abby sat and blinked, orienting herself, holding the sheet to her naked body. The night came back to her on a sensual wave of memory. She thought of the total abandon with which she had given herself to Brock, and how the fact that she was engaged to be married hadn't entered her mind until afterward. Even the last time she and Brock had made love, she'd never once thought of her fiancé. What kind of woman was she?

Distant gunshots reverberated, rousing her from her reverie. They echoed again, and she wondered who had cause to be firing a gun on Sunday morning. This close to the house, they wouldn't be hunting.

Abby discovered a note from Brock on the bureau, assuring her she was alone upstairs and letting her know he'd heated a tub of water for her across the hall.

Abby donned the borrowed wrapper, gathered her clothing, the soap and towels, and ventured across the deserted hall. An inviting bathing chamber surprised her, and the water he'd promised was still warm. She sank into it and enjoyed the luxury.

Everett didn't carry a gun. He didn't try to charm her or seduce her. He had a stable position in town, was a responsible citizen. She had wanted to marry him because he didn't make her lose her head; that was the truth of it. She'd felt safe with him because he couldn't possibly hurt her. No matter what he did, he'd never break her heart...because she would never give it to him. He didn't have the power.

That was why Brock frightened her. He had the ability to crush her heart to a pulp.

But only if she gave it to him again. Her future happiness depended on keeping herself safe from that possibility. So far she hadn't done so well in resisting him, and her weakness was scandalous. Why, then, did being with him seem so right...so pure?

She dried off and surveyed her clothing, which didn't look too bad. Refreshed and dressed, Abby straightened Brock's room, made his bed and hung her towels to dry before making her way down the stairs. The house was silent, her steps creaking the floorboards as she checked for signs of the Kincaid family or her son.

A kettle of hot water sat on the kitchen stove, so she made tea and sipped a steaming cup. The back door opened and Brock came in from outside, cold air swirling in around him.

He looked so incredibly good with his skin ruddy from the cold, his hair tossed around his face—a tall, beautiful man who filled a room with his presence. A smile broke across his familiar face when he saw her, and her recalcitrant heart fluttered. "You're up."

"Shamefully late," she agreed with a blush. "I can't imagine what your family thinks of me."

"They think nothing, because they all left early to visit the reservation."

"Jonathon, too?"

"Jonathon, too. He'll love it. Zeke will introduce him to his cousins. There's a plate in the oven for you. Eat and then I'll take you for a ride. I've even hitched a buggy. One of the hands was heading toward Whitehorn and I asked him to pay a call on Sam, see if he'd go over to the store and let Dilly out."

"Oh, Dilly!" she said with another twinge of guilt. "I forgot."

Brock went to the oven, pulled out her plate and stuck a couple of bricks in. "For your feet," he said.

"You'll spoil me." She tasted the frybread and spicy potatoes, finding them delicious.

Brock leaned over her, his coat brushing her shoulder, and said beside her ear, "You deserve to be spoiled once in a while."

Warmth spread through her limbs. Abby turned her face to see his eyes, so blue, so seemingly earnest, and wished with all her heart that this was what her life could be like forever.

He kissed her lips, and she watched his lashes flutter down. His mouth was cold, his hair and skin smelling of outdoors.

But forever was a risk she wasn't willing to bet on. She had a son to think about now, besides herself, and she hadn't done a very wise job of making choices for him so far. As usual, when Brock was around, she lost her perspective. Everett came to mind, and she ended the kiss to eat her breakfast.

Once she'd finished, Brock gathered her warm outer clothing, helped her with her boots and carried the hot bricks out to the waiting buggy.

A solitary black mare had been harnessed to the rig, and she stepped out at a brisk pace at Brock's prompting.

"Where are we going?" Abby asked.

Brock glanced at her lovely face, her curious, yet troubled green eyes, and gave her a smile. "Not far. You'll see."

She rode beside him, snuggled into the blanket he'd wrapped around her, and from time to time pointed out a bird or a small animal. Once they saw an old bull elk watching them from a stand of bare cottonwoods.

Brock guided the rig to the settler's cabin and stopped in the clearing. Animal tracks led back and forth in the snow, and a squirrel chattered at them from a nearby limb.

"This is my land," he told her, watching her face for a reaction.

She glanced around and back at him. "Yours?"

He nodded. "The sections I inherited from my father. I've mapped them out and made plans for spring."

"What kind of plans?"

"A house. New barns and corrals." He jumped down and came around for her. "Not much to see yet, I guess." He glanced at the scenery he'd been so enamored with since deciding on this place. "Want to walk some?"

She let him help her down, her boots immediately becoming engulfed in the deep snow, her dress hem dragging.

"I picked this spot for the water and the windbreaks. The house will face south...over here. With a big wide porch for sitting in the summer."

She surveyed his land, her nose red from the cold, but she said nothing. What had he wanted her to say? He'd wanted to show her this. Show her he was staying. Convince her. Maybe she wouldn't believe him until the house was built and the ranch was in operation...after it was too late and she'd married Matthews. She was just stubborn enough to continue with her plans, even though he'd proved to her that she wanted him.

"Be a good place to raise a family, wouldn't it?" he asked, surveying the mountains.

"It would," she agreed. "What is this place?" she asked, gesturing at the cabin.

"It's been here for years. Probably before Kincaids owned the land. I plan to use it while the house is being built."

He watched her exhale white clouds into the air, and realized that bringing her here didn't prove anything, least of all his dependability. He would have to earn her trust. "Abby?"

She turned luminous green eyes on him.

She'd changed since last night; she held herself less rigidly, hadn't said a heated word yet. She was somehow softer, more vulnerable, and he remembered her agonized tears. He'd never felt so close to anyone in his life—and it wasn't just the sex. It was the intimacy of sharing what had been held so tightly inside, recognizing how he'd hurt her, and admitting his regret.

Could she forgive him? He didn't know how to ask.

She was waiting for him to say something. Instead he shook his head and looked away, feeling inadequate, angry at himself.

A brisk wind tugged at his hat and he secured it.

"Well, I'm sure it's a nice place for a house," she said at last.

He studied the mountains, the bare trees and the snow-laden ground before turning back. He didn't know what he'd accomplished by bringing her here; it had just seemed crucial to do so.

The horse neighed and shook her head, jingling the harnesses. She reared up suddenly, bucking the buggy precariously. Brock darted forward to calm her, but she shied away from him and continued her nervous prancing. He grabbed her halter and pulled her head down, placing his hand over her nose.

He scanned the nearby shrubs and spotted the source of her agitation. A lean gray wolf surveyed them from a distance of twenty feet. Holding the horse with his left hand, Brock drew the .45 from his right hip. "Abby, move slowly and come around behind me. Don't get too close to the horse."

She spotted the wolf and alarm crossed her features. She did as he asked, but instead of avoiding the horse, she stepped to the other side and took hold of the halter, soothing the more with soft words.

"Stay between her and the wolf, so she can't see it, and keep your hand over her nose."

"Are you going to shoot it?" she asked, using the same calm tone he had.

"Not if I don't have to. Maybe it'll move on."

"What if it has a pack nearby? Maybe we should unharness the mare and let her run."

He didn't spare her a glance. "Then what will we do?"

"Then you can go get her when it's clear."

The horse reared up and it took both of them to keep her from overturning the buggy.

"Or maybe we should just get in the buggy and leave," Abby suggested.

"Not as spooked as she is," he replied. "She'd spill us out in no time."

"Well, then, what do you suggest?" she asked.

"That you have a little patience and shut up," he told her.

Chastened, Abby kept silent and watched the wolf. By and by, two more joined it, both smaller, one obviously nursing pups.

Brock cursed under his breath. The click of his trigger being thumbed back was loud. The hair on her neck rose and Abby held her breath in trepidation.

# Chapter Fifteen

Brock's gaze narrowed.

Abby contemplated his impassive expression.

"Wolves kill calves, Abby," he told her.

She knew. "Yes."

"I'll only get one and the others will run."

"Don't kill the mother," she pleaded.

"I really should, you know."

"I know," she said again.

Without seeming to take aim, he raised the gun and pulled the trigger. The gunshot reverberated loud in Abby's ears. Barks and yelps echoed. The horse whinnied and sidestepped and Abby hung on. She had squeezed her eyes shut, but opened them to see the male wolf lying lifeless on the snow, a neat hole in his head, the others nowhere in sight. Her heart raced as though she'd been running, but relief sliced through her cold limbs.

Brock holstered his gun and calmed the horse. Abby looked from the dead predator to Brock's grim face. The regret in his eyes made it plain he hadn't wanted to do it, but shooting the wolf had been his only choice. She'd seen that look once before—the day he'd shot Guy. How had she ever imagined Brock and her brother as being the same? Her only excuse was foolishness, youth. Brock wasn't the man she'd made him out to be all those years.

"I—I heard shots this morning," she said, and her words sounded funny in her ears.

He nodded once and met her eyes squarely. "I was teaching Jonathon to shoot a rifle."

A resigned sadness filled her chest and her heart. A year ago—a month ago—she would have shrieked and stormed and accused him of leading her son along a deadly path of destruction. She'd heard all of Brock's arguments and they had never made a difference—until now. After this, after seeing the need for safety, which she already knew, but had denied, she understood the necessity for self-defense.

What if Jonathon had been with them and Brock hadn't been wearing a gun? What if the horse had run off with the buggy and they'd been left here without protection? She'd always known. A man could be thrown from his horse and left on foot. There were a hundred dangers in this untamed land, the least of them wild beasts. "A boy should learn how to take care of himself," she said finally.

Brock's usually stoic expression revealed his surprise at her accepting words. Of course he'd be shocked; she'd berated him at every opportunity for carrying a gun. A person could get hurt with a knife or an ax, too, but that didn't mean they weren't necessary tools. She'd been a foolish, spiteful, hurt girl for a lot of years. For her son's sake, she had to let the fear go.

Once the mare was calm, Brock lifted Abby into the buggy and headed back to the ranch. She waited in the barn with him while he unhitched the horse, brushed and fed her. Jonathon's gelding nickered on the way past.

"Jonathon rode to the reservation with someone else?"

"With John," Brock answered.

Abby stopped to greet the horse. "Has he named him?" she asked, scratching the animal's forehead.

"He wanted to name him Jack. I told him to think some more."

"Why's that?"

*"Jack,"* he explained. "After the gunfighter in the dime novels."

"Oh." She tilted her head. "And you wouldn't like that?"

"I didn't think you would. Besides, those stories are just glorifying a job that isn't all that glamorous."

"Spoken like one who knows."

He shrugged and leaned a shoulder against the stall.

"You've read them?" she asked. "The books?"

"James loaned me one."

"I asked Asa to stop reading them to Jonathon," she told him. "Do you think that was wrong?"

"I don't know," he replied. "Boys like to hear about adventures. Robin Hood was an outlaw."

"You don't think the stories would influence him to want to take up that kind of life? Like…like Guy did?"

Brock's blue eyes were penetratingly dark in the shadowy barn. "You're asking me as though you care about my opinion, Abby."

Ignoring him, she looked back at the horse and gave him a final pat on the neck. Brock took her hand and led her from the barn.

The family returned within the hour. Jonathon wore a beaded necklace given him by a new friend on the reservation. He excitedly showed Abby and proceeded to tell her about the food and the tents and the fires, and described the children Zeke had introduced him to.

"I hope it's okay that Jonathon went with us," Ruth said as Abby helped her prepare a meal. "Brock thought you could use the rest."

Wondering if Ruth knew Brock had been with her in her room last night, Abby's cheeks grew warm. "I didn't mind a bit."

Many of the townspeople snubbed Ruth and John, but the Kincaids surely knew by now that Abby wasn't one of them.

After supper, Caleb helped his wife clean up the kitchen. John and Zeke played a game of checkers, and Brock showed Jonathon a treasure trove of wooden toys stored in a window seat. "They belonged to me and my brothers when we were your age."

Abby smiled at Jonathon's delight at playing with the miniature carved soldiers. He built a fort from notched blocks, and Brock helped him with the stockade.

"I'd better get you home," Brock said at last, ruffling the boy's hair and glancing up at Abby.

Jonathon turned a pleading gaze on his mother.

"You have school tomorrow," she reminded him.

"Can Mama come back again?" he asked, his blue eyes wide and sincere. "She likes it here, I think."

"Your mama can come back anytime she likes." Brock gave Abby a warm smile.

Coming back probably wasn't a good idea. She was already terrified of Jonathon becoming too attached to Brock. They needed to put a safe distance between them for a while—she needed to distance herself because she had no stores of reserve when it came to the man.

Abby thanked the Kincaids and accompanied Jonathon to the yard, where Brock had stopped the buggy.

"I thought we'd ride!" Jonathon said.

"It's cold tonight, partner," Brock replied. "We need to keep your mama warm." He helped them into the vehicle and tucked blankets around mother and son.

The moon reflected from the glistening countryside, while a light dusting of new snow fell and created a magical world. They drew close to town and, for the first time in years, Abby felt as though the streets and buildings were an imposed restriction.

With a bittersweet feeling in her heart, she approached the hardware store, the place that had been home for nearly eight years, but that now seemed like an end to something she had hoped for, but had never been able to grasp. With Brock standing on the boardwalk below, she and Jonathon climbed the stairs.

Jonathon pulled his hand from Abby's and clambered back down to throw himself against Brock and hug him. Abby couldn't see Brock's face, but she didn't miss the tender gesture as his huge gloved hand pulled Jonathon against his chest.

The embrace ended, and with a wave, Jonathon returned to Abby. She turned the key in the lock and entered their quarters.

For two days, Abby thought of nothing except her part in what had happened between her and Brock. She'd been an eager participant, just as he always accused her, only this time she didn't blame him. She blamed herself.

Everett played on her mind, too, and she was glad he didn't show up to ask her why she hadn't been in church on Sunday. None of this was fair to him. She was going to have to do something.

Wednesday night, she bundled up Jonathon and went to visit Laine. Abby hadn't slept well since Sunday. She had pledged to marry Everett. The entire town expected them to say their vows on the appointed day. She had lied to herself and done a pretty good job of it. She'd believed that he was everything she wanted. She'd convinced herself that marriage to a man like him was her desire.

At least Jed had been kind and loving and considerate, a wonderful father to Jonathon. Everett had shown himself only to be tedious and bigoted and self-serving, and maybe he'd been that way all along, but it had taken Brock to make her see it.

Even if the man had been on fire for her, she could have seen some potential for their future, but not this way. Not with *nothing* between them.

She could never thank Brock for opening her eyes, because she hadn't wanted them opened, but now that they were, she had to deal with the cataclysmic results.

Laine welcomed them in and gave Jonathon a set of carved ships he loved to play with. She heated water, and she and Abby took seats on comfortable cushions on the floor.

"What troubles you, my friend?" Laine asked.

"How do you know something is troubling me?"

Laine smiled and poured green tea into tiny cups. "Call it intuition."

Abby made certain Jonathon was occupied. "I've been pretty confused lately."

"I have noticed that you were quiet. Is your confusion created by Mr. Brock?"

"It certainly is." Collecting her thoughts, Abby took a deep breath. A decision had been clear to her for the last few days. Now she had to face it. Voice it. "I can't marry Everett."

Laine blinked, her lovely almond-shaped, dark eyes puzzled. "You cannot?"

Abby shook her head. "I was fooling myself. He's not what I want at all."

"I am happy you realized that now—before the wedding."

Abby agreed. "But it will be so humiliating to call it off."

Her friend raised an ebony eyebrow. "What would be worse?"

"Marrying him, I know."

"So you've come to me for…reassurance?"

"I'm doing the right thing."

"If you do not love him."

"Is love always so important?"

"Not to a father," Laine scoffed. "My father wanted me to marry as a young girl. One less mouth to feed. I resisted and managed to bring in enough to pay my own keep. I believe love is important."

Abby observed her son playing quietly.

"Mr. Matthews is not what you want. And you do not love him, is that correct?"

"I don't love him," Abby agreed.

"And you know this now because Mr. Brock is what you want, and you do love *him?*"

She couldn't let Laine jump to wrong conclusions. "Brock is not what I want, either."

Once she'd said it aloud, she examined the meaning of those words. "I've changed my thinking about him, yes, but not to that degree. My anger has been diffused. But he still lacks the qualities I think are vital."

"Which qualities?"

"Dependability."

"Because he left a long time ago. Haven't you both made mistakes?"

Abby nodded. "And he told me he regretted that. He accepted the blame for everything that went wrong."

"Is the fault all his?"

"No," she said, barely above a whisper. "I chased him away. And I resented him for staying away—leaving me alone to deal with my father. I thought Brock was such a coward. He admitted that he was."

Laine refilled Abby's cup. "He did not know that your father was not still alive, did he?"

"What do you mean?"

"When he came back. He might have returned to face

your vengeful father. He had to face his brothers—both of them. And you. Perhaps it took more courage to return than you are giving him credit for.''

Thinking over Laine's words, Abby had to agree. Brock hadn't known what awaited him when he'd returned to Whitehorn. He hadn't denied Jonathon; in fact, just the opposite was true. He'd embraced the boy as his son, had been irritatingly possessive. ''Perhaps it did.''

''And you recognize the feelings that are missing with Mr. Everett, because you love Mr. Brock.'' Laine was not letting go of her inquisition.

As a woman, Abby had never allowed herself to think in that direction. Perhaps as a girl she'd fancied herself in love with him, but she was a lot smarter now. ''Even if I did love him,'' she began, ''it would be fruitless.''

''Because he does not love you?''

He desired her. He wanted her. For now. Desire hadn't been enough in the past. Why should she believe it would bind him to her now?

''Because we have no future. I will not risk my heart or my son's heart.''

''What will you do now?''

''I guess I'll have to tell Everett that the engagement is off.''

''When will you tell him?''

She hadn't thought too much about when or how. ''As soon as possible, I guess.''

''How about now? Jonathon can stay with me.''

Perhaps it was best to get the unpleasant deed over with quickly. It was a short walk to the boardinghouse, and the evening was still early. Abby accepted the offer, kissed Jonathon and went out into the cold.

With each step, she considered her forthcoming words, imagining his reaction, wondering how her life could have taken such a confusing turn. At the boardinghouse, Mrs.

Harroun answered her knock and welcomed her inside. "Mr. Matthews isn't here," she replied to Abby's inquiry. "He's never here of an evenin'."

"Do you know where he might be?"

She was clearly flustered, her head wobbling on her neck as if it were loose before she managed a reply. "Seems I've heard he frequents the Double Deuce mostly."

Absorbing that information, Abby thanked her and walked along the street lit by gas lamps. She drew close to the saloon and recalled thinking she'd seen someone who resembled Everett in passing. She stopped on the boardwalk. Now what was she to do? A lady didn't walk into a drinking and gambling establishment without setting tongues to wagging, without ruining her reputation.

She pulled her coat tighter and waited.

Several minutes later, a boy of about twelve ran toward her, headed for the door.

"Are you going in there?" she asked.

"Yes'm. I'm sellin' cigars for my pappy."

She dug into her pocket and found a nickel. "Will you please send Mr. Matthews out? Do you know who he is?"

"Sure I do." He snatched the coin from her hand and disappeared inside, the opening and closing door allowing her a quick glimpse of the smoky interior.

She waited several minutes and had begun to think that perhaps Everett wasn't in there, before the door opened again.

"What are you *doing* here?" He hunched into his coat.

"I wanted to speak with you."

*"Here?"* The cloying smells of smoke and whiskey clung to him.

"Well, this is where I found you."

"What were you doing, checking up on me?"

"I wasn't checking up on you. I went to the boarding-house to speak with you."

"I told you I didn't spend my evenings there."

"You neglected to tell me you spent them *here*."

"It's unusual to find me here," he claimed, taking her arm and guiding her away.

She pulled her sleeve from his grasp. "I don't care. That's not why I'm here."

"Why are you here?"

"I told you I need to talk to you."

"And it's so important you have to call me away from a good hand? I work all day. I deserve a little relaxation of an evening."

"I told you—I don't care."

"Well, what did you want?" He stopped and faced her.

Confronted with the question, she glanced around. Was this the right time? There was no right time. It simply had to be said. "I've been doing a lot of thinking," she began. "I've come to an important decision. One that wasn't easy, but that will prevent us from making a mistake, from winding up miserable eventually."

"What's this big decision?"

"Everett, I admire a good many things about you." Or she had until she'd gotten to know him a little better. "And I would never want to do anything to hurt you. I don't want to get hurt, either. That's why this has been so hard."

"For heaven's sake, woman, what are you trying to say?"

"Everett, I can't marry you."

Roughly, he grabbed her arm through her coat sleeve. "What?"

"I can't marry you. I've thought it through. The past month or two has shown me it was a mistake to think it could work."

"Abby!" he said, plainly aghast at her announcement. "You said yes. We set a date. I made plans."

"I was wrong."

"Wrong? What do you mean, wrong?" He gripped both shoulders and gave her a little shake. "You're breaking a promise here. You made a promise to marry me."

"I'm sorry, Everett, really I am." She jerked from his hold and backed up a few steps. "I should have known you'd be angry. But you're going to see that this is for the best. Truly it is."

"I want an explanation," he demanded.

"I've thought it through. It's not what I want."

"What you want isn't good enough. What about what *I* want?"

She was getting angry now. Raising her gloved hands in an irritated gesture, she said, "You can't make me marry you." She turned her back and headed the direction she'd come. "That's it. That's all."

"This is not all," he said. "Don't walk away from me!"

She kept going. At the corner, she turned back to catch him going back inside the Double Deuce. All the way back to Laine's, she wondered if she'd handled it badly, if she'd said the wrong things, if she could have waited, chosen a better time.

"There was no better time," Laine assured her after she'd told her what had happened. "You had an unpleasant task to do and you handled it."

"I feel bad."

"You would feel a lot worse if you woke up beside him ten years from now and knew you had never said the words when you should have."

Abby hugged her impulsively. "You are so right. Thank you."

She gathered Jonathon and they walked home.

Abby had a dream that night. The scenario was hazy, the colors dark and the faces blurred, but she knew who each person was. She and Jonathon had become lost from a group of people traveling from a barn raising, and as she tried to find the way home, a pack of wolves slunk after them. The animals' teeth were yellow and their snouts snarling. Jonathon got tired and lay down, crying. With a jagged stick, Abby tried to keep the wolves away from Jonathon's feet.

A knock wakened her, and she was grateful for the interruption and the quick trip back to the reality of her warm bed. The knock came again and the dog woofed quietly. She grabbed her wrapper and groggily pulled it on as she made her way to the kitchen, Dilly loping ahead of her.

Brock had shown up many a time in the evening, sometimes even late, but never in the middle of the night. Opening the door, she wondered what in the world had brought him this time.

Everett pushed past her.

Dilly's low growl should have warned her that the nocturnal caller wasn't Brock, but her head hadn't been clear. "What's wrong?"

"You know what's wrong. You delivered the news that our engagement was off barely hours ago. What do you think is wrong?"

"I don't mind speaking to you if you want to discuss things civilly, but I didn't appreciate the way you spoke to me earlier."

"I'll talk to you any way I see fit. Suddenly you're better than I am—is that it?"

"Of course not. Everett, be reasonable."

"Reasonable? I'm not the one who broke our engagement in front of the Double Deuce."

"That's where I found you."

"I have a right to be there."

His thinking confused her. She held her tongue.

"What does Brock Kincaid have to do with you not wanting me anymore?"

"Nothing."

"Come on, Abby. I'm not stupid. Or blind...or deaf. Since he came to town, people have been talking. And now you've suddenly decided that you don't want to marry me. Isn't that too much of a coincidence?" He took her arm and leaned over her, and she smelled the smoke and the liquor on his clothing and his breath.

"Maybe it is."

"The hell it is! You threw yourself at him once and you're doing it again, aren't you? Aren't you?" He shook her.

"No," she said, struggling to pull away. Dilly growled and yipped at his heels.

"What is it about him that you like better?" he asked, and his mouth curved up in a leering smile that turned her stomach. "I tried to treat you like a lady—even when I knew you weren't."

Stunned, she didn't have a reply, and struggling against his strength was taking all her concentration. He jerked her hard and she lost her balance. He used the opportunity to yank her toward the bedroom.

Abby wanted to scream, but she didn't want to awaken Jonathon. She bit Everett's arm and he pulled it away with a growl. "Is that it?" he asked. "Maybe you don't like to be treated like a lady. Maybe you'd like me better if I weren't a gentleman."

He flung her on the bed, and she instantly bounced back up and made a run for the doorway. Dilly barked. Everett caught her by the back of her nightdress and hauled her back, pushed her down on the bed and held her in place with a hand in the middle of her chest and his knees on either side of her hips.

Truly frightened now, she conserved her strength and stared at him as though she'd never seen him before. She hadn't. Not like this. Not the real him.

"Did you allow him ungentlemanly behavior, Abby? Did you? Did you like it?" He leaned down and spoke over her, his eyes gleaming.

"Where is this going to get you?" she asked, speaking calmly and hoping to reach the logical side of his brain. "What can you be thinking?"

"I'm thinking you wanted to be my wife until that two-bit gunslinger showed up!"

"And this is going to change my mind?" she shouted back. "Get off me, Everett."

"Where is he now, that wonderful man of your dreams?"

"Let me go."

"You've had him here in your bed, haven't you? You took up with him just like before. Didn't you? *Didn't you?*"

"No."

"You're lying. Just like you've lied about everything, to everybody. You let him have you when you were just a girl, didn't you?"

Abby couldn't disguise the gasp that tore from her throat.

"That kid of yours is his bastard, isn't he?"

"Get off me!" she screamed, and lunged upward, dislodging him. She got out from under him and rolled toward the edge of the bed.

He held her by the hair and jerked her back. "Isn't he?"

She slapped at him and grabbed her hair to keep him from pulling it. "Get out of my house!"

Dilly barked and made darting nips toward Everett's legs.

"You were his whore before you ever married Jed, and you've become his whore again."

Rage like she'd never known welled up inside her at his inflammatory words. She swung her open palm over her shoulder and it connected solidly with his face. "How dare you speak to me like that!"

Immediately, he jerked her head back and pressed his face up against her cheek. "Because you're going to marry me, that's how."

"I told you I'm not going to marry you."

He bracketed her face with his hands, gripping her cheekbones painfully, his hold on her tender scalp relentless. "You'll marry me," he said in a frighteningly quiet voice. "You'll marry me or I'll tell the whole damned town your dirty little secret."

Abby's whole body stiffened.

# *Chapter Sixteen*

Abby's first horrified and incohesive thoughts were of the people of Whitehorn hearing the truth and gossiping about her—about Jonathon—spreading rumors and calling her son names. Her greatest fear would become a reality because of this man's cruelty—if she didn't comply with his threat.

"They should know, don't you think, that the prim little proprietor of the hardware store spreads her legs for the man with the big guns?"

Abby clenched her teeth and dug her nails into his hands and wrists. He squeezed her cheekbones all the harder.

"Mama?"

If she were a fainter, she would have blacked out at the alarmed sound of her son's voice. He mustn't see this! In a desperate silent plea, she begged him to go back to his room, but knew he had just become involved in something ugly. Her heart wrenched.

"Let go of my mama!"

Abby couldn't see him because of the hold Everett had on her head, but she heard the tremor in his brave command.

''Your mama has some thinking to do. And an apology to make. Don't you, *Mama?*'' He made the name sound like a profanity.

Abby pulled herself together. If her son was going to see this, he wasn't going to see her bullied without a fight.

''Go to hell,'' she managed to gasp through achingly clenched teeth. His fingers were bruising her face. The other hand yanked her hair. Her eyes stung from the pain.

''Uh, uh, uh,'' he warned. ''Be nice, Abby. Be nice or I'll tell everyone.''

He would do it, she had no doubt. He would reveal her private shame and heartache without a qualm. In the midst of her tumultuous thoughts floated the memory of Brock's admonition that people probably knew more than she'd let herself think. He'd pointed out Jonathon's uncanny resemblance to him, the fact that people could put two and two together on their own.

She'd realized that Caleb knew, but she'd blindly ignored the possibility that others might, too. The whole damned town probably knew anyway, so the hell with Everett's threats. ''I'll never marry you,'' she said through gritted teeth. ''I don't care what you do.''

If there were people who would be shocked by the truth, she would live with that. Her son was as good as anybody, and she'd teach him to believe the best about himself.

''You care,'' Everett said. ''And you'll care more when the town shuns your bastard son.''

In a fury, Abby used both fists to beat him in the head.

Dilly barked and lunged for Everett.

Everett screeched and released his hold on her hair and face to kick at the dog. Dilly yelped.

Jonathon howled with fright.

Breathless, Abby escaped and sprang up from the mattress. If she had a gun, she would shoot him in the heart without a qualm. The violent thoughts shocked her. She glanced wildly about for a weapon to use to defend herself and her son.

Everett stood and straightened his clothing and his collar, as though he'd only just finished a cup of tea. Red marks dotted his hands from Abby's fingernails, and he bore a welt on one cheek. Adjusting his tie, he turned his spiteful gaze from Abby to Jonathon. "You look just like him, you miserable little rat."

Confused, his blue eyes wide with fright, Jonathon cast Abby a pitiful glance. His lower lip quivered.

Abby picked up the nearest heavy object, the pitcher on her washstand, and swung it toward Everett's head.

Seeing it coming, he raised his arm and deflected the blow. The pitcher fell with a crash and broke into several pieces. He held his forearm against his middle, a look of pain distorting his vengeful features.

"Get out of my home!" Abby yelled.

"Your home, your precious home. What did you do to earn this place? You just waltzed in and seduced a rich man, then inherited everything when he kicked off. Not a bad trade for a few years in the old guy's bed."

"You don't know what you're talking about. Get out of here."

"Did you let him think the kid was his? Were you that good? Didn't he ever figure it out?"

"Get out!" she screamed, and dimly thought she heard knocking.

"Thought you had everybody fooled, didn't you? Too bad the kid's the spitting image of his murdering father." He turned to Jonathon then and the boy cringed. "That's right," he said, stepping over the pieces of broken pottery. "Your father is a murderer, kid. He killed your uncle."

"It was self-defense," Abby declared.

"My papa never kilt no one," Jonathon denied.

Pounding sounded on the interior door. The Spencers had heard the commotion.

"That old man wasn't your papa," Everett said with a sinister smile. "Your real father is a worthless, no-good coward who ran away."

"No he ain't!" the boy shouted, his face red with indignation. "Why's he thayin' that thtuff, Mama?"

"Becauth it'th the truth," Everett said, leaning toward Jonathon and mocking his speech. "Brock Kincaid is your father. Your mama is his whore."

Abby picked up the bowl that remained and lunged toward Everett, raising the heavy crock and bringing it down with a sickening thud on the back of Everett's head.

He crumpled to the floor.

Crying, Jonathon ran to Abby. She dropped to her knees and folded him in her arms. Whining, Dilly licked his face.

"He's a bad man, ain't he, Mama?"

"Yes, darling, a very bad man."

"He's a liar, ain't he?"

*The truth, Abby.* All the damage had already been done. And she'd hidden her secret for long enough.

"He's a liar sayin' my papa wasn't my papa. Why'd he say that?"

"He said it because he's mean and he wanted to hurt me. But..." She pushed him an arm's length away and studied his precious, tear-streaked face.

"Abby!" Daisy's alarmed voice registered now, along with the frantic pounding.

Glancing at Everett's prone body, Abby stood and pulled Jonathon along with her to the hallway door. He might rouse, and she'd better be gone if he did. She yanked open the door.

"For heaven's sake, what is going on in there?" Daisy

wore her flannel wrapper, and her silver-streaked blond hair flowed across her shoulders. "Are you all right?"

"It's Everett," Abby said. "I hit him and he's on the floor…in my bedroom."

"Asa went for the sheriff." She moved past Abby, revealing the derringer in her hand. "Is he dead?"

"Lord, no! I don't think so, anyway."

"Well, we'll wait for the sheriff."

Abby nodded her agreement. Jonathon still clung to her side, his body trembling. She rubbed his shoulder and bent to kiss the top of his head. "We have a lot to talk about."

Some time later, after Abby narrated her abbreviated story and Daisy and Asa backed it up by telling what they'd heard, James took Everett, handcuffed and unconscious, to jail. Abby locked her doors tight and made Jonathon hot chocolate.

He sat at the kitchen table, a wary expression on his young face.

"Jonathon, there's something you need to know."

"What is it?"

"Your papa was a good and kind man who loved you very much. He provided for us and took care of us and loved us. He loved you and nothing can ever change that."

Her son studied her solemnly, a chocolate mustache rimming his upper lip.

"But he was not your true father."

Jonathon's eyes were wide and blue, and he had never reminded her more of Brock than he did at that moment. "He wathn't?"

She shook her head. "I met your real father many years ago. I thought I loved him very much."

"But you din't?"

How could she ever explain this to a child when she

could barely understand it herself? "No, I did," she assured him, knowing it was true. She had adored him, all those years ago. "I did love him very much."

"Mr. Matthews thaid Brock is my father."

"Everett was right about that part. But before you think that Brock wasn't here for you or that he didn't want you, I have to tell you what happened…and why he never knew about you until this very year."

As honestly and simply as she could, she explained that she and Brock had loved each other, but that her brother hadn't approved of their love and had come after Brock, intending to shoot and kill him.

The most difficult thing to explain was her part in driving Brock away, but she did her best, assuring Jonathon that Brock hadn't known about him. Once he had learned about Jonathon, he'd done everything he could to claim him as his son without hurting either Jonathan or Abby.

"Is he still my father?"

She studied his innocent features. "You can't change who your father is. You can have a new father if your mother marries, which is how Jed became your papa. But the man who helped create you will always be your real father. And Jonathon," she told him, "being a true father means caring for you and loving you. Jed loved you very much, just as Brock does now. So you're a pretty special boy because you have had two fathers."

"But Brock is my real daddy."

"Yes."

"And you're my real mama."

She smiled. "Always."

He thought a minute. "Can a kid have two mamas?"

"Well, I guess he could. His mother could leave or die, and he could get a new mama when his father married again. Zeke had two mamas, remember?"

"I'm only gonna have one."

"That suits me just fine."

He yawned and blinked sleepy eyes.

"You need some sleep, little fellow." She removed their cups from the table.

"Are you gonna sleep, too?"

"I'm going to try. There's still a couple of hours before daylight."

"Can I sleep with you?"

"Sure." She took his hand and they scurried into her room and cuddled beneath the covers. Abby smoothed his hair and rested her palm above the steady rhythm of his heart.

"Mama?" he asked some time later.

"Yes?"

"You're not gonna marry Mr. Matthews no more, are you?"

"Certainly not."

"Good. Me'n Dilly don't like 'im."

"I don't like him, either."

"He won't hurt you no more, will he?"

She hated that her child had witnessed that terrible scene. "No. He's in jail right now, and he'll have to deal with the circuit judge."

"Brock's teachin' me how to shoot a gun. I could get a gun and keep it under my bed."

Abby's heart fell at his words. She had never wanted him to have thoughts like those, but how could reality be avoided? "Brock is also teaching you that guns are necessary, but to be used only when there is no other choice, right?"

"He said a smart man knows when to leave his gun in the holster, but a man who fires at everythin' is marked for death."

Abby studied the ceiling in the darkness. *Like Guy.*

"He's a wise man," she told him. "You pay attention when he tells you things."

"I'm too big to be thleepin' with my ma, ain't I?" Jonathan said a few minutes later.

"Do you think you're too big?"

"I think I'll be too big tomorrow. Tonight it'th okay."

"I think you're right. You're doing a lot of growing up tonight."

He fell still and silent, and his breathing deepened. Abby released him from her embrace and lay on her back. Oddly enough, she felt as though an enormous weight had been lifted from her chest. And it wasn't that circumstances had changed as much as it was that she had changed. At long last, she had been honest with herself, and with Jonathon. He deserved to know the truth. She would have chosen another way to tell him, but the end result was what mattered now.

Wondering what would happen with Everett, she knew James Kincaid wasn't the kind to spread malicious talk. But others would gossip; it was natural. News would spread.

She owed it to Brock to tell him what had happened before he heard it by some other means.

The following morning, she kept Jonathon home from school and took him to Laine's for the morning. Leaving Sam in charge of the store, she trudged to the livery. Surprised to see her, Lionel Briggs rented her a horse and helped her into the saddle by offering her a step up on his laced fingers. He wiped his palms on his pant legs. "You sure you know how to handle 'im?"

"I'm a rancher's daughter, Mr. Briggs," she assured him. "I've been riding since I was barely able to walk."

With a shrug, he waved her off.

Her confidence wavered momentarily when she had to get her bearings and assure herself she was headed in the right direction. She'd been to the Kincaid ranch recently, and she would simply remember to keep the mountains at her left shoulder. Sure enough, the landmarks were familiar, and before long, she recognized the copse of trees Brock had pointed out as marking their property border.

She thought briefly of the wolves, and decided not to borrow trouble by imagining the worst. The ranch house was a little east of where she thought she'd find it, but the smoke and tracks led her right to it.

John Whitefeather spotted her immediately and rode out to meet her. "Mrs. Watson," he said politely.

"Good morning, John."

"Ruth will be pleased to have company."

"Actually, I've come to see Brock."

John leaned back in the saddle and pointed to a horse and wagon a measurable distance from the corral. "That's him."

She thanked him and nudged the horse forward.

Brock was hammering at a section of fence, his coat and hat slung over the back of the wagon. He wore a thick sweater, dungarees and boots, and of course, the ivory-handled revolvers.

Catching sight of her from the corner of his eye, he straightened, the hammer falling still in his gloved hand.

Abby rode close and reined in.

"This is a surprise," he said.

She was probably the last person he'd expected to see riding here today. She threw her leg over and dismounted, and he dropped the tool to help her.

A line of worry furrowed between his brows. "Is Jonathon all right?"

"Jonathon's fine."

Quick as a snap, his expression changed and his whole body seemed to come to attention. His gaze had focused on her face, and he ripped off a glove to cup her chin and tilt her face up. "What the hell happened to you?"

She had forgotten the rows of bruises on her cheeks, which had been barely visible in her mirror in the bleak morning light. If they looked anything like they felt, they had probably turned a vivid purple. "Do I look bad?"

"You look like a prizefighter after a match. What the hell happened? This looks like—Lord, Abby, these look like finger marks!"

"There's something I have to tell you."

"Damned right you do." He released her chin and stepped back. "Did that son of a bitch Matthews do this to you?"

"Yes, but—"

He cursed and punched the air, muttering a string of profanities.

"But he's in jail," she assured him, grabbing his arm and silencing him. "The sheriff locked him up."

Pain was evident in his eyes when he turned them back to her, as though he couldn't bear to look at her injuries. His tone of voice had softened to one of almost agony. "What did he do to you?"

"He got angry because I told him I wasn't going to marry him."

Brock let the words sink in to make sure he got the information right. "You did?"

She nodded. "I made a decision yesterday."

He inspected the bruises marring her beautiful face and drilled his gaze into hers. His chest grew tight. The sweat under his clothing chilled now that he'd stopped working, but he ignored the cold and hung on to her words.

"I realized that I couldn't marry him. Actually, I made the decision in my heart a few days before, but it took a while to get to my head. I shared it with Laine, and she encouraged me to go tell him right away—get it over with.''

The joy of knowing she had changed her mind—that she wasn't going to go through with the wedding—mixed with the fury of knowing the detestable man had harmed her. "And he did this to you?"

"Not right then. I found him at the Double Deuce, told him on the street out front. He came over later—during the night. I wouldn't have opened the door, but I guess I thought it was you."

"I told you to ask who it was!"

"I know, I know. But I still wouldn't have thought him capable of what he did. I probably would have let him in anyway."

"What else did he do?" A horrible thought crossed his mind, an unacceptable image of Matthews forcing himself on Abby. "Did he—Abby, what did he do?" Waiting was agony.

"He was angry—he'd been drinking. He shouted and said horrible things."

"What things?"

"Things about you—about us—about Jonathon."

Her skin was pale in the cold, making the bruising look all the worse. He wanted to pull her close and comfort her, but he didn't want to stop her talking.

"Jonathon woke up and was scared." Her chin trembled then.

Brock held himself still and waited.

"Everett told Jonathon that Jed wasn't his father."

Brock's heart hammered against his breastbone.

"He told him that *you* were—and that you were a murderer."

Clenching his jaw against the anger and pain, Brock imagined his little boy hearing those hateful words, imagined the confusion he must have felt. "I'm so sorry, Abby."

It came out a choked whisper.

She blinked. "The blame isn't yours!"

"I'm responsible. Way back then I made bad choices."

"Not just you," she told him sternly. "I blamed you for so long that I never took time to admit my part in what happened. I'm responsible, too. Maybe more than you. I knew you were unhappy and confused, but I let myself think that I could be the answer to all your problems. What kind of girlish foolishness was that?"

He shook his head, no reply forming. "What did Jonathon do? What did he say?" He brought a hand to his temple. "I can hardly stand to think of it."

"It wasn't so awful," she told him gently. "Well, Everett was awful. But I knocked him out and—"

"How?"

"With my washbowl."

He pictured it. Amazement washed over him.

"Asa and Daisy had been knocking on my door. When I was able to let them in, Asa went for help and the sheriff took Everett away. After that Jonathon and I had a long talk and I told him the truth."

An unexpected satisfaction flooded Brock at the knowledge that his son knew about him now. Now he could be free to love him, to express himself as he hadn't been able to. "Is he okay?"

"He's an amazing little man," she said, pride lacing her tone. "He accepted the news surprisingly well." A brisk wind caught Abby's turned-up collar and blew it against her face. "I also told him about my part in making you go away. I assured him that you didn't know about him when you left—and that I made you leave."

After all that she'd been through, after condemning and hating him, she'd taken the blame upon herself in Jonathon's eyes. Had she truly had a change of heart? Refusing to marry Matthews must have been a result of her transformed attitude.

"Why did you take the blame?" he asked.

"Because it's the truth. And it's past time that the truth be uncovered." She explained the remaining details and assured him that Everett hadn't seriously harmed her. "I think you should talk to him now," she said, referring to Jonathon.

"When?"

"Whenever you want."

"How about now?"

"That would be fine."

He turned, tossed tools and wire on the wagon bed and got his coat and hat. "Let's get you to the house and warm you up first."

To his amazement, Abby was frank with Ruth, explaining the situation and the bruises on her face.

Ruth made a poultice and asked Abby to allow her to treat her while they talked. The hot packs removed much of the pain and swelling from her face and jaw. Caleb entered the house at eleven, and while they ate, Abby thanked him for his years of silent support and consideration, and explained the situation to him.

"The entire town will be buzzing in no time," she told them, "so the more people who hear the truth from me or from one of you, the better."

"This is very brave of you," Ruth told her.

"Not so brave," Abby denied. "Just not as cowardly as trying to keep secrets."

"I'll ride back to Whitehorn with you," Brock told her. "Let me go up and change." He dipped a bucket of hot water from the well in the stove and left.

Caleb headed back to his work.

"You are free once again," Ruth said. "Does this mean you will be thinking about marrying Brock?"

No one had mentioned a word about a future for the two of them, least of all Brock. "He's never spoken of wanting to marry me," she told her. "And even if he did, I don't have it in my heart to trust him."

"There is more trust in your heart than you are willing to look at," Ruth replied. "You are no longer that wounded girl. Brock is no longer a young boy. Believe in the man he has become."

Abby thanked her for the healing poultices and the understanding friendship, and joined Brock for the ride back to town.

Etta Larimer was sweeping the boardwalk in front of the newspaper office when they rode past, and she paused in her task to observe.

Brock touched the brim of his hat politely. Abby waved.

Etta waved back hesitantly, then returned to her sweeping.

Brock met Abby's gaze. Had news spread already or was she imagining the curious look? Abby out riding of an afternoon instead of at work in the store was probably an oddity in itself.

A loaded wagon sat before the dock, and Mr. Meeks and Sam were unloading the supplies.

"Where are your helpers?" Abby called, dismounting and tying her horse to the rail.

"Boys have a fever," Meeks told her. "Their mama wanted 'em home today."

Abby started toward the heavily ladened wagon.

"I'll help," Brock offered. "I might as well hang around until you get Jonathon."

He pitched in and, with his help, the job progressed

quickly. Abby checked over the invoice sheet and paid Mr. Meeks for the trip from Butte.

"Sam," Abby said directly, once the three of them were alone and the door was closed. "You're going to hear some things, so I want you to hear them from me first. The right way. The truth."

Her employee and friend looked from Abby to Brock. "All right."

"Brock is Jonathon's father," she said simply, then hated the rush of discomfiture that brought heat to her face. This was a difficult admission to make so boldly. "Things didn't work out for us back then...a lot of misunderstandings and hurt feelings...and pride. But Brock has come back to start over in this town, and I want him to be a part of Jonathon's life."

Sam's expression showed only interest. "Thank you for telling me, Abby. I've heard talk, but never gave it much thought." He and Brock exchanged a look. "Guess we're both new fathers, huh?"

"Guess so. Congratulations, by the way."

Sam reached a hand forward and Brock gripped it in a firm shake. "You, too."

And so it began, this revealing of the truth, and with it a newfound freedom. There would be those who looked down on her or shunned her, but she would deal with them with her head held high.

She went to Laine's for Jonathon just before time for school to get out. Back at the hardware store, she took their coats and watched the boy scamper toward the rear of the building. He came to a halt in his tracks before he reached the counter, where Brock stood with a mug of coffee. Abby noted his hesitation, but trusted Brock to set him at ease.

"Daisy sent cinnamon rolls over this morning," she said, finessing a measure of privacy for the two of them.

"Jonathon, why don't you take Brock upstairs and share a couple? Zeke can help me with a few chores when he gets here."

"Okay." Quite naturally, Jonathon reached for Brock's hand.

Abby watched her son and his father head for the back stairs.

## Chapter Seventeen

No part of Brock's body had ever taken such a beating as his heart was taking right now. "Did you have a nice time at Miss Shan's?"

"Yeah."

He walked behind him up the stairs and followed Jonathon into the kitchen.

Jonathon paused and looked from Brock to the covered plate on the table. "You want milk?"

"I'd like some milk."

"I can get it."

"Okay." Brock perched on a chair and watched the boy carry a pitcher from the ice box, then pull out a chair to reach two cups from a cupboard shelf. Watching his son perform these simple, yet somehow grown-up tasks gave Brock pleasure he hadn't expected. He'd spent so much time regretting what he'd missed that he hadn't taken time to appreciate the fact that from now on he was part and parcel of the boy's life.

Jonathon poured milk, spilling only a few drops on the tabletop, and placed a small plate in front of each of them. Then he peeled the napkin away from the plate on the table, revealing the gooey rolls. "Go ahead."

Loving his child more each second, Brock took a roll. "Your mother told me everything that happened last night."

Jonathon met his gaze. "Mr. Matthews is a really bad man."

"Yes, he is," Brock replied, noting Jonathan's careful pronunciation.

"He called my mama bad names." He placed a roll on his plate and licked his fingers.

"That must've hurt her feelings a lot."

He shook his head. "Nope. Made her *real* mad."

Brock had thought this was going to be a serious and difficult discussion, but already the boy had him smiling. "How about you? Were you mad, too?"

"Yup. And so was Dilly. He kept bitin' his legs and feet and stuff."

"Good for Dilly."

"He's a good dog, ain't he?" Jonathon took a big bite.

Brock agreed, before asking, "And your mama told you how it was between us?"

He swallowed. "She said you're my real father."

Brock's throat tightened at the words. "Yes," he managed to answer.

"She said you love me a lot."

There was only one other person he'd ever loved as much. "I do."

"Can you teach me to protect my mama?" he asked, as if he'd already accepted Brock as a parent, and his love as due.

"That's what a father's supposed to do, I guess, huh?"

"I reckon. She din't get mad about you showin' me how to shoot the rifle."

Brock had been amazed about that himself. "I know."

"Maybe you can show me how to shoot those Colts." He gestured to Brock's revolvers. "Them's just like the ones Jack Spade has. Billy Warren says his papa thinks *you're* really Jack Spade, not that Manley fella.''

"If I was Jack Spade, what would I be doing working on a ranch and nursing sick dogs and helping your mama in her store?''

The boy shrugged. "I guess even Jack Spade needs a holiday.''

"Wouldn't he travel to Europe or somewhere exciting if he needed a holiday?''

"I reckon.'' His voice held disappointment.

"You know, Jonathon, those Jack Spade stories are only partly true. A lot of that stuff is made up to make for a better story.''

"But there really is a Jack Spade.''

"How do you know?''

"Everybody knows. They wrote about him in the newspapers, and those people really seen him do stuff.''

"What people say isn't always what really happened,'' Brock reminded him. "Just like you might hear people talking about your mother, or me and your uncle Guy. But only we know the real story.''

"You gonna tell me?''

Brock nodded. "I think your mama and I will tell you together…tonight.''

The boy's eyes sparkled. "Like a family, huh?''

Brock couldn't answer. He scrubbed his hand over his chin. Inquisitive, yet trusting, bright and charmingly innocent, with an elfin chin and round liquid eyes, this boy was more than any father could hope for. Brock would prove himself worthy of the boy's love; he would make up for the past.

It would be easier to accomplish that with his son than it would be with Abby. Jonathon already accepted him with childlike faith; Abby still didn't know she could trust him.

From a distance, the sound of the bell in the store clanged.

"Don't ya like the roll?" Jonathon asked.

Brock had been so engrossed in the boy, he'd forgotten to eat. "I like the company better."

Jonathon grinned.

Since she wanted to make a few purchases at the mercantile, Ruth came for Zeke. Abby held Bart while Ruth got Zeke into his coat, and then waved them off.

Later, after the store was closed, and Brock had purchased dinners from the hotel for their supper, the three of them sat upstairs near the hard-coal heater and sipped from steaming mugs.

"Mama makes the best hot cocoa in the whole world," Jonathon declared.

"I'll have to take your word for it. I've only tasted hot cocoa once or twice."

"What did you always drink to keep warm?"

"Coffee."

"Oh."

Brock exchanged a glance with Abby.

"Wish we had a fireplace," Jonathon said wistfully. "Like at Zeke's house."

"Jed thought this was the modern way to heat," Abby said to Brock. "And it is. But it's missing the coziness of a real fire."

"Are we gonna talk about everything together?" Jonathon asked then. "Mama, Brock said—" He stopped midsentence. "Am I apposed to call you Brock? I mean, since you're my real father an' all?"

"You can call me anything you're comfortable with," Brock told him.

"Don't seem like you're a papa," he said, one side of

his mouth twisted in thought. "Papa was…well, he was older."

"Jed will stay your papa," Brock assured him, not wanting to take away anything Jonathan had shared with the man who had raised him as his own. "He was a good papa to you."

"What did you call your father?" Jonathon asked.

"I called him sir," Brock replied. "You would have had to know him."

"I remember him," Abby said. "Years ago our families were neighboring ranchers," she told her son.

"And you knew each other a long, long time ago?"

"We did," Abby replied. She told him about her brother, Guy, about how he'd fancied himself a fast shot and had been hot-tempered and quick to draw his gun for any small reason. Her story was related with no animosity toward Brock. When she said that Brock's leaving was her fault, he interrupted to share the blame.

"And you see," Brock told him, "that those dime novel stories might be exciting and sound adventurous, but when men get killed, the people left behind who loved them are hurt."

"I never thought about that," Jonathon replied.

"And even if the dead man was an outlaw, the man who killed him still has to live with the fact that he took a life."

Abby studied Brock as though considering him from a whole new perspective. Bringing a finger beneath her eye, she quickly brushed away moisture and looked away.

Jonathon lay with his head in Abby's lap and absorbed the story of his uncle and the lesson it had provided. His eyelids grew heavy. "I think just Pa," he said out of the blue.

"What's that?" Abby asked.

He sat and took stock of Brock. "I think I want to call you Pa. That sounds grown-up, don't it?"

"It just sounds good to me," Brock managed to answer, around a lump in his throat.

Jonathon got to his feet, leaned over and kissed Abby on the cheek. "'Member I'm grown-up today?"

"I remember."

"I'm gonna get ready for bed so Pa can tuck me in."

Abby thought of him snuggling with her just the night before, and knew he was making some adjustments toward maturity. "I'm sure he'll like that very much," she told him.

"Come to my room in five minutes." He held up his hand with all five fingers outstretched.

"Five minutes," Brock agreed.

Jonathon ran from the room with Dilly on his heels.

When Brock found him in his room, pajamas buttoned up crooked, the covers under his armpits and Dilly lying on the foot of the bed, he grinned. When he bent to tuck him in and Jonathon reached to hug him around the neck, an incredible warm feeling touched his heart and brought tears to his eyes.

"I love you, Son," he said, drawing away and looking into the eyes so like his own.

"I love you, too…Pa."

Brock clamped down on the emotion and smiled through the blur. He extinguished the lamp, gave Dilly a final pat and left the room. He stood in the hall for a few minutes, dealing with the new emotions.

Abby was rinsing their cups in the kitchen when he found her, and he stopped a few feet behind. "You've done a great job…with Jonathon," he told her.

"Jed helped," she said.

Brock accepted that, was grateful for it, even. He had wondered once if he could put his past behind him to become the man he wanted to be. He knew now that he would—because he wanted to be a good father to his son. If he could have a part in raising a fine boy—making a difference in his life—he could at last live at peace with himself. Even if Abby never let him make up the past to her, he could start over with Jonathon.

But he hoped she would.

She turned around, found him close, and took a cautious step away, obviously distancing herself.

"Abby," he said softly.

"I'm a stronger person now," she told him with a little shake of her head.

"You were always a strong person. I liked that you had a mind of your own—knew what you wanted."

"No," she stated. "I was always weak. I let everything get out of control because of it."

"Because of me, you mean."

"Because I let things happen."

"*Things?* Like what we've done together?"

She only nodded.

"Since we're being honest and getting everything out in the open, there's something I have to ask you," he said.

She brought her luminous gaze to his, her hesitation apparent.

"Can you forgive me?"

The question hung in the air like the retort of distant gunfire. A minute ticked by and he waited, her silence ringing in his ears.

"I don't hate you," she conceded at last. "I don't think I ever did. I just hated what I'd become because of you—or maybe because of my reactions to you—to us."

"We're really something together," he said softly.

Her cheeks reddened with embarrassment—or shame?

"Do you think it's a weakness to want someone?" he asked.

"If they don't want you back," she declared.

"It's never been that way between us. I've always wanted you just as much. More."

"No." She shook her head. "Desire. You *desire* me. It's different."

"You desire me, too. Right?" She could confuse him easily this way.

"It's different," she argued. "I *wanted* you!" Her voice broke. "Wanted you to stay, wanted you to love me, wanted you to make a family with me." She moved away and wrapped both hands over the back of a chair.

He studied the lustrous braid that hung down her back, the delicate curve of her bruised cheek, the coil of fine hair at her neck. Just looking at her, he could smell the delicate lilac scent of her skin, though the smell had to be imprinted in his memory because he was standing too far away.

She was a woman of strong passions: love, hate, resentment, desire. A woman of strength and fortitude, a prickly woman when defensive. But like a porcupine, she had a vulnerable underbelly.

He understood now. Since her passion for him had been so strong, her loss had been agony as well. He regretted ever hurting her, ever making her lose her trust, cursed himself for crushing her girlish fancies.

"I'm asking you to forgive me for being a fool," he said. "I didn't know what I wanted back then. I wouldn't have made a good husband. I shouldn't have taken advantage of you, because I knew you were in love with me. I knew I wasn't capable of being what you wanted, and that scared me.

"I've admitted I was a coward. I've done everything but stand on my head and spit nickels to change your mind about me. I'm just damned sorry, Abby. What more is there?"

She turned halfway back, glanced at him and away. "It's over," she said. "It's past and behind us. Let's forget it."

"And you've forgiven me?" he asked.

"Why do you have to make me say the words? Can't you just let it go?"

He didn't know what to make of that question. He couldn't make her forgive him. Perhaps asking forgiveness was for his own selfish peace of mind. Maybe he didn't deserve absolution. What he'd really been asking was if there was hope, and she wasn't giving him any encouragement. "All right."

He ambled to the hooks near the door and got his hat and coat.

"Brock?" she said.

He turned back.

"Um, thank you for supper."

"You're welcome." Shrugging into his coat, he left.

Abby bolted the door, leaning against it for a moment. Finally, she turned down the wall lamp and carried another lamp to her room. She had only a few shreds of self-defense left, and she couldn't afford to let him rip them away. Depending on how long he actually stayed in Whitehorn, she might have plenty of opportunities to resist him, and she couldn't do that if things were all neatly tied up between them.

All she had left was this last meager shred of defense. And she wasn't letting go to forgive him.

At the bottom of the stairs, Brock turned left and entered the alley, as he always did when he left Abby's. The hair on the back of his neck stood up, and he removed his glove and opened the front of his coat. Drawing one .45, he let his eyes adjust to the darkness.

At the back corner of the building next door, the orange

glow of a cigar caught his attention at the same time he smelled the aroma of tobacco. His wariness eased somewhat, because obviously the person in the darkness wasn't trying to hide.

"Evenin'," Brock called.

"Warm one," came the reply. He'd heard the voice before, but couldn't place it.

This alley was an odd place for a man to stand and enjoy a smoke, so Brock left his hand on the revolver. Matthews was still in jail, but this was below Abby's home. "Got business here?" he asked.

"Maybe."

Brock came to a stop six feet from the indistinguishable man. The moon was up, but the figure was shadowed by the looming hardware store. "What might that be?"

The man took a few steps forward and Brock made out the hat and coat, the lean face and the dark mustache. "Manley?"

"Spade?"

Brock's instincts took over, his mind and body functioning as one, deadly calm, alert, focused. "Name's Kincaid," he replied.

This wasn't the way a flashy gunfighter like Linc Manley called a man out. There was no crowd, no one to witness the heroics he thought he possessed, no one to carry the story to the papers. He hadn't come here tonight for a showdown, but he had come for a reason. Brock was sure on both counts.

"There seems to be a lot of speculation over which one of us is Jack Spade," Manley said. "Amusing, isn't it?"

"Not particularly."

"Oh, come now. Surely you can see the irony in the fact that you're trying to lose a reputation and I'm looking to gain one."

"It's the looking that will get you killed," Brock warned him.

"Such concern for my welfare is heartwarming. Who would have thought that a famous fast draw like you would be concerned for a stranger?"

"You don't know what you're talking about."

"I'm talking about Jack Spade. The man who fights for law and order, the man who strikes fear into the hearts of the dangerous men he hunts down. The man who seeks justice with a pair of deadly blazing .45s."

Brock actually chuckled. "You've been reading too many dime novels."

"Writing them, actually."

That brought Brock up short. "You've written stories about Jack Spade?"

"Jack Spade, Wyatt Earp, the Rock Canyon Kid—all of them. I've traveled the West in search of stories, and told them to thousands of readers."

"Half that stuff isn't true," Brock pointed out.

"That's why it's fiction." The tip of his cigar glowed as he drew on it.

In the back of his mind Brock was thinking that Manley might be trying to trick him into saying something he could use against him. "So you're famous yourself."

"I write under the name L. M. Hayes, but nobody remembers my name. They only remember Jack Spade's."

"What do you want from me?"

"The name."

"What name?"

"Jack Spade. You're done with it. You're starting over here."

This could still be a trick to draw him out in the open.

"I covered your back with the last one," Manley added.

"What do you mean?"

"The shooter outside the restaurant. Followed him and took care of the situation."

The information didn't sit well. More than one person had already tracked him here. This man and the shooter.

"Figure I've already started earning the name," Manley said.

Without acknowledging the man's admission, or the fact that he believed him, Brock shook his head. "Guess you don't need my permission to call yourself anything you want to." Brock took a few steps past the man and stopped. "But you'd be inviting trouble if you chose to use that name. Men and boys will track you down to try to get the drop on you. Someone will always want to be better. Faster. More famous."

Manley touched the brim of his hat. "Warning taken."

Brock strode through the alley, the exchange troubling him. Reaching the livery, he saddled his horse and headed for the ranch. Had Manley set out to find Jack Spade or had his arrival in Whitehorn merely been a coincidence? If one man had looked for the gunslinger here, it meant others could, too. Others who wanted more than just a chat. Had it been foolish of Brock to come here? Was he placing his son and the woman he loved in danger?

Just when things had turned for the better. Just when it had begun to look as though there might be a future for him here, just when he and his son had formed a tenuous bond... A terrible heaviness weighed his heart.

As much as the thought tore him apart, he gave it consideration: maybe leaving again would be his only choice.

The second thaw came a week later, the snow melting and rushing down from the mountains in a torrent, overflowing creeks and riverbeds. The ranchers and hands from the higher country went to help others in danger of losing cattle, as well as aiding the business owners in

Whitehorn, who sandbagged their buildings against disaster.

In the midst of the confusion, the circuit judge arrived and held court. Abby testified against Everett, and the judge gave him thirty days in jail.

For the most part, the population was sympathetic toward Abby, and several of the women voiced their support. Those who had bought into the rumors and snubbed her she recognized as never having been friends.

Sheriff Kincaid came to tell her one evening that Everett was planning to head East after he'd served his sentence. He'd been strongly encouraged to do so by the Kincaid family.

The river had risen to a dangerous swell and then, as if a dam had burst somewhere downstream, it gradually lowered. Abby breathed a sigh of relief. Standing on her dock beside Laine, who wore a man's Hudson Bay coat, she shaded her eyes against the glare of the sun and listened to the report of the cowboy who rode down the muddy street calling the news. The town was a flurry of activity, accommodating the added business of having emergency help on hand.

Up and down the street, the buildings were surrounded by piles of strategically stacked sandbags, customers climbing over them to enter stores and businesses.

"The river is down," Laine breathed.

"Thank God," Abby replied.

Across the street, Sam and Brock wearily perched on kegs on the boardwalk. Linc Manley, dressed in his long black coat and wearing a red satin bandanna, smoked a cigar and carried on a running conversation with them. Sam and Brock had been hauling bags of grain and seed up a ladder to the Dillards' loft all morning.

Suddenly, gunshots echoed from another street.

"Someone is celebrating the flood missing us," Laine suggested.

"Seems they could clap or sing or something, wouldn't you think?" Abby asked, cringing at the sound.

Several men on horseback rode toward them, mostly ranch hands, but at the front of the group was a young man who didn't look like he'd come to Whitehorn to work. He wore no coat, but sported pistols tethered to his thighs and a pair of thin leather gloves.

The horses couldn't hold their footing in the slick mud, and the young man impatiently waited for his mount to obey his commands.

From behind them, a commotion rose, and a throng of people appeared, most on the boardwalks to stay dry, but some running through the ankle-deep mud.

"Jack Spade!" the kid hollered, the shout echoing.

The crowd murmured. Some folks moved backward, others scrambled forward for a better look.

"Nobody here goes by that name," Brock called back, slowly standing.

"Don't matter what name he's goin' by, I reckon. I come to send him to glory. Him and anybody else who gets in my way."

"That's big talk," Brock called.

Horror engulfed Abby's senses, numbing her scalp, ringing in her ears. What was Brock doing? *Stay out of it!* she wanted to shout, but her lips were frozen, as if she was having a nightmare.

Sam stood, too, but he moved back against the wall.

Linc Manley crushed out his cigar with the toe of his boot and draped his coat back, away from his holsters. "Better think twice, kid. You've got a lot of years left for card games and pretty women."

The kid laughed. "Guess your days are numbered, though, eh, Pop?" The kid dismounted, dropping his horse's reins and taking a couple of steps forward. He stood wide-legged, facing Brock and the man in black. "Either of you got the gumption to draw?"

Abby's scalp prickled with horror. *Get away from there, Brock! Get back!*

Brock's coat still covered his guns, and he wore a pair of work gloves.

Abby's stressed brain likened this moment to another many years ago, a day when her brother had looked just as cocky and sure of himself as the boy who stood in the street right now.

Fast as lightning, the kid drew both his guns.

# *Chapter Eighteen*

Shots rang out, and immediately the kid dropped a pistol and held his hand to his chest, his face contorted with pain.

Linc Manley lay on his back in the street, one boot on the wooden stairs, his hat fallen away. He held a gun lifelessly in his gloved hand.

Brock had one hand on his gun, too, but Abby didn't know if he was drawing it or putting it away; it had all happened too fast. He was alive and that was all that mattered.

People crushed in around the fallen gunfighter, and someone called for a doctor. "That's you, Laine," Abby said.

Laine's almond-shaped, dark eyes blinked in dreaded resignation. She took Abby's hand and they hurried through the slippery mud to the other side of the street.

Blood bubbled from a hole in Manley's brocade vest. His breath wheezed from his throat. He looked at Brock and tried to say something. Abby covered her mouth with her hand and shuddered with the remembered horror of watching a man die.

Laine took an apron that Tess Dillard handed her and

pressed it to the wound. Even Abby could tell it was a hopeless act.

"Like you said," Manley rasped, and blood trickled from the corner of his mouth.

"Don't talk," Brock told him, leaning forward.

He took Brock's collar and pulled him down. "One of us is dying here."

Brock met his eyes.

"Someone...will always...want to be faster...." He chuckled, a ghastly, choked sound. When he coughed, Brock helped him turn on his side to spit out blood. Bile rose in Abby's throat.

"Don't let anybody take my guns," Manley said, a vein bulging in his temple with the strength it took to speak.

Brock assured him.

His eyes rolled back.

Laine placed her fingers on his neck. "He is dead."

The crowd murmured, and men turned to talk to each other.

Brock leaned over Linc Manley's body with the front of his coat open, and Abby thought she saw him tuck something into the other man's coat. Brock straightened, and his grim expression distracted her.

He bent at the waist, unbuckled the holsters from the man's body and held them for a moment. Turning, he walked toward the kid, who stood surrounded by another, smaller crowd. Bart Baxter and Will held him between them. "His hand's shot," Will said.

"Good." Brock leaned toward the boy and poked his chest with Linc Manley's gun belt. "Maybe that'll keep him from killing more people."

The boy cringed and whined, "One o' you sons of bitches shot me!"

"You're lucky that bullet isn't between your eyes," Brock growled.

Sheriff Kincaid showed up then, raising a hand to silence the dozen voices talking at the same time. "Quiet!" He turned in a half circle. "Who saw the whole thing?"

Twenty voices declared they had.

"Who shot Manley?"

"He did." In a consensus, they pointed to the kid.

"And who shot you?"

"Jack Spade," he said, cradling his hand. Laine hadn't made a move to help him. "I killed Jack Spade!" He glanced at Brock with uncertainty.

"You don't know for sure he was Jack Spade." James glanced toward the man lying in the street. "He's dead?"

Laine and Brock affirmed that he was.

"Somebody take him to the livery, then. Briggs can lay him out."

Brock handed his cousin the gun belt.

Sam came out of the hardware store with the makeshift stretcher they'd used to transport Mr. Waverly. "Somebody give me a hand."

George Lundburg moved forward, and with another two men, they got the body onto the stretcher. Manley's coat gaped open in the process.

The butcher leaned over his prone form. "I'll be damned!"

Heads turned.

"Look at this!" He slid a small stack of colorful playing cards from Manley's vest pocket and splayed them for everyone to see. Every one of them was a jack of spades.

Conversation rose all around them.

"Told ya I killed Jack Spade," the kid bragged.

Brock drew back his fist and slugged him in the jaw with a sickening crack. The blow elicited a howl, but effectively shut him up.

James placed a restraining hand on Brock's chest. "Can't let you beat up any more prisoners."

"Lock him in there with Matthews, will you, James? Let them kill each other."

Abby elbowed her way to Brock's side. "What did he mean by that? Have you talked to Everett?"

"Briefly. He'll be heading out of town as soon as his jail time is up."

"I hope you slugged him once for me."

He slanted her a glance.

She'd been terrified of him getting caught in the middle of a gunfight. Seeing him standing here in the sunlight, as handsome and vital as he'd ever been, she breathed a prayer of thanks. "For a few horrifying seconds there, I thought I might lose you."

Something flickered behind his blue eyes. "So did I."

She had the feeling he didn't mean it in the same context she had. Around them, paying Brock and Abby scant attention, neighbors talked and gestured and prepared to move on about their business. The gossipmongers had something more absorbing to dwell on now.

Laine hurried home to get supplies for the kid's hand. Brock walked Abby toward her store and watched her climb the stairs, then stop and turn back.

"You put those cards in his vest pocket, didn't you?"

His expression didn't change. He was good at hiding what he was thinking. The only times she'd ever seen a reaction on his face were when they'd been involved intimately...and when he looked at Jonathon.

"Jack Spade is dead now," she said.

He nodded.

She remembered the lightning-fast speed with which he'd leaped from her divan and held a gun to her head. She'd known then, she supposed. She'd known in her heart every time she looked at those guns, heard the regret in his voice, read the reactions only she could pick up on.

"You stayed away to protect your family," she said, thinking aloud. "To protect me…and the son you didn't know you had. It took more courage to stay away than to come home, didn't it?"

He wasn't answering. His face revealed nothing.

Over his shoulder, she saw Sam approaching. "Watch the store for a while, will you?"

Brock turned.

"Sure," Sam replied.

"By the way," Abby asked, "how's that girl from the reservation working out? A big help with the baby?"

"A godsend," Sam replied, then passed her on the stairs and entered the store.

"Come with me," she said, and stepped back down and around the corner. Brock followed her up the stairs and inside her kitchen, pausing in the doorway to glance back down at the street.

"They have better things to talk about today," she assured him, closing and locking the door. Abby removed her coat and took Brock's. "I have something to say."

"Okay."

"Let's have tea—or coffee, you like coffee."

"Let's get to the point. Everything's a work of art with you."

She filled the enamel pot with water and added a log to the cook stove. "Trying to make me mad?" she asked, measuring grounds.

"That's something I don't have to work at with you." He leaned back against the counter and crossed his arms over his chest.

She offered him a smile and a slice of corn bread.

He accepted the plate. "You can't make me say anything I don't want to."

"It's my turn to say something," she told him. Behind her the coffee boiled, the aroma filling the air.

Brock took a few bites of the corn bread and set the plate aside.

Abby removed the pot and poured two mugs full, spooning sugar into Brock's.

"You laid it all out for me," she told him. "Shared your regret and your feelings and apologized...and I couldn't take those extra steps. I was too afraid. Afraid you'd leave again, but more afraid of how powerful these feelings are."

"I understand, Abby."

"I know you do. And that's why I was afraid. That and a lot of other reasons. If I couldn't love you, I had to hate you—I had to hate myself. You said I was strong because I knew what I wanted. But what I wanted I couldn't have, and so I told myself I didn't want it. I told myself I didn't love you. I told everyone I could that you were a detestable, vile excuse for a human being, and then I started to believe it.

"Until you came back...until I was forced to see who you really are and what I'd become."

"You were hurt," he said. "Hurt and young and scared, that's all."

"But you see," she went on, "if I forgave you, then I would have to forgive myself. And if I forgave both of us, then I would risk loving you again."

"And you love me, don't you?"

"Sure of yourself, aren't you?" she asked, tears threatening.

"About some things." Stepping toward her, he took her hands, and she knew he could feel her trembling. "I'm sure I can stay here now. Nothing will ever make me leave again. Nothing."

"I believe you." She'd seen him slip those playing

cards into Linc Manley's pocket so that it would look like the man who had died was the famous Jack Spade. Why would he do that unless he was Jack Spade and he wanted to put that entity to rest once and for all?

She had never wanted anything as much as she wanted this man in her life, wanted him to have and to hold forever.

"Forgive me," she begged softly. "Like I've forgiven you."

Brock wrapped his arms around her and pressed her to his chest comfortingly. "You don't need my forgiveness, Abby."

She pulled back enough to slug his chest with a closed fist. "Don't tell me what I need! I know what I need. I held on to those feelings of anger and resentment, and I talked bad about you to everyone. I blamed you for things we did together, without taking responsibility, and I *need* forgiveness!"

He grabbed her hand. "All right, woman, I forgive you."

She laughed, but it came out a sob. "That's better."

"Shall we drink our coffee now?" he asked, his expression almost teasing. "That is why you brought me up here, isn't it?"

"I brought you up here to tell you I forgave you and that I love you, but you make everything so—so difficult."

His face did change then, a perceptible flutter of eyelashes and the flare of a nostril. It was a heady feeling to crack the steel-plated armor of a man like Brock Kincaid. Abby experienced the satisfaction of a personal victory.

"I love you," she said again, testing the power of those words.

A luminous sheen in his blue eyes told her she'd shaken him, but he said nothing. Her heart softened. Fluttered.

This fearless man, who fought outlaws and faced down gunfighters without a quiver, trembled when she made love to him...wept when she professed her love. Yes, he loved Jonathon—but he loved her, too. Had loved her first.

She smiled through her own tears and framed his beloved face in her hands. "I love you," she said again, this time a heartfelt promise, rather than a confession or a test. "And I want you. Forever."

He hauled her up against him and kissed her hard, parting her lips, tasting her, leaving the buttery taste of corn bread on her tongue. This kiss was a melding of souls, a blend of cleansing and forgiving in the form of a greedy consummation. She released his cheeks to wrap her arms around his neck and cling to him. That he could really be hers at last was a joy that filled her mind and her heart.

Experiencing the liberation of not hating herself for wanting him like this, she gave herself over in newfound freedom. Happiness welled from the depths of her being in the form of tears.

Brock released her and, holding her hands, knelt and gazed up. "You'll marry me, Abby."

The laugh she emitted sounded more like crying. "Was that a question?"

He gripped her hands. "You know I love you—say you'll marry me."

That was the best proposal she could hope for, so she nodded her agreement. Threading her fingers into his silky hair, she leaned forward and pressed her lips to his, kissed his eyes, his forehead. He gripped her bottom through her skirts and petticoats, forcing her to straighten, and pulled her hips toward him, pressing his face into her skirt.

Abby's heart pounded.

He got to his feet and pressed himself against her.

She reached for the buttons of his shirt.

"I probably smell like I've been working all morning," he said.

She continued to open the front of his shirt. "I have hot water and soap."

"That's sounds like a proposition."

"If I'm going to trust you, I want you to trust me, too," she said.

"I trust you."

"Then show me your gun."

He stilled, as if wondering what she was asking.

"Show me that one," she said, pointing to the revolver at his right hip. The one she'd seen his hand on.

Hesitantly, he drew it from the leather holster.

"Now show me the bullets."

He knew now what she was asking to see; she recognized the decision he made to comply.

He turned the barrel away, deftly thumbed the release aside and revealed the ends of the bullets in the cylinder.

"Turn it all the way around," she said, with a vague idea of how the cylinder held the bullets and how the repeat action turned it to place another bullet in front of the chamber.

Brock turned it slowly, the ends of the bullets moving past, until an empty chamber came into view.

He had fired a bullet. The one that hit the kid's hand. And his gun had been back in his holster before anyone had time to realize what had happened. She would bet the store that Linc Manley's gun hadn't been fired.

Brock raised his gaze to hers.

"Thank you," she said.

Without looking, he slid a bullet from his belt, fed it into the empty chamber, flipped the cylinder back into place and holstered the gun. Just as she'd known, he kept all the chambers full.

"You can take that off and put it under my bed," she suggested.

"Am I going to make it to your bed?"

"Well..." She continued unfastening his shirt, pulling the hem out of his pants, and stripped it down his arms. He wore a flannel union suit. "This is interesting."

"It's cold out."

She unbuttoned that, too, and his pants, while he lay the gun belt on the table. "Remember that day in here—the day we kissed?"

"I remember."

"I thought of pushing you right down on the floor and..."

"And?"

"And you still need to wash, right?"

She left him standing with his pants open, his union suit unbuttoned, and poured warm water into the sink.

"Want to take those boots off, cowboy?"

He made quick work of the boots and the pants, his underwear folded down over his lower body.

Abby soaped a cloth and handed him a towel. She washed his face, pausing to kiss him tenderly. He closed his eyes and released a deep sigh. After soaping his hands and arms and chest, she rinsed the cloth and removed the suds, having him lean forward over the sink so she could rinse him. Drying his shoulders and chest, she kissed the warm damp flesh, tasted him with her tongue.

"I think these got wet." She indicated the underwear.

"You're still dressed," he said.

With a seductive smile, she unbuttoned her shoes and kicked them aside, rolled down her stockings and slid them off her feet. After undoing the buttons of her shirt-waist, she removed it. Brock kissed her neck and touched his tongue to her collarbone, while unfastening her skirt, untying her petticoats and shoving them out of the way.

He had knelt to help her out of the layers, and without rising, pulled her to him, crushing her to his bare chest. With only the thin layer of her cotton underclothes between them, Abby felt the heat and strength of his hard body. She ran her hands over his arms and shoulders, and shuddered with anticipation when he buried his face against her breasts and cupped her bottom.

"How can it be so wonderful each time?" she asked incredulously. "Will it always be this way between us?" Truly amazed and overcome by the power of sensation and desire that raged unchecked between them, she closed her eyes and soaked Brock in through her pores.

He opened her chemise and suckled her breasts, and pleasure rippled through her, an erotic expectancy so sweet and intense, she bit her lower lip and groaned. He cupped her through her drawers and she ground herself against his palm.

She wanted to kiss him. She bent forward and covered his mouth with hers. She wanted him inside her, filling her. Pushing him back, she tugged his underwear down at the same time he disposed of hers, and she straddled him quickly, urgently, watching his expression as her body took his.

She kissed him. He moved beneath her.

She stroked his chest. He cupped her bottom and gazed at her breasts, her face.

Her braid fell over her shoulder and he used both hands to remove the tie and work the hair loose, spreading it over her shoulders, her breasts.

She kissed him. He grasped her hips.

She ran her finger across his lips. He drew it into his mouth and sucked it.

She held her breath. He smiled, slow and lazy and oh so brazenly. He knew he turned her inside out. He knew she loved it. Knew she loved him. And that was okay. He should know. Anyone who was loved as much as this man should know.

"I love you," she said.

He reached up and cupped her face, a smile reaching his eyes. "And you do it so well, my Abby, my love."

She loved him unashamedly, without reservation, without fear.

He held her still for a moment, meeting her gaze. "This time we might make a baby, Abby."

She smiled and moved sensuously against him, knowing she was pushing him to the edge. "This time you'll be here when he's born."

She watched emotion and pleasure cross his features, shared his release, and wiped the perspiration from his forehead with her rumpled petticoat.

"There isn't another woman like you in all of Montana," he told her, a tender smile on his lips.

"And you would know," she teased, kissing him.

"Nor in all of the West, actually."

"My, your conquests are broad."

He chuckled. "I love you, Abby."

"Yes," she said. "I believe you do."

# *Epilogue*

"He'll never shoot with that hand again," Ruth told Brock and James. Upon Laine's request, she had visited the jail and assured the Chinese woman that she'd done all she could to heal him. Without a surgeon, luck wasn't on the kid's side.

Or perhaps it was. At least he'd stay alive for a while.

"He'll learn to use the other one," Brock told his cousin and Caleb.

"Not for a long time," James assured them. "He killed a man in cold blood in front of fifty or more witnesses. He's going to die in jail."

Brock looked through the bars at the young man they spoke about. Stupidity. Foolish youthful stupidity. A wasted life.

The kid glared at him.

"What if he escaped?"

"He's not going to escape. I take him to court, he gets sentenced. He'll probably go to Helena."

"Somebody has to take him, right?"

"A marshal will come for him."

"You could hire me. I've marshaled."

Ruth gave him a sideways stare. "Your wife would kill you."

"Not if she doesn't find out."

"You're talking crazy here," Caleb said.

"Not at all. I take him, but he gets a jump on me, escapes. Nobody's ever the wiser."

"Except us," James objected. "I can't let a prisoner escape deliberately."

"What is he, seventeen?" Brock asked. "Look at him."

"You can be seventeen and still kill men."

"Not if you're scared spitless."

"And you're going to scare him spitless?"

"If you let me."

"No. Absolutely not."

Benji Buchanen awoke with a start. Handcuffs weren't the most comfortable bed partners. And this Kincaid fellow was so crazy, Benji slept with one eye open, watching him.

Now he was moving around the campfire, fishing in his saddlebags. He stepped over to Benji and knelt over him. "So, you wanna take your chances with me?"

Benji squinted up at him. "What're you talkin' about?"

"You'n me. A shoot-out. Winner leaves free and clear. Loser…well, dies."

The man had already shot his hand, but Benji had been too embarrassed to tell anyone. He'd let 'em think it was Jack Spade, but truth was, Spade hadn't even cleared his holster. This maniac, on the other hand, had fired and sheathed his gun just like nothin' had ever happened. Benji still couldn't figure that one out.

"What do you say, big gunfighter? You game?"

"I can't draw now. You shot my right hand."

"You can use your left, can't you? You wear two guns."

"Yeah, I can use it, but what kind of match is that—against a man with two good hands?"

"Hey, that's a chance you take in the business you're in. You get caught in a crossfire and get shot, you've still got to keep firing or you die."

Seemed Benji didn't have much choice. Still wasn't much of one.

"Okay, we'll make it fair. I'll wrap my right hand up and keep it behind my back. Suit you?"

Refuse and live his life in jail, Benji thought. Go along and at least he had a fifty-fifty chance. He'd seen the man shoot, though. Maybe not fifty-fifty. But at least a chance. "Okay."

He was sweatin' by the time Kincaid had him released and handed him his guns. How he'd come by those, Benji couldn't figure. Except that the sheriff had the same last name. Didn't look nothin' alike, though.

Warily, Benji strapped on his guns. What if he didn't have any bullets and the man shot him to pieces?

"Go ahead," Kincaid said. "Look."

He checked for bullets: loaded. His heart hammered and his skin felt clammy.

Kincaid wrapped a strip of cowhide around his fingers and thumb, wrapped his whole right hand up and tightened a knot with his teeth. He placed the hand behind his back. "This is it, then."

Kincaid backed up, his ivory-handled revolvers gleaming in the firelight. Wasn't very good light to shoot by.

"Maybe we should wait till mornin'," Benji suggested. "When there's more light."

"Gunfights don't happen under perfect conditions," Kincaid told him. "Sometimes it's raining. Sometimes the dust is blowing in your eyes. Sometimes you got more than one shooter aiming for you. Sometimes you get shot.''

Benji swallowed.

''Killed many men yet?'' Kincaid asked conversationally. He was crazy.

''Just the one. Jack Spade.''

''Thought you'd start out with the best, eh? Where you going to go from here? Nowhere to go but down.''

''Why don't you shut your trap and let's get to business.''

''Okay, okay. I was just trying to be friendly.'' He shook his left wrist and took a loose-legged stance. ''Ready when you are.''

''You gonna talk the whole damned time?''

Kincaid shook his head and showed he was ready.

Cold sweat poured from every pore in Benji's body.

He observed the other man's calm expression, the way he waited like a snake ready to strike. Benji shoulda stayed in Nebraska, and none of this woulda happened. He shoulda listened to his aunt Neda and his pa and stayed to plant. Now he might never see them again.

His only prayer was to shoot this crazy man and ride outta here and never look back. He calmed himself. Thought back over all his practice. All those bean cans and squash he'd murdered easy as you please. He might be able to do it if he didn't throw up first.

This was it. Live or die. A twist of fate made in a second. His head grew light. He steadied his hand, calmed his nerves and cleared his mind.

He reached for his gun.

Bullets pelted the ground in front of him, spraying dirt and pebbles across his pant legs and boots. One bullet caught the end of his boot, another his sleeve. Benji jumped back, hobbled, and fell on his butt.

''You're crazy!'' he screeched, in shock that none of

the shots had hit him. He hadn't even gotten his gun out of the holster. He couldn't think. He looked at himself. Nothing hurt.

"See that stain on your heel?"

"What?" He raised his boot to look.

Kincaid fired, hitting his boot and knocking his foot back with a stinging jerk. Benji yanked his wild gaze from the man to his boot, where a bullet lodged. The man could have killed him in a heartbeat.

"Why didn't ya kill me?"

"I killed a boy your age before. It broke his father's heart—his sister's, too. And I've lived with it for nearly eight years. I'll live with it until I die. Just like you're going to live with the death of that man you killed in Whitehorn, wondering if he had a family, if they know what happened to him, if they'll come after you."

"You ain't gonna kill me?"

"No." He unwrapped his hand and tossed the leather away. "Did you give the sheriff your real name?"

"No."

"What is it?"

"Benji."

"I'm setting you free, Benji. And I think you're just smart enough to go home and make a new start."

"I am. I'm real smart." Tears of relief sprang to his eyes and he cried like a baby.

Kincaid strapped a bedroll to one of the horses, added a canteen and a saddlebag. "You got family at home?"

He nodded. "My pa. And my aunt Neda."

"Well, you give your aunt Neda a hug. And be a good son to your pa. A father wants to be proud of his son."

"I will. I swear I will."

"I know you will."

Benji pulled on his coat and hat, mounted the horse and

looked down at the man who had just given him a second chance at life. "I won't forget this, mister."

"I don't suppose you will."

The stars stretched in all directions across the Montana sky. Wide-open spaces. Freedom. He turned the horse's head toward Nebraska.

Brock watched the kid ride away, a feeling of rightness giving him peace about what he'd done. He and James would handle this with the marshals and the judge.

It was Abby to whom he had a lot of explaining to do. Chuckling, he threw dirt on the fire. He couldn't wait to make up.

\* \* \* \* \*

*Be sure to look for*
*John Whitefeather's amazing story,*

***WHITEFEATHER'S WOMAN***

*by Deborah Hale,*
*available in October 2001.*

*Please turn the page for*
*a sneak preview…*

# Chapter One

*May 1897*
*Whitehorn, Montana*

A frontier saloon was just about the last place on earth Jane Harris had ever expected, or wanted, to find herself. Why, Mrs. Endicott and her Ladies' Temperance Society back in Boston would have been properly horrified. They'd have been more horrified still by the knowledge that Jane had stolen and sold a brooch of Mrs. Endicott's to get here.

The jarring notes of a tinny piano pummeled Jane's throbbing head, and the reek of raw spirits and tobacco smoke made the flesh at the back of her throat constrict. If she'd had anything to eat in the past twenty-four hours, the stink, the noise and her own overwrought nerves might have conspired to make her violently ill.

Perhaps it had been a harsh blessing that she'd run out of money for food back in Omaha.

"Kin I pour ya a drink, little lady?" bellowed the man behind the bar, his voiced laced with genial mockery.

Jane gasped, her heart hammering against her corset like the pistons of a runaway steam engine.

"N-no thank you, sir." She raised her voice louder than she'd ever spoken in her life, to make herself heard above the *music* and the babble of voices. "I'd be most obliged if you'd point out the foreman of the Kincaid ranch to me. The gentleman at the telegraph office told me I might find him here."

As she turned to speak to him, the bartender flinched. At the sight of her face, most likely. She'd hoped the bruises and cuts would have healed by the end of her long trip West. They must still have a ways to go if her appearance distressed a man who worked in such a rough establishment.

"Yep, ma'am. I seen him come in a while back and he ain't left that I know of." The bartender squinted through the haze of smoke around the cavernous room, with its sinister shadows and a huge, glowering buffalo head mounted behind the bar.

Raising a gnarled finger, he pointed to one particularly murky corner. "That's John Whitefeather, over there. He don't come in here much as a rule, but when he does it's always off by hisself."

Jane heard nothing after the bartender spoke the name. *Whitefeather?* An Indian! Her knees commenced to tremble beneath her skirts and petticoats.

Back in Boston, Jane's sole dissipation had been reading Western dime novels from Beadle's Library. Along with stories of legendary gunslingers like Jack Spade, they often featured lurid accounts of Apache atrocities. Were there any of that fierce tribe this far north? Perhaps she was about to find out.

"Thank you...sir. I—I appreciate your assistance." As much as a condemned prisoner appreciated a deputy's *assistance* to climb the scaffold.

Jane tried to smile at the man, but between her mounting agitation and the still healing gash on one side of her mouth, she didn't make a very good job of it.

Step by halting step, she crossed the saloon floor, painfully conscious of curious, predatory eyes following her movements. Had young Daniel felt this way walking through the lions' den? Probably not, for Daniel had been a man, and he'd had the Lord on his side. With the sin of her desperate theft weighing on her conscience, Jane was certain she'd left any slight protection of the Almighty far behind her in New England.

John Whitefeather sat at a corner table, all alone, his back to the wall, as though he did not care to turn it upon the denizens of the Double Deuce. The bartender's pointing finger must have alerted the man that she wished to speak with him, yet he did not rise or otherwise acknowledge her approach.

Reason assured Jane that the Kincaids' foreman was hardly apt to pull out a tomahawk and scalp her in the middle of a crowded saloon. But her tautly stretched nerves refused to unwind for logic. She stopped before his table and stood like a convicted felon in front of a hanging judge. For a wooden nickel she'd have turned and fled, but she'd been told the Kincaids lived miles outside of town. John Whitefeather might be her only means of reaching them.

For perhaps the hundredth time since stealing out of Boston, Jane wished she'd been able to spare the money for a wire to advise her new employers that she was on her way. Mrs. Kincaid might have come to the depot to meet her, or at least have sent her a less alarming escort to the ranch.

"A-are you Mr. Whitefeather, the Kincaid foreman?"

The man gave a slow nod. Jane sensed his gaze sweeping over her, but unlike the bartender, he betrayed no sign that her battered face affected him.

"What can I do for you, ma'am?" His voice, a soft rumble with a queer melodic inflection, was barely audible over the raucous hubbub of the saloon.

"I'm Jane Harris, Mr. Whitefeather." She tried to sound competent and businesslike to convince him of her identity, but her words came out stiff and prissy instead. "I've arrived from Boston to work for Mr. and Mrs. Kincaid, taking care of their boys."

Her syllables began to trip over one another in her haste, and she had to pause frequently to gasp for breath. "I regret that I was unable to send a wire to announce my arrival. I'd be most obliged if you could arrange my transportation to the ranch."

He muttered something to himself, but what Jane could hear made no sense to her. Was he speaking some Indian dialect?

Draining the contents of a tall bottle, he rummaged in his pocket and tossed several coins onto the table. Then he scooped up his hat, pushed back his chair and stood.

Jane's last sound nerve shattered.

He was so big. John Whitefeather towered over her, his shoulders alarmingly broad under an enormous duster coat that fell almost to his ankles. And his hands—Jane nearly swooned to imagine the horrible damage they could inflict on a woman's vulnerable face and body. Emery Endicott had been a runt compared to this giant. Before she'd run away to Montana, though, her fiancé had managed to beat her badly enough to put her in the infirmary.

"I expect you'd better come along with me, ma'am."

Any man who spoke so softly and with so respectful a tone could never harm her. Jane didn't really believe it, but the alternative was too terrible to contemplate. He brushed past her, a man-of-war in full sail, while she bobbed along in his wake like a dinghy swamped by his bow wave.

To her surprise, John Whitefeather held the saloon door open for her like the most fastidious gentleman. Squinting against the bright setting sun, Jane stepped outside onto the boardwalk that ran in front of the businesses on Main Street. The air was dry and dusty, but otherwise clean. The rowdy noise of the Double Deuce immediately muted to a faint echo.

Behind her, John Whitefeather's voice rumbled, ominous, yet absurdly reassuring in its hushed tone. "Are your bags at the stage office, here, or still back at the rail depot in Big Timber? Either way, we probably ought to leave them be until you've talked to Caleb and Ruth."

She spun around to face him. "I—er—don't have any bags."

Before she had time to lose her nerve, or recover her scruples, she rattled off the lie she'd carefully rehearsed all the way from the Atlantic.

"One of the trains got derailed just outside Chicago, you see. We passengers were thrown around the car, which is how I came by my—injuries. Then the baggage car took fire. I believe a lamp fell and burst when we went off the tracks. My trunk and both my valises were burned to a cinder, but of course I was relieved to have escaped with my life."

Quite against her will, the inflection of Jane's voice rose at the end of her account, as though questioning whether her listener was prepared to swallow this barely probable tale.

"That's too bad about your train, ma'am. Do you have any money to tide you over?" He took a few long strides down the boardwalk that abutted the false-fronted buildings of Main Street—a hardware store, a butcher shop, and an alarming number of saloons.

Jane scurried to keep up with him. "M-money? What makes you ask?"

Why she clasped her reticule to her bosom, Jane wasn't sure. It contained nothing more valuable than a pair of damp, crumpled handkerchiefs, the pawn ticket for Mrs. Endicott's brooch and a newspaper cutting of the Kincaids' original employment notice.

"I'll be getting room and board working for the Kincaids, and they'll be paying me wages. I can get by until then."

John Whitefeather stopped in his tracks and glared at her with a sullen severity that almost brought tears to her eyes.

Oh dear. Had she offended him by implying she feared he might steal from her?

He didn't raise his voice. If anything it grew quieter. The temperature of it dropped, too, until Jane fancied his breath frosted the air. "Forget it."

Her eyes were becoming accustomed to the sun's glare. At last she was able to take in more about the Kincaids' foreman than his general shape and size.

Beneath a battered brown hat with a broad brim, John Whitefeather's coal-black hair was tied back with a leather cord and cascaded down past his shoulder blades. He had skin the color of oiled teakwood, with the dark shadow of whiskers on his firm jawline. Above high, jutting cheekbones blazed deep-set eyes, the startling blue of an infinite Montana sky.

His fierce, intensely masculine beauty unsettled Jane almost as much as his height had. What a mousy, battered eyeful he must be getting by comparison.

Heaving a sigh from deep within his vast frame, John Whitefeather made a subtle movement, as though adjusting an awkward load upon his powerful shoulders. He untied the reins of a tall, white-spotted horse from the hitching post, then started across the hard-packed dust of

Whitehorn's main street with his mount in tow. Not knowing what else to do, Jane followed.

Over his shoulder the Kincaids' foreman called, "I reckon we'd better get you out to the ranch so we can sort all this out."

*Sort what out?* What was there to sort? Even if she'd had breath left to speak, Jane would not have dared ask. But she disliked the sound of it. She'd come West in answer to the Kincaids' letter, to work for them. Far from Boston. Far from Emery. Far from danger.

Except that Whitehorn, Montana, didn't seem very far from danger at the moment. Was there a safe haven for her anywhere in the world? Jane wondered. If there was, she'd barter her very soul to find it.

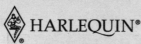
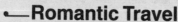